Hold on to your seat. . . .

At least my car was still in one piece. I was now facing the direction I had just come from and struggling to undo my seatbelt when a well-manicured hand reached in and touched me on my shoulder.

"Are you okay, miss?"

"Daaaamn," I replied in the most inappropriate manner. The brother was hittin'! Time for the checklist—nice haircut, good edge, goatee not too hairy, over six feet, smooth brown skin . . . Wait a minute! This was the guy in the BMW. Shit.

"Huh?" he replied with a wrinkled brow at my remark.

"Umm. I meant, 'Damn, my head hurts.' "

"Do you need me to call an ambulance?" he asked while opening my car door to assist me. Such a gentleman. I'm glad I had my clean drawers on. Maybe he would get a chance to see them. . . .

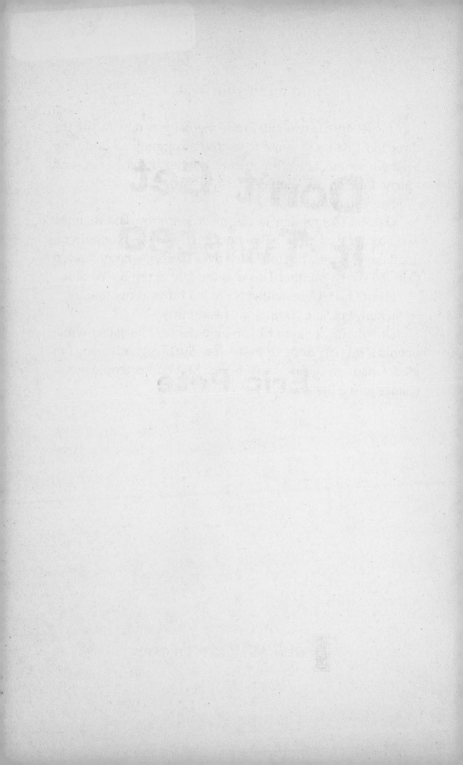

Don't Get It Twisted

Eric Pete

 NEW AMERICAN LIBRARY

New American Library

Published by New American Library, a division of
Penguin Group (USA) Inc., 375 Hudson Street,
New York, New York 10014, USA
Penguin Group (Canada), 90 Eglinton Avenue East, Suite 700, Toronto,
Ontario M4P 2Y3, Canada (a division of Pearson Penguin Canada Inc.)
Penguin Books Ltd., 80 Strand, London WC2R 0RL, England
Penguin Ireland, 25 St. Stephen's Green, Dublin 2,
Ireland (a division of Penguin Books Ltd.)
Penguin Group (Australia), 250 Camberwell Road, Camberwell, Victoria 3124,
Australia (a division of Pearson Australia Group Pty. Ltd.)
Penguin Books India Pvt. Ltd., 11 Community Centre, Panchsheel Park,
New Delhi - 110 017, India
Penguin Group (NZ), cnr Airborne and Rosedale Roads, Albany,
Auckland 1310, New Zealand (a division of Pearson New Zealand Ltd.)
Penguin Books (South Africa) (Pty.) Ltd., 24 Sturdee Avenue,
Rosebank, Johannesburg 2196, South Africa

Penguin Books Ltd., Registered Offices: 80 Strand, London WC2R 0RL, England

First published by New American Library, a division of Penguin Group (USA) Inc.

First Printing, October 2005
10 9 8 7 6 5 4 3 2 1

New American Library and logo are trademarks of Penguin Group (USA) Inc.

LIBRARY OF CONGRESS CATALOGING-IN-PUBLICATION DATA:

Pete, Eric.
    Don't get it twisted / Eric Pete.
       p. cm.
    ISBN 0-451-21654-7
    I. Title.
    PS3616.E83D66 2005
    813'.6—dc22   2005010860

Printed in the United States of America

Acknowledgments

God, thanks for granting me another day to see another one of my babies take flight.

Marsha, thanks for giving me the encouragement with the first "Beep, beep, beep" of *Real for Me* and for pushing me to let these dreams go beyond my mind and onto the pages where I would later share them with the world. Thank you for being by my side through both the tremendous highs and abysmal lows a writer in this industry can go through. Guess I got a "ride or die chick," huh? One day, I hope to make all your dreams come true.

Chelsea, your daddy is so proud of you. I've watched you grow into quite the young lady. You will go far in this world and do great things. Remember this.

Mom, to go what you've gone through and still radiate warmth with your smile is a testament unto itself. I love you.

To my family both of blood and of the bonds of friendship, which is sometimes stronger, thank you for the support, encouragement, companionship, camaraderie, shelter, and advice along the way. You know who you are and how I feel about you.

To the readers, book clubs, bookstores, fellow authors, and media out there who've welcomed me so warmly, thanks. A lot of you are included in the last group.

A nod and tip of the hat to my agent, Elaine Koster, and

the folks at Penguin Books/New American Library: Kara Cesare, Rose Hilliard, Kara Welsh, Anthony Ramondo (thanks for the slammin' covers, bro), and the rest of the staff, in New York and in the field, who work behind the scenes to make this happen. Thanks for having my back.

To everyone whose path I crossed, but would not have if not for this leap of faith I took, I thank you allowing me into your lives.

To the readers of my previous works, *Real for Me, Someone's in the Kitchen,* and *Gets No Love:* Thanks for coming back. I know there are a lot of options available to you. I'm just honored to be one of them.

In closing, I give special thanks to Christine Mandubourg, my high school counselor. Thanks for being such a positive force during a rough time in a young man's life. I'll never forget.

It's probably best that I close now so this book you hold in your hands makes it to press. But, you know what's coming. If not, ask somebody. . . .

"Can't stop. Won't stop. Believe that."—Eric

Where we're at

"911. How may I help you?"

"I need the police!"

"What's the nature of your call, ma'am?"

"Can you please just send the police! And an ambulance too!"

"Ma'am, please stay calm. I just need to get some information from you. Is someone hurt?"

"Yeah, you could say that. A couple of people."

"What happened?"

"What happened? Lady, will you fuckin' hurry up! People are hurt and bleeding!"

"I'm dispatching them to your location in Long Beach as we speak. I need for you to remain calm, okay?"

"Okay! Okay! I'll try."

" Now, I need to ask you a few questions. Do you know who is responsible for this?"

"Yeah. Me."

"Ma'am? Ma'am, are you still there?"

"Yeah. I'm here."

"I need your name."

"Isrie. Isrie Walker."

PART I

It's Just Emotions . . . (Where It All Began)

1

Isrie Walker

"Hello?" I said into the receiver. Nothing. The caller ID showed a blocked number. Should've known it was nothing but trouble.

I called out again and was met with still more silence. As I went to hang up, I heard laughter—a woman's laughter. I would've hung up—no, *should've* hung up—but now I was curious. "I can hear you on the phone, so you might as well say what you have to say."

There was a click as she put her phone on speaker. Blocking out everything, I could now hear a man's steady breathing. There was a rustling sound as if sheets were sliding around. The woman groaned, not from pain, but from pleasure. He was fucking her. Ryan was fucking her and they had the nerve to call me to hear.

I can't believe this shit, I thought to myself.

"Oh, yes! Get that shit. Get that shit, daddy," she urged him. Damn. I knew he would get it too. That was never my problem with him.

Ryan and I had been seeing each other for the past five months. *Had* is the operative word. I'd dumped him last night. Tonight, we were supposed see that Denzel Washington movie. Instead he was fucking the girl who thought she'd won the ultimate prize and I was on the phone like a fool.

"Ooh!" she gasped, startling me out of my funk. "No, no. Don't do it like that. Ryan, you're gonna make me scream."

I knew what *that* was and had had enough. "You're welcome to my seconds, bitch!" I was about to click my phone off, but raised it back to my mouth. "And for the record, I dumped him!"

Rebelling against my parents' nagging to find a man and settle down, I'd met Ryan. He was my date on one of those television dating shows where they pay you to go out with a complete stranger. Turned out Ryan was no ordinary date, but a flashy record producer out for some publicity.

I was extremely skeptical when I met him, but those dreamy green eyes and peanut-butter-smooth skin had me ignoring the obvious. Ryan was a bad boy. The good that came with that in the bedroom . . . and on balconies . . . and in a restaurant bathroom once also came along with the paternity tests and threats from crazies like the one on the phone. Ryan had too much ego. It was that ego that caused me to let him go last night after complaining I was fed up with the loose ends, or as I preferred to call them, tired ass hoes. His ego lost, but why was I the one feeling so ripped up over it? I was never one to depend on a man to define who I was, so I decided to brush my shoulders off like the pimp that I was.

I dumped the pint of Ben & Jerry's in the sink and went to change. Some Italian mules, a pair of my favorite denim jeans, topped off with a black long-sleeve tee, and all that was left was my grille. I went into my bathroom, turned on my makeup light, and went to work.

When finished, I was dressed and made up with nowhere to go. I still could have gone to the movies without Ryan, but decided to have a drink at a local spot. I wasn't one for drinking alone, so the call went out.

I speed-dialed a number, then waited. My girl, Deja, was always working late on her photo assignments, and it was easier to page her and let her get back to me. Five minutes later, my phone rang on cue.

"Hello?"

"What's wrong, Isrie?"

"You know me too well, D-Square." Ms. Deja Douglas got her nickname from both her initials and her cup size, although she was actually a large C or small D.

"I thought y'all were going to the picture show tonight." *Picture show*. Deja always had to be different.

"No. I'm about to go have a drink, though. Want to come?"

"On a Monday?"

"Look, I'm dressed up and don't feel like staying in the house. Are you coming or what?"

"Alright. I'll keep you company, but I'm not drinking anything heavier than water with lemon. I have a shoot in the morning. Look, I've got one more roll to develop. How about in thirty minutes?"

2

Isrie

I was at the bar nursing a watered-down cosmopolitan when Deja walked into the Neon Owl on Wilshire Boulevard, which was right down the street from the spa where I was employed as a massage therapist.

Deja and I had been good friends since back in the day. I used to live in the same Ladera Heights town houses as her before moving into my studio apartment on Seventh and Bixel in downtown LA. I had offered to go in on a two-bedroom unit and split the costs with her, but she chose to stay put. I didn't blame her though. My new surroundings came with a heavy price tag, but my hard work was starting to pay off and I deserved some pampering every now and then.

"Hey girl," Deja said as she placed her large black handbag on the bar. Deja was wearing a black two-piece skirt set with one of those little matching fashion cowboy hats, which was no surprise. A truly eclectic person, that girl was. Deja was a plus-size girl with a face like the actress Tatyana Ali, but with a short haircut. My girl was a cutie, but was self-conscious about her weight. To those that didn't know Deja, her bubbly personality concealed it well.

"You sure about that water with lemon?" I asked while ordering another cosmopolitan for myself.

"Yes. I haven't drunk enough water today," she replied while reshuffling things in her handbag. "What's up?"

"I dumped Ryan."

"Whaaa? Ah, no!"

"For real. Kicked his ass to the curb, girl. Last night."

"What happened?"

"You know how Ryan was. It was only a matter of time." I slipped a tip to the bartender as he brought my fresh drink. "Hmph. My parents were just adjusting to him."

"But you said he was good in—"

"That's the only thing that kept him around this long. Too bad he felt the need to *share the love*. He's sharing it right now with some bitch."

"You don't know that, boo."

"Yes I do. They called me so I could hear."

"Da-yum, that's some sick freaks for you."

"Tell me about it. I suddenly feel like doing shots. You game?"

"Girl," she said as she laid her hand on my arm, "stick to the cosmos. That wannabe Suge Knight ain't worth your liver. He should be called Suge Light." She chuckled at her own joke. "I don't know why you went on that TV show in the first place. I know your momma's still talkin' about that."

"Don't remind me. Brothers still come up in my face. 'Excuse me. Don't I know you from somewhere?' "

"Hell, send 'em my way. I can be your screener, y'know."

She'd made me smile like I knew she would. "Thanks for coming, girlfriend," I said as I raised my glass in a friendly toast.

"You know me, Isrie. I don't have a life. Looks like you might be in the same boat now too."

"I'm through sweating these little boys, D-Square. Seriously. I've got a great paying job, great apartment, new sofa—"

"New sofa. That's important." Deja chuckled as she interrupted my monologue.

"And *finally* a dependable set of wheels. That should be enough."

"Isrie, you forgot the best part."

"I did?"

"Yep," she beamed with glee, as if holding back some great secret.

"What did I forget?"

"That you get to rub on men all day."

"Yeah, and get paid!"

"Legally!" she added. Our laughter drew the attention of other bar patrons, wondering what we were drinking.

"Okay. I'll admit that some of the men I see are better left clothed."

"And what do you say in a situation like that?"

"Hmph. Not a damn thing. You think I'm crazy? I just do my job and get them out of there. I get more women than men as customers anyway. The job doesn't come with a choice. Speaking of jobs . . . you're the one with all those *hard* bodies, Ms. Photographer."

"I'm not even studying them, Isrie. Don't get me wrong. They are *hella* fine, but they're either too vain or they're gay . . . or both. Actually, there are a couple of male models that—"

"Whaaaaat?"

"Nothing. Nothing," she said with a dismissive wave of her hand. "How long do you plan on staying here?"

"Just for one more drink."

"I'll join you for one." She held the single finger up to make sure I got it. "You buyin'?"

"Sure. I dragged you out here tonight, didn't I?"

"Then I'll have one of those pretty things you're drinking."

3

Deja Douglas

I was running late for work on Tuesday morning. Being a self-employed photographer had its advantages in situations like this. I got out of my work what I put into it, though, and this sister wasn't sleepin' on anything.

I'd been fortunate enough to land a photo shoot along Pacific Coast Highway for *Rider Life*, one of the local urban lifestyle magazines. I had already worked with most of the models on jobs around town, so I figured they had put in a good word for me.

This was a hard industry for a woman to break into, and being a black woman had cut my chances in half. I wasn't about to stop, though. As a little girl growing up in Compton, I knew I enjoyed anything having to do with pictures; it was just the other side of the camera that I preferred. I was always on the chubby side and never the most popular, so while my girlfriends at Centennial High were getting pregnant or hooking up with gangbangers and whatnot, I got into things like the high school yearbook. My interest in pictures carried me through to photography school even though my grandma wanted me to attend junior college. I interned with a few of the local newspapers before branching out on my own. To earn a buck, I now split my time between photo shoots for various magazines and businesses and taking family portraits from my small office I had converted to a studio.

The money wasn't always consistent and some months were downright scary, but this was the path I chose. Hell, I really wanted to share a place with my girl Isrie, but had to pass. I never told her about my two near-evictions while she was still staying in the Heights.

"Need a hand?" I heard from behind me as I unloaded my equipment from the back of my old white van. It was my bronze Adonis and favorite subject, Ivan Dempsey. He was clad in some white linen drawstring trunks and his bare chest was glistening in the morning sun.

"Here. You can carry this tripod. I'll get the box," I replied as our eyes met, and I felt that feeling of cold iced tea on a hot day that often came in his presence. I was sure Ivan had something to do with my getting this job. Ivan was six foot five inches of tight ass, chiseled abs, broad shoulders, and Tyson Beckford eyes that dared any woman to get lost in them. One day at my studio, I'd caught a glimpse of my boy's magic wand while he was changing, and it is right on time I tell you. Ivan was definitely not the shy one, and he had no reason to be with all these beautiful women pumping him up. With all that said, Ivan still managed to keep a humble quality about him, which I admired maybe more than his physical attributes.

The other models—an espresso-drinking social climber named Lauren, a professional catalogue model named Ron, and this sister, Sophia, who belonged on *Baywatch*—were standing around wondering what Ivan was doing helping the crew. They were wearing those fake smiles that told you they liked you but still had better things to do than wait around for an overweight photographer all morning.

"Thanks for landing me this gig," I said as the two of us approached the shoot site. One of the assistants hired by *Rider Life* had already set up the dressing room tent and I could hear the handlers yapping it up inside.

"How do you know I'm responsible, Deja?"

"C'mon now, Ivan. *Look* at them. You think any of those three really want me here, let alone enough to have requested me? Especially big forehead Sophia," I whispered as I smiled and didn't break a step.

"Okay. You got me. You do good work, girl. You need to ease up on Sophia, though."

"Why? 'Cause you're sleeping with her?" My feet formed a trail in the sand as I trudged steadily ahead. "I can't help it if you have a taste for big foreheads."

"See, you need to stop that, girl. I defend her just like I defend you when people say you're always late to your shoots."

"That's why I love you, babe. You always give it to me straight. I wouldn't be late so much if I had dependable transportation. Now, are you going to be a doll and help my late ass set this stuff up?"

"I will," he said while extending the legs on my tripod and planting them in the sand near the rocks, "but you're going to have to pay me."

"With what? You're the one making all the money these days. I can only give you love and free passport photos."

"Or you can go out with me."

"*On a date*? Yeah, Ivan. Whatever," I replied as I pinched him on the cheek. "Boy, you need to stop. You're used to them sticks like Sophia over there. I'm not giving up the nana, and if I did I might wind up breakin' your pretty-boy ass in half with what I got."

"I'm serious," he replied with a chuckle. "You always say no. Let me take you out. Once."

"No. Go away, boy. I've got everything under control now. Go get ready with your *friends*."

Ivan shrugged his shoulders, giving up. I adjusted the settings on my Olympus, smiling as I followed him through the lens as he entered the tent with the other models.

4

Isrie

As I sped east on the San Bernardino Freeway Saturday morning, Tamia's melodies played loudly through the speakers in my burgundy Scion. It was getting a little hot as the sun came over the mountains, so I closed the sunroof and turned up the air conditioner. I had some time off from the spa this weekend, so that sixty-mile trip out to San Bernardino to see my parents was a nice break from the usual hustle and bustle of my life these days.

Let's get things straight. I was a true daddy's girl in every sense of the term, but it was my mother that I shared that special bond with. I think she saw a lot of herself in me and in some of the choices I had made in my life. That still didn't stop her and my dad from pushing for me to be an *honest woman*. Funny, I always thought that being true to me was being an honest woman, but my cousin who married and moved to Arizona to start a family had ruined it for me. We were living in the twenty-first century, but to some it could've been the nineteenth century.

My parents had moved into their new home on Scotch Pine Way, just off Kendall Drive, about a year ago. The single-story, four-bedroom home was my dad's surprise to my mom for her years of patience and support. My dad was semiretired, but still turned out his mystery novels that I never read. My mom did some volunteer work at Loma Linda Medical Center to keep herself active when her knee wasn't bothering her. The two of them had been happily married for forty years and still carried on like newlyweds, which really made me wish they'd calm down sometimes. I didn't need a little brother or sister popping up unexpectedly at my age.

When I drove up the driveway to the Spanish-style home with ceramic roof shingles, my mom's car was in the driveway and the garage door was up. My dad must have just cut the little patch of grass he called a lawn as I saw the recently cleaned lawn mower resting where my mom's car would normally be. I decided to walk in through the garage since it was already open, laughing to myself as I strolled around the still-warm lawn mower. It was a little strange coming home to this house, since all I had ever known was our more modest home back in Bellflower, but my parents had been nice enough to keep a room for me here.

"Hey, baby girl!" my dad said in surprise as he opened the door to the garage and bumped into me. My dad, Harold, was wearing his favorite pair of blue jeans and his old FREE O.J. T-shirt. He may have been in a new neighborhood and new town, but he would always be the same old Harold Walker. The world would change before he did. Believe that.

"Hi, Dad," I responded as I gave him a big hug in the doorway and kissed him on his graying scraggly beard. My dad reminded me of that old basketball player Bill Russell, even though my dad was a hell of a lot shorter.

"Ella!" my dad shouted into the house with his hoarse voice, "Isrie's here!"

"How's the book coming along, Dad?"

"Absolutely marvelous, girl. Mosley ain't got shit on me," he replied with a hearty laugh. "Your mother's in there somewhere. Go on in. I gotta turn on the sprinklers. You might get some water on your little car. Want me to move it for you?"

"Nah. It's dirty anyway."

I left my dad to his yard work and entered the kitchen just past the laundry room. I still didn't see my mom, but heard the sound of paper rustling in the living room.

"Mom!"

"Isrie, baby! How you doin'?" my mom replied from the earth-tone sectional she was sitting on. Her drugstore reading glasses rested on the end of her little nose, and she had the monthly bills sprawled out in a pattern that made sense only to her.

"Fine, Mom. I missed y'all."

"Well, you know you welcome here anytime, baby. Come give me a hug."

I eagerly complied with my mom's request and ran around the sofa and into her arms.

"I still wish y'all hadn't moved so far away from the city."

"Baby, San Bernardino *is* a city."

"Mom, you know what I mean. Save the tourist commercial for someone else."

Ella laughed. "I know, I know. Your father couldn't pass up a deal like this out here. Besides, he likes the atmosphere for his novels."

"What atmosphere? Coyotes, desert, and brush fires?"

"Behave, Isrie June. We get warnings when the brush fires get bad. You're not too old for me to put you across my knee, y'know."

"Just kidding. How's his book coming along?"

"You know your father don't tell me a thing. He just locks himself in that den and chugs away. You're his baby girl, so I'm sure he'd tell you. He was in there this morning, but stopped to cut the grass. He's probably out there now on the side of the house. Tryin' to smoke a cigarette on the DL. *Like I don't know,*" she huffed.

"You know your husband too well, Mom."

"You stayin' the weekend, baby girl?" my mom asked as she held my face in her weathered hands and tried to read my mind.

"I don't know. I don't have any pressing business in the city."

"No date with Ryan?" My mom hated the way I met Ryan and *really* hated what he did for a living, but once she and my dad met him, they came to like him. My mom also thought he was a cutie, to boot.

"Umm. That whole thing is over with."

"Huh? I *know* you didn't run that boy off. Isrie . . . talk to me."

"Yeah. It's over. He wasn't the one." I wisely chose to spare her the details.

"Girl, you're not getting any younger the last time I checked."

"Mom!"

"Relax, relax, baby. I'm sorry. I just don't want you out there desperate in your later years, that's all."

"Mom, you know you raised your daughter better than that. I've still got many good years ahead of me," I replied with a subtle cringe at my mother's suggestion. I'll admit I was fearful of doing the singles thing at forty. I saw how happy my parents were together and that set the standard for me. The problem with such a standard was that it made it hard for any man ever to measure up. At least, that's what I told myself was the problem.

5

Deja

I had been up till two in the a.m. finishing some family portrait packets. The last thing I wanted to hear was a knock at my door five hours later. I tried to ignore the continuing knocks in the hopes that whoever it was would realize they had the wrong apartment and move the fuck on.

"Shit," I muttered to myself from under my comforter. I had so planned on sleeping in this Saturday morning. Isrie was visiting her parents in San Bernardino, so I knew it wasn't her. Maybe it was Ivan wearing nothing but a loincloth and carrying roses. Hell, a sister could wish, but that kind of wish could be dangerous. I held off a few seconds longer as the knocking kept up, constant and steady, before I gave up and hauled my ass out of bed.

"Who is it?" I asked with a snarl of disgust mixed with weariness. I was too tired to look through the peephole and hoped that I would recognize the voice on the other end.

"Open the door, girl." It was a familiar voice, but one I didn't expect to hear. I sighed and adjusted my black robe before turning the latch.

"Good morning to you too, Theron," I said as I swung the door wide open. My hardheaded baby brother had showed up from out of the blue, just as he had through most of my adult life. It had been almost three years since I had last seen him before this go-round. He had the same droopy eyes but he'd put a few pounds of muscle on his tall, lanky frame, and the walk was different too—more upright and with more confidence in his stride.

"New clothes? Just tell me you're not in trouble again. Okay, little brother?" Theron was taller than me by about six inches, but he would always be my little brother.

"Nah, girl. No trouble. I'm just stoppin' by to visit. You not happy to see a nigga?"

"Yes . . . I am happy, Theron. You just caught me off guard. Don't you ever call first? I was sleeping."

"You sure you ain't got a man with you in that room back there? Wearin' that black silk shit 'n all," he mumbled, which was accompanied by a chuckle. I didn't realize how much I had missed the gruff little laugh that was my brother's signature.

"No, I don't have a man in my room. I just like to wear sexy stuff when I sleep. A sister can't feel good about herself?"

"I guess. You got something to eat?"

"*Well, hello to you too*, bruh. Can I at least get a hug?"

"I'm sorry, sis. C'mere."

I was sleepy as all hell, but fixed Theron some bacon and eggs, which he devoured while talking with his mouth open. I *hated* when he did that. My brother shocked me when he told me he had joined the Army. That explained his being all "swolled up" now and his change in demeanor.

Theron was never one to stay put for long, so when he first disappeared at seventeen, it came as no surprise to me or our grandma, who raised us. It was right after he got his GED and I had completed photography school. He wound up living with a thirty-year-old woman and her two children in Ohio that time. That lasted for a year before Theron showed up again, but only for a couple of months. I think his disappearance that time had something to do with the law or somebody he owed money to . . . or both. I never asked him when he next resurfaced, knocking at my door just like today.

"So, fill me in on the haps. Where'd you go? What'd you see? How long are you staying? Got any babies?"

"Okay, okay! Slow down, girl. I'll be around a while, so I'll answer all your questions in due time. I'm on leave right now and wanna wind down."

"Leave? Some of y'all still get that with what's going on?" Seeing so many of our soldiers killed daily in Iraq because of Dubya's recklessness made me fearful of my brother's decision. I bit my tongue, though, because I was proud of him for doing something positive for a change.

He hesitated, then removed his cap. His prized braids were gone, replaced with a bald scalp. "Yeah, believe it or not. Which brings me to my question. . . . Can I crash here?"

"What do you think, little brother? Where's your stuff at?"

"Heh," he chuckled. "Right outside your door."

"Figures. I think you're familiar with the sofa. Go get your shit."

"Thanks, Deja," Theron said as he popped up to attention and marched toward the front door. I was yawning and stretching while thinking about resuming my sleep when my phone rang. Damn. Was everybody up this morning?

"Hellooo?" I answered in my fake cheery business manner.

"Hi, Deja."

"Oh. So you want to call me instead of showing up. What happened to the loincloth and roses?"

"Huh?"

"Nothing. I'm just acting crazy. What do you want, Ivan?"

"I just wanted to see how you're doing."

"Fine. Sleepy, but fine. Why is everybody awake? Tell me, please."

"Umm. Did I catch you at a bad time?"

"No. I'm sorry, dear. I was up late working."

"Oh. That's why you never called me."

"*I was supposed to call you?*"

"Yeah. About our date."

"Boy, please. I told you to kill that noise."

"I'm serious, Deja. Just one little date."

"You don't quit, do you?"

"You want me to beg?"

"Why, boy? *Why?*" Theron was dragging his suitcase and duffel bag in the door. I intentionally lowered my voice and turned away from him. My brother had a habit of staring in your mouth when you were on the phone, and now was not the time.

"I'm about to start begging. I can't believe you're going to make me beg."

"Stop it, Ivan."

"Five."

"Stop it!"

"Four."

"You are crazy."

"Three."

"I'm about to hang up on you, boy."

"Two."

"Ivan, stop! I'm serious."

"One."

"Okay! Okay! I'll go out on the damn date with you. Now I gotta go. I've got company and you're embarrassing me," I whispered harshly over the line at Ivan's pretty ass.

"Alright. Next weekend?"

"Yeah. Sure. Bye."

"Bye, Deja."

I hung up the phone and set it on the table. I shook my head and laughed to myself. I gave Ivan a hard time, but I did like the attention he gave me. I hadn't had any man give me what I needed in a long time, let alone a gorgeous one like Ivan. I still wondered what his angle was, but he hadn't done anything to betray my trust yet. He still had his women, but nothing serious. Besides, this was only going to be a single date—and a non-nookie one at that.

When I turned around I realized that Theron was standing there the whole time. His bags were neatly arranged in the far corner of my living room and he was laughing.

"Aww, sookie-sookie now! That was your man, Deja?"

"No. Just a friend. I don't have a man."

"Sounds like somebody *wants* to be your man, though. At least from what I heard on this end. So, what's up with this nigga? He *is* a black man, right?"

"Yes, Theron. He's a *brother* . . . and we're just friends."

"Uh huh. I need to check out this fool. Make sure he's got good intentions 'n all. *Knowhutimsayin?*"

"Please. You've got your life all together in the Army and all of a sudden you want to come back and run *my* life? You just take care of yourself, bruh. I've got this under control."

"Damn. This is me backing off right now, sis. So what else do you feel like doing besides talking about your boyfriend?"

"Theron, I just want to go back to bed."

6

Isrie

Sunday morning, I awakened in my old bed. Old bed, different room. It didn't have that musty smell I'd grown accustomed to as a little girl back during poorer times in our old house, but it was my bed and all was well with the world. Most of my old furniture was here too, untouched by time, except for my Jodeci and Tupac posters I'd had since Mayfair High. I'm sure my dad was the one to throw those out with the trash upon their move. Nothing but a bunch of thugs, he used to say. He would've stroked out knowing I'd tried mailing my panties to those "thugs" back then.

My mom and I had stayed up most of the night in the living room while my dad was inspired in his den and cranking out pages on his computer. We played some checkers and reminisced about the old hood and my childhood years for the first couple of hours. The last few hours consisted of my mom grilling me about what happened with Ryan and my *manless* future while she brushed my hair for me.

"Girl, don't ever cut your hair," she said, brushing with the same soft, gentle strokes I remembered. "I remember you were a little bald-headed girl when you were born. The men must love seeing this when you walk into a room."

"Mom, I don't think it matters how long my hair is. They've got a lot of women with short hairstyles who are doing just fine. Look at Halle Berry."

"*What about her?* She without a man now. And even she

added some hair to her head. Hmph. I saw her on *Entertainment Tonight* lookin' like she grew a mane overnight."

"Whatever, Mom," I mumbled. "To tell you the truth, I've been seriously thinking about cutting this. Just for a new look, y'know?" My mom froze in the middle of her brushing. She must have been about to faint or burst a blood vessel.

"I know I can't tell you what to do, but I think you'd be making a mistake. I shouldn't have said that because you'll probably go ahead and do it now just to spite me."

"Mom, I'm older now. I think I've outgrown that stage." *Even though the thing with Ryan and that dating show was kinda like that.* "I just feel like a change, that's all."

Those words from last night resonated through my head as I brushed my teeth in front of the bathroom mirror. I gave a quick thought about where I was going in life and in general, then spit.

I hadn't spent much time with my dad this weekend and I was already preparing to head back to LA. Surprisingly, he was out of his self-imposed exile in his den this morning. He and my mom were in the kitchen and I could hear him whispering sweet nothings in her ear as she giggled.

"*A-hem,*" I said as I entered the room. "Why don't y'all get a room?"

"We already got one, girl," my dad answered without taking his eyes off his bride. "We're just waiting for you to leave."

"Aww! Trying to run your dear, sweet daughter off, huh? You don't love me anymore, Daddy?"

"You know I do, puddin'. You still need to keep out of grown folks' business, though."

"*And if I don't, old man?*"

"Then I guess I'll have to kick your young ass out of my damn house," he answered laughingly as he raised his hand up in a mock gesture.

My dad and I joked around like this, but it was never serious. He had busted his hump to give his family a better life, and his love was unquestionable.

"You want breakfast before you leave, baby?" my mom asked as she separated herself from my dad's grasp and adjusted her clothes. Ella's small frame was adorned with her floral house-coat this morning. I detected the embarrassed blush on her face beneath the head full of green plastic rollers that was covered in a scarf.

"Sure, Mom. Let me put my stuff in the car first." My dad cut a wink at my mom on that, but I didn't know why.

I walked outside through the front door to find my car clean and sparkling. Knowing my dad, it probably had a full tank of gas.

"You like?" he asked as he strolled out behind me with my mother in tow. He had his chest poked out in pride at his hand-iwork.

"Dad, you shouldn't have," I said as I set my stuff down in the walkway and gave him a kiss on the cheek. "When did you have time to do this?"

"I took a break from my writing this morning. I knew you weren't going to clean it, so I did it while you were sleeping."

"You spoil me too much."

"Well, somebody has to. That boy Ryan must not be doing his job. Leaving a new car dirty like that is a sin."

"Um . . . me and Ryan aren't together anymore, Dad," I said while looking at my mother. I assumed she had filled him in al-ready, but obviously she hadn't.

"Oh," my dad said with a trace of disappointment. "Since when?"

"Last weekend."

My dad sighed and looked toward the Mrs., who simply shrugged her shoulders. In an effort to drop the subject, I inten-tionally didn't say anything as I loaded my stuff into the back of my Scion. I saw my dad whispering under his breath to my mom, though. I could tell breakfast was going to be an uncom-fortable experience, as I, the grown woman, was going to be made to feel like a thirteen-year-old. No matter what kind of success I was having in all other endeavors, it was always the state of my relationships or lack thereof that brought the drama. Why couldn't I be a nun?

Fast-forward several hours to Sunday afternoon. I'm away from San Bernardino, back on my turf with a full tank of gas, and heading to my apartment. I'm playing the prank call through my head, which is stinging again after my dad's inquisition about Ryan. My back's also cramping from the drive, and worst of all, I have to go to the bathroom—bad combination. What made the combination worse was that I was speeding through an intersection just then. Oh, by the way—did I mention my light was red?

When I realized my light was red, it was too late. I was already in the middle of the intersection. I saw the silver BMW coming from my right and tried speeding up to clear it. No luck. The squealing of brakes announced the meeting of a fifty-thousand-dollar car with the back of my ride.

The hit knocked me sideways and sent my car into a spin. I was lucky my air bag didn't pop out and hit me in the face. As I was bouncing around, all I could think of was my coworker whose face looked like a busted sack of potatoes after an air bag pop.

My world stopped spinning and I pulled my heart back down from out of my throat. I wasn't dead because I could hear the sound of loud music from a truck that went around me before disappearing down Olympic Boulevard. As it passed, I heard one of the surfer punks inside yelling, "Aww! That's fucked up!" as they laughed and stared at my stupid ass. At least my car was still in one piece. I was now facing the direction I had just come from and struggling to undo my seat belt when a well-manicured hand reached in and touched me on my shoulder.

"Are you okay, miss?"

"*Daaamn*," I replied in the most inappropriate manner. The brother was hittin'! Nice haircut, good edge, goatee not too hairy, over six feet, smooth brown skin . . . Wait a minute! This was the guy in the BMW. Shit.

"Huh?" he replied with a wrinkled brow at my remark.

"Umm. I meant, 'Damn, my head hurts.' "

"Do you need me to call an ambulance?" he asked while opening my car door to assist me. Such a gentleman. My mom would approve.

"No. I'll be okay. Is *that* your car?" I asked with a point of my finger and an apologetic look on my face. It looked like he had only a busted headlight and scuffed bumper, but on his car was probably equivalent to two months of my salary.

"Yes. What were you thinking?" He was finally showing the signs of anger that I would have expected in this situation. It wasn't rage, but rather a controlled burn that I could see in his brown eyes.

"I dunno. Hell, I wasn't thinking. Look, I'm sooo sorry."

"Alright," he said while sizing me up with an intense gaze. "I'm going to get my insurance information from my car. I'll try to call the police again too. My phone hit my windshield and is acting funny now."

I should have been concentrating on getting my paperwork out of my car, but I was too busy watching him walk to his. He wore a dark blue dress shirt with black pants. A platinum chain dangled on his wrist as he held the cell phone at his side. He had one of those proud walks that said he was used to having women eye him. Most importantly, he was *hella fine*, as Deja would say. I continued keeping my eye on the new man in my life while fishing for my paperwork in the glove box.

I stood up and began walking over to the stranger. He was standing next to the open door of his car, still fumbling with his phone. His left hand was draped over the door and I looked for the tan line where a wedding ring would have been. All clear, I thought. I thought I caught a hint of a tan line, but wasn't sure if it was my imagination.

"Here's my insurance information—"

"Michael. My name's Michael. And you are . . . *Isrie*?" He had stopped dialing on his phone and was trading looks between my insurance card and me. He let out a light laugh before extending his hand.

"Yeah, that's my name," I answered in a low voice with false modesty. I tried to run my hair back over my right ear in a vain attempt to look sexy all of a sudden. Michael had a firm grip and his hands were lightly callused. Good. That showed he wasn't just eye candy.

"Pleased to meet you, Isrie. Um . . . can I tell you something?"

"Certainly. What?"

"This card is expired." He then slowly turned my insurance card into view to further convince me.

"No," I said in a low tone as my mouth dropped.

"Yes," he said, thrusting the card closer to my face. I was already convinced. I had fucked up. I'd been so busy, I had forgotten to renew my insurance. I had switched agencies six months ago to save money, but I didn't remember their sending me a bill. Upon further thought, it came to me. I had forgotten to send them a change of address card and my mail was no longer being forwarded.

"Look, Michael . . . I am so sorry." I had said that a lot already, but I couldn't think of anything else to say.

"Is that all you can say?" he said with a laugh that was more one of disgust.

"See . . . I moved and . . . and . . . You don't want to hear this, do you?"

"No," he answered with a chuckle. "Not really."

"I am going to be in so much trouble when the police get here. Shit."

He started dialing again, as if intentionally ignoring me, then suddenly stopped. He then handed me my worthless insurance card back, and smiled.

"Go."

"Huh?"

"Go. I'm about to finish dialing."

"Is this some kind of joke?"

"Your car's driveable, right?"

"Yeah, but—"

"Get out of here. My damage isn't that bad. I'll say it was a hit-and-run, and that I can't identify the car."

"A-are you sure?"

"Looks like you've got a lot of stuff on your mind. I don't want to give a pretty lady like you any more problems." True. I was a pretty lady, but it still was a cheesy line. Michael's good looks made the line very acceptable, though.

"Okay. Look, I owe you for this. Big-time."

"No. You don't, Isrie." His saying my name gave me chills.

I wanted to hug him, but that would have been very inappropriate. I had to think of something. I noticed Michael rubbing the back of his neck, so I ran back to my car, aching head and all, and dug in my glove compartment.

"Here," I said as I shoved my business card into Michael's face.

"Your business card?"

"Yep. I'm a massage therapist."

"I see. Not one of those *massage parlors*, huh?" he said with a half laugh.

"No," I shouted emphatically as I swatted playfully at his arm. "It's legit. A *spa*."

"I told you don't worry about it. I'm not going to call you for any money or anything."

"The card is for you to get a complimentary massage. Uh, that means free."

He laughed.

"It's the least I could do. I know you have to be sore, because my head is still ringing." I ran a light; now I was running game. Aww, don't you just love it?

"Alright. I accept, Isrie." Again those chills.

"I'm still sorry about what happened."

"Okay. I accept your apology, but you better go. Unless you want to lose your driver's license for a year." If I did, would you give me a *ride*?

I kept my dirty thought to myself and simply smiled. I gave Michael one final thank-you before turning my car around and jetting away. For all I knew, Michael might still turn me in to the police. I decided against telling my parents about this. My apartment was only a few blocks away and I was going straight there. If this had happened on a weekday, the police would have been in the area already and I would have been straight busted. First thing Monday, I was getting insurance on my car again—if I wasn't sitting in jail.

7

Deja

I still hadn't gotten a chance to hang with my brother since his surprise return. Sunday I had some work to do at the studio. On Monday, I didn't get back until late. Both times, he was already asleep when I got home, so I didn't disturb him. Theron still hadn't told me where he was stationed or anything about what he'd been up to for the past few years. If I wasn't careful, he was going to up and disappear in his normal manner before I knew it.

I busted ass and wrapped up things early Tuesday, planning on spending some overdue quality time with him. I was going to call Theron to let him know, but decided to surprise him instead. As I pulled into my parking spot, my thoughts were split between catching up with Theron and my upcoming "date" with Ivan this weekend, which still had me nervous . . . and somewhat geeked.

Before I got to the top of the stairs, I heard my stereo blaring. Some things about Theron would never change. He was playing my Jagged Edge CD, my favorite. Rather than fumbling for house keys in my overfilled black bag, I just decided to knock for Theron.

No answer. I knocked a little harder the second time and waited for about a minute. I looked at my watch. It was noon. It wouldn't come as a surprise to me for Theron to have been asleep on the couch, even with the music turned up. I set my bag

down and found my house keys resting at the bottom, beneath
a wrinkled program guide from a fashion show I had attended
last month. I *really* needed to clean this bag out.

"Theron?" I called out after closing my front door, expecting to
hear an answer. The ass had jetted and left my stereo on. Probably
running the streets, I thought. Regrets about not calling him crept
in as I wondered if he'd hooked up with trouble from the old days.
Theron could be loyal to a fault when it came to his boys.

I lowered the volume on my stereo as the track "Walked
Outta Heaven" was coming on. I was thirsty, but also hot and
sweaty, so I decided to handle the latter and headed to my bedroom. Because of the type of person I was and type of job I held,
I always wore interesting and edgy clothes, but it sometimes felt
good just to slip into a T-shirt and shorts. One day, I would have
my weight under control and would wear *less* in public. It just
wasn't going to be today. I knew I wasn't ugly, but the echoes of
"chubby," "fat ass," and "big girl" lingered from childhood. I always took that hurt and flipped it into laughter in front of
everyone. "Never let 'em get you down, baby," my grandma
used to say.

I smiled to myself as I turned the knob to my bedroom door.
Thoughts of my grandma were always refreshing and uplifting.
Those thoughts went by the wayside as I walked in.

"What the fuck?"

The naked sister with brown braids and big tits screamed at
the sound of my voice. I couldn't believe this shit. Theron was
humping this chickenhead doggy style . . . on *my* water bed.

"Get the fuck out!" I shouted at the top of my lungs. She was
having trouble balancing herself on my mattress while attempt-
ing to remove herself from Theron. The girl, probably in her
early twenties, looked toward Theron for advice while fumbling
for her clothes on the floor. Rather than looking at her, he instead
turned to look back at me like a fox caught in the henhouse.
Things were still going too slow. On my bed. No, no, no. If it
hadn't been so long since last seeing him and if he had some-

where else to stay, I would have thrown his ass out with the trick.

"Now!" I shouted to speed up the girl's departure. She hadn't finished putting her clothes on, but instead grabbed her shoes and what was left and scurried past me.

"I'll call you," Theron halfheartedly called out to her just before my front door slammed shut. I don't think she heard him. He had put his little brown Army drawers back on and was scratching his head.

"Boy, can you be any more rude?"

"Sorry."

"*Sorry?* Nigga, that's my bed you were . . . were spewing all over! You're gonna clean this shit up. Now!"

"You're home early" was his odd response to my screamfest.

"Yeah. I came home to spend some time with you, bro. This is what you've been doing while I've been working, huh?"

He chuckled. "No. Just today. She works at Costco. Need anything from there?" Theron had begun pulling the sheets off my bed and was gathering them up in a ball.

"That shit ain't funny. Why couldn't you do this shit somewhere else?"

"I said I'm sorry. Hell. She said she never done it in a water bed before. I was gonna change your sheets anyway."

"Whatever. I just hope your ass used a condom."

"You think I'm stupid? See?" He held up his evidence.

"Boy, I don't want to see that! You're sick."

"Yeah, yeah. Still feel like hanging, sis?"

"Finish cleaning my room and we'll see."

"You know I love you, sis."

"Here," I said while picking up Theron's plastic-coated chain and tags that were on the floor at my feet. "Dog tags for a dog."

"Roof! Roof!"

8

Isrie

Earlier in the week, I expected to hear from either the LAPD or Michael. I would have preferred a call from the luscious chocolate man in the Beamer, but neither came. I'd driven around town paranoid, limiting my trips to work and back, until getting some insurance again. When the lady asked if my car had been in any accidents, of course I lied and said a polite no. She was too lazy to get up from her desk to check, but believed me since I batted my eyes and paid out the ass.

Wednesday morning I was wearing the usual work attire—blue and white linens—and my hair was down. I had just finished a sixty-minute massage session and was looking at my hair in the mirror, still thinking about how it would look short.

"Isrie, the eleven fifteen is here. Mr. Ross," came over the intercom from the front desk.

"I'll be right down," I replied into the speaker. I released the strands I'd scrunched in back of my head, letting my hair fall back into place, and donned a pair of eyeglasses. I normally didn't wear them, but they helped change my features. Ever since that darn TV show, I'd had a few wannabe macks trying to run game up in here.

My appointment was seated in the lobby of the spa, entertaining himself with a copy of *Cosmopolitan* I knew he didn't want to read. He was here for a thirty-minute deep-tissue massage and had requested me. I assumed he was a return customer. Return customers were what could make you or break you in this business.

"Mr. Ross?"

"Yes." He lowered the magazine from his face and I blinked with recognition.

"Hi. I'm your massage therapist, Isrie," I said in my cordial professional voice. "You requested me?"

"Yes, I did," he replied as he set the magazine down and stood up to greet me. "You've come highly recommended."

"A thirty-minute deep-tissue?" I always confirmed what the customer requested, and paid for.

"That's it," he responded with a smile and nod. Even though this spa was more on the high end, we still got a few cheapskates that would try to get extra time for free.

"Okay. Right this way, sir."

I led Mr. Ross behind the walled art deco facade and up the glass-lined stairs to the massage booths. We called them booths, but they were actually rooms. At least here they were. The Calming Images Spa on Wilshire always kept a full schedule of clientele, from wannabe stars to the Hollywood A-list. We were a full-service spa, complete with saunas, whirlpool, shiatsu, and some serious wax jobs. Oh. Did I tell you our hot-rock treatment was to die for?

"Neck and back?" I asked while making sure everything was in place on the table. I lit a few candles, then lowered the lights to set a relaxing mood.

"That's it," he said with that same smile and a wink for added measure.

"Okay. Well, I'll step out to let you change. Just make yourself comfortable and I'll be back."

"Alright. Can I ask you something before you leave?"

"Sure."

"Do you always wear those glasses, Isrie?"

"No, I don't, Michael."

"Maybe you should have worn them Sunday."

"Cheap shot. You know I already feel bad about that. You don't want me screwing up your back too. Now get undressed and I *might* be back."

Of course, I was certainly coming back.

I had barely closed the door when my emotions erupted. With a whoosh of air, I released the breath and the straight face I'd been holding. I wrung my hands and shook my arms to remove the remaining jitters. "He's here. Damn. He's here," I said to myself with a pleased grin. I looked at my watch. Another few minutes, I'd give him . . . and myself.

Michael was on the table and resting comfortably on his back when I returned. His eyes were shut and the heated blanket covered him to his waist. I lightly traced my fingers across his thigh, more interested in the slight bulge in the middle of the blanket.

"You're not asleep yet, are you?"

"No. Just resting my eyes, Isrie." I was the one dressed, yet felt those chills. "The view just got better, so I guess I can open them again."

"Flatterer."

"Hey. Just speaking the truth. Remember, you're the one who could screw up my back. I know better than to piss you off."

"Well, thank you, I guess. How have you been?"

"Sore. Extremely sore. I got my car fixed, though. Picked it up this morning. How about you?"

"I know you're tired of hearing me say this, but I am so sorry. Did you have to go to the hospital?"

"No. I've felt worse before. My neck's sore but getting better."

"Well, I'm glad you came by for your complimentary massage today. I'll be sure to go easy on you. Now close your eyes and let me make it up to you."

I put on the sounds of waves crashing on a faraway beach and had Michael inhale my custom-made aromatherapy to relax him. I never let my personal life or feelings flow into my business, but I was enjoying the thought of running my oiled hands all over his body. I grasped his forearm and worked toward his hand, being certain to check again for a sign of wedded bliss. I nodded to myself and smiled as I began doing my thang.

"*Oooh*. Damn, that feels good," he said at the first bit of pressure applied to the base of his skull.

"You should have come in sooner, then."

"Can I let you in on a secret?"

"Shoot," I replied as I walked my fingers across the muscle tissue that made up his neck and shoulders. Between his shoulder blades, my fingers slowed at the long scar in the middle of his back, as if wanting to commit it to memory. I wanted to know more about this man.

"I came here yesterday."

"Huh?" He broke my concentration on that one.

"Yeah. I came by yesterday . . . for my massage. I didn't make an appointment and you were with somebody."

"Oh?"

"Uh huh. This woman, Kendra, offered to take me."

"*I'll bet she did.*"

"What did you say?"

"Nothing. Relax. Your muscles are all tensed up."

"That's what she said yesterday."

"Kendra was right. Now turn over facedown and stop talking."

"Y'know, in prison that phrase wouldn't sound too comforting."

"Shush."

I really wanted Michael Ross to be quiet to give me time to think. He had showed up at my job twice in two days—and was paying for this visit. I still wanted to keep this on a professional level, so I tried to ignore the obvious—there was chemistry here. Besides, I had just dumped an asshole last week. I didn't need to rush headlong into the house without checking to make sure it wasn't on fire, or already occupied. Ryan had taught me that.

Michael was silent through the rest of his session. I loved a man who followed directions. I could actually see the scar now and wanted to ask about it. Time was up, though.

"Hey," I whispered in his ear seductively. "I'm going to leave you now. Take as long as you want to get dressed."

"You can stay, y'know." He took a deep breath, then looked at me.

I shook my head, but smiled at his suggestion. "This is my job, y'know."

Michael put clothes back on that gorgeous body of his, and I led him downstairs after giving him a glass of water to help him detox.

"Do you know who you look like?" he asked, stopping on the stairs.

"No, but I'm sure you're going to tell me."

"That girl in the Kanye West video—Stacey Dash."

"I think I'm taller than her. Don't have those eyes either."

"Yeah. I know that, but you still resemble her."

"It's the hair. I'm thinking about cutting it."

"Don't."

"Excuse me?"

"I mean . . . I like it. Just the way it is."

"You sound like my mom with that noise."

"Then she's a smart woman."

I smacked my lips.

"Well, I guess this is it," he said as we reached the front lobby.

"Yeah," I replied softly, keeping my professional stance, I didn't want my fellow employees knowing my business. "Thanks for bailing me out . . . again."

"Thanks for today. My neck feels much better."

"We aim to please, Mr. Ross." *Get his number,* I thought.

"I guess I'll see you around, Isrie." Goose bumps surfaced again at the way he said my name. This time my nipples hardened too.

"Definitely," I replied. *Get his number.* I ignored the little voice again. If he was interested, he'd ask for mine, I said to myself in a defiant old-school moment.

I watched Michael's white oxford shirt and gray slacks as

they jiggled out the front door. He wasn't one of my usual thugs, but there was an air of mystery that turned me on just the same. I didn't know what he did, where he lived, or if he was involved. The only thing I was certain of was that I wanted to know more.

9

Deja

Needing to talk to my girl, I took off a little early from a job in Huntington Beach. I sped my van north up the Harbor Freeway from the San Diego Freeway, leaving a cloud of smoke behind me. Orange County, as tidy as it was, was a little too mild for my tastes, and frankly I was glad to be gone. I cranked up KJLH on my radio and sang along with Usher to drown out my noisy muffler. I knew I was going to get stung on my next emissions inspection.

Calming Images Spa was my destination, but I didn't have the ends to shell out for a massage today. I was going to be spending enough money for an outfit to wear on my date with Ivan. I really didn't want to go when I initially gave in to him, but now I was looking forward to it. I just needed my girl to co-operate.

Since I was just running in to holler at my girl, I flirted with the valet so he'd let my van stay put. The college student named Armando smiled and gave in to me, but told me to hurry up. He was another CNB, Cutie with a Nice Booty.

Once I confirmed she wasn't in the middle of a session, I had the receptionist at the front desk page Isrie, but I told her not to say who the visitor was. Over the speaker, I heard my girl pause, then perk up before agreeing to come downstairs. I wondered if she knew it was me. I smiled. Her good mood would make what I was going to ask of her a lot easier.

"Oh," Isrie said as she came down the stairs and saw me. She was in the middle of taking her work glasses off and skidded to a halt when she realized I was her visitor.

"Damn. Hello to you too," I said with a laugh and a little bit of hurt in my voice. "Expecting someone else, huh?"

"Nooo. I just thought you were in Long Beach today, that's all."

"Huntington Beach. And I *was* there. What you doin' for lunch?"

"Nada plans, D-Square. What's up?"

"Girl, I'm starvin' and I need to have a little talk with you."

"Alright, where do you want to go? Mariana's?"

"Nah. We go there too often. That place is getting played out. How about Templeton?"

"Okay. That's close by too. You driving?"

"What? You don't want to take *your* car, Isrie?"

"No. Not today. I need to tell you about that."

"Alright. If you don't mind my junk and the loud noise."

"Girl, please. Let me get my purse."

Armando the valet was just coming inside to tell me to move when the two of us walked out. He had been so nice that I gave him a tip just for letting me park in front. Isrie thought I was crazy and accused me of checking out his ass. She was right.

Templeton was a cafeteria-style diner where you still had to slide your tray along as you told the cook behind the glass what you wanted. It wasn't pretty, but the cook put her foot in whatever she cooked. Translation: Shit was *hella* tight! Most places, I watched what I ate. But here I had to let my hair down and give in to the character of the place. I was more comfortable here than spoiled-ass Isrie. She preferred those chichi high-end places like Mariana's downtown or Heaven, that NFL guy's joint over on North Robertson, but still she took everything in stride. I never had the men pampering me nor the funds myself to hit those places on the regular.

We got lucky and found a parking spot right in front. That made me feel at ease as I had a lot of camera equipment thrown in the back of my ride. I was still smarting from a break-in a few months back.

"Wanna try some of my pork chop?" I asked Isrie while taking a swig of my water with lemon. "It's really good today."

"I'll pass," she replied. She was twirling her baked spaghetti on her fork. She knew I had something on my mind. "What's wrong?"

"Nothing's wrong."

"Oh. When you said you needed to talk to me, I just assumed—"

"You know what they say about assuming." I played with my potatoes before continuing. "Anyway, my brother's in town."

"Theron, right? That's good news! You haven't seen him in a while, huh?"

"Yeah, girl. Showed up at my door Saturday morning. Blew back into town with the wind."

"He's your baby brother, right?"

"Yep. By three years. The boy up and joined the Army."

"Oh? Brave man, the way things are going down. How long is he staying?"

"Tell you the truth, I don't know. He's been tight-lipped about that and I've been so busy this week with work and all. Speaking of that—"

"Uh oh. Here it comes," Isrie said as she cut me off and folded her arms. We know each other too well.

I was about to get down to it when we were interrupted. A fine motherfucker in baggy jeans and a white T-shirt walked over to our table. He had that day-old beard and braids thing going on—rough, rugged, and raw. His eyes were focused on Isrie and I knew what he was gonna say before his lips parted.

"Excuse me. I don't mean to bother y'all, ladies, but don't I know you from somewhere?" he asked while staring Isrie down. There he went. It would have been a tired line, but he was a catch. Besides, he probably saw her on TV that time.

"No. I don't think you do," Isrie said with a smile that was polite but dismissive.

"No. Seriously. Aren't you on TV or something." I held back a snicker as Isrie made eye contact with me.

"Nope. Just moved here. Wouldn't be me. Sorry."

"Well . . . um . . . I'm sorry to have bothered you ladies. Enjoy your lunch."

"You lying cow," I spit out at Isrie once the jilted one had moved out of earshot. "You let *that* get away?"

"Girl, please. I've got other things on my mind."

"Other things? Or other *people*? Details."

"No. There are no details. I wrecked my car."

"What? When?"

"Sunday. Coming home from my parents."

"That's why you didn't want to drive."

"Yep."

"You okay?"

"Yeah. Lucky."

"Whose fault was it? Is the other person alright?"

"I wasn't paying attention. Stupid, stupid, stupid," she said with a slap to her forehead in disgust. "He's a little sore." Isrie split her meatball with her fork and took a bite.

"He? White? Black—oops—*African-American*? Other?"

"He's black. Now what were you getting to before we were interrupted?"

"Ivan asked me out." The rest of my pork chop was getting cold, but I had come mainly to talk anyway.

"The pretty boy? He's been asking you out." A lightbulb came on over Isrie's head. "Wait. Oooh, you accepted!"

"Yeah. He called me at home right when Theron got there. Caught me all sleepy and at a moment of weakness."

"Sounds like you're ready to give in to that weakness, D-Square."

"No nana. Just a little date. I need a small favor, though."

"I know we're friends, but I'm not sleeping with Ivan for you.

No matter how much you pay me, I'm not doing it. So my answer is no."

I flicked some of my water at her. "You done bein' a dumb-ass?"

"I guess."

"Um, I haven't had much time with my brother yet and—"

"And?" There went those arms again, folding tighter than Michael Jackson's ass cheeks on his first day in prison.

"And I was thinking that maybe all four of us could hang Saturday. That is, if you don't have any plans. It would be fun."

"So you want me to babysit your drifter brother? And keep tabs on you and Ivan?"

"No. Just enjoy our company. And my brother ain't no drifter. He's being all he can be now."

"I don't know what I'm getting into, but okay. You ready to bring me back to work?"

"Well, let us be off in my Porsche then. Come."

10

Isrie

By Saturday night, I had gotten over my paranoia of driving my wrecked car. I opened my sunroof to let the night's cool air flood in with the sounds of a city that was gearing up for another wild weekend. As I passed through the intersection responsible for the "big bang," my phone rang. I wished it was Michael and I'd regretted not giving him the digits. I still couldn't believe that he had let me just leave the accident like that. He was nice as they come, but he had to have an ulterior motive. There I went. Looking for excuses to keep from admitting I was attracted to the man. This was too soon after the business with Ryan, and maybe I was just confusing my feelings of gratitude with something else. I snagged my phone and answered just as my voice mail was about to kick on.

"Hello?"

"Going out? I hear noise."

"It's my sunroof. What the fuck do you want, Ryan?"

"Just checking up on my girl."

"I ain't your girl. And that speakerphone shit was childish."

"That wasn't my idea."

"I really don't care. Look, what do you want, nigga?"

"I want to know if you're serious."

"About?"

"About us."

I laughed at the nerve of him. "You are sick. You know that, right?"

"I know you don't mean it. That's why I'm offering you another chance."

"Want to hear my decision?"

"Yeah."

Click.

I set my cell phone to vibrate for the rest of the night as the streetlights sped by.

Deja wasn't sure where we were going tonight, so I decided to wear my black Marc Jacobs blazer and pants with burgundy mules. It was comfortable yet dressy enough for most places that we might wind up. I wore my hair pinned up in back with the ends dangling on both sides.

When I arrived at my old apartment, I parked in my familiar spot next to Mrs. Winfrey's station wagon. Her car alarm still went off at the slightest sound, causing most of the residents to ignore it. Amidst the blaring and honking, I took one last look at my reflection in my car window before taking my gum out and strolling toward Deja's unit.

It was unusually dark around the stairwell to Deja's, which made me slide my hand inside my purse for my mace. It never hurt to be careful around this town. I noticed a shadow overtaking mine and kept looking straight ahead as I walked to play it off. I had only about ten feet to go before I reached the steps. Whoever followed me was a smoker, their tobacco scent giving them away as they got closer. It took all I had not to break into a full sprint. I was placing my foot on the first step when I thought everything was going to be okay. Then I felt it, a man's hand on my left arm . . . and I lost it.

I tried to break free as I darted up the stairs, but the grip tightened. I started slipping and began to lose my balance. I would have used my free hand to steady myself, but it was already pulling the mace out instead. Whoever it was actually held me from falling back. Bad for him. Without looking back, I brought my little can up over my shoulder and unloaded a squirt dead in his face. The man instantly let go and fell down, cursing and yelling as he covered his face. I broke into a full sprint, taking two steps at a time as I headed for Deja's door.

"What's wrong with you, girl?" Deja asked as I ran past her screaming.

"Close the door! Close the door!"

"Okay! Okay! What happened?"

"I—I—this guy. Out there," I gasped as I caught my breath. *"Huh?"*

I pointed to her door just as someone began pounding on it. My eyes grew wider as I pointed once again for emphasis and shook my head for her not to open it.

"Open the fuckin' door!" said the harsh voice outside.

Deja looked toward the door and back at me once more as if in thought. Then she acted.

"No!" I screamed as Deja turned the latch on her door. I moved to stop her, but it was too late.

Without looking to see who it was, Deja let the door swing open. An angry tall brother clad in black and tan Rocawear gear with red eyes and a scowl on his face was still cursing. He appeared to be in his early twenties and didn't look at all like the mugger type. He just stood there staring at me, and my fear slowly turned to embarrassment.

"Isrie, I'd like you to meet my brother, Theron," Deja said with arms folded as she gave me the *stupid-ass* face. "I sent him downstairs to wait for you."

I had been finding myself apologizing a lot lately.

"I can't believe you maced my bruh." Deja was putting the finishing touches on her makeup in her hand mirror. Theron was washing his eyes out in the bathroom, so my girl had to make adjustments. Ivan was on his way over.

"I said I was sorry, girl. He just spooked the hell outta me. I feel bad enough about it."

"Relax. I'm just giving you a hard time. Theron can handle himself. He probably deserved it for something else he'd done in the past."

Deja was looking surprisingly voluptuous for her date. An exotic woodprint dress that hugged her hips and came to rest just above her knees was accentuated with gold bangles and matching sandals. All that was missing were her Chanel sunglasses to complete her star getup.

"Where are we going tonight anyway?" I asked her.

"Yeah, Deja. Where are we going with this pretty boy?" Theron had barged in from Deja's bathroom. His eyes looked much better and he was no longer cursing me out loud or under his breath. He referred to Ivan as pretty boy, but, wait till he actually meets him, I thought. I had seen Ivan at Deja's studio once, and he was definitely a piece of work, even though I knew I shouldn't have been thinking like that. I hoped he wasn't playing head games with her. If he was, he'd have to answer to me.

"To tell you the truth, I'm not quite sure. I left all those details to Ivan," Deja replied to her brother.

"We should just pick up something from Woody's or Marilyn's on the 'Shaw and bring it back here. I've been missin' that shit," Theron said, the craving apparent in his voice. He was obviously referring to Woody's Barbecue on Slausen or Chef Marilyn's over on Crenshaw, a few blocks from us. I used to eat at both places when I lived here. Great food, but I didn't put on this outfit just to sit around the house. Even if I was doing Deja a favor, I still wanted to have *some* fun.

"Theron, we're not hanging around this place tonight," Deja replied while giving me a reassuring glance. "We are all going out and are going to have a good time. Now would you go wait in my living room, please?"

"Whatever, sis." Theron gave me a wink before walking out while dragging his fingertips overhead along the bedroom ceiling.

"I can tell this is going to be a crazy night," I said with a huff as I sat on Deja's bed.

"Oh, girl, just relax. Ivan will be here any minute and we'll be off." Deja finished up her face in the bathroom mirror and applied multiple sprays of Escada to her wrists, neck, chest, and up under her dress. I let out a laugh in response to that.

"Hey, a girl can never be too careful," she replied with a laugh.

"Yeah. Ivan just might fall over and his head accidentally land between your legs."

"Girl, you know we be havin' earthquakes and shit. It could happen."

We joined Theron in the living room and were watching a *Fresh Prince* rerun on TV when Deja's prince charming arrived. I was sitting closest to the door when we heard the knock, but Deja beat me off the sofa. I let her win and chose to observe from my ringside seat. Theron stayed put on the floor in front of the tube. He briefly cut his eyes at his sister's behavior, but then went back to watching Will Smith as if unfazed. He still wanted some takeout.

Ivan greeted Deja with a polite kiss on the cheek, followed by a hug. A single yellow rose was in his hand, which contrasted nicely with the purple jacket he was wearing. Underneath his jacket, he wore all black. Beneath his shirt you could tell his abs and ripples were dying to bust out. Fine man, that boy. It was dark, but Ivan wore eyewear with tinted lenses to match his jacket. *"Coooordinated,"* as John Witherspoon would say.

"Thank you for the rose, Ivan!" Deja gushed as she led him inside. "Let me introduce you to everybody. You've met my best friend in the whole world, Isrie."

"Hello, Isrie. Long time no see. Nice to meet you again," he said in a pleasant manner. I waved from the sofa.

"And this is my brother, Theron," Deja said as she led Ivan by the arm over to Theron, who was still in front the TV.

Theron broke from laughing at Carlton doing his dance with Tom Jones long enough to acknowledge Ivan and eye him up and down before looking back toward the TV. Theron's not-so-

subtle diss put a chill in the air and left Deja fidgeting uncomfortably with her bangles until I decided to move things along.

"Okay, Ivan. What's the big surprise?" I asked while spring-
ing off the sofa. "Where are we off to tonight? Deja told us you
were the man with the plan. I'm starving."

"Well, before I knew we were all going out," he said with a
jab at Deja, "I had made arrangements at Heaven, a little place
owned by my boy Fred Hinton, who plays for the Colts. Is that
okay with y'all?"

"Is that okay? That's perfect! I love their fried green tomatoes," I said.

"Yeah, Ivan. That's one of Isrie's favorite places. You've already won points with my girl if not my silent brother over
there," Deja said with exaggerated disgust.

"Well, that's a start. I made reservations, so we need to get to
Beverly Hills now," Ivan said with a glance at the Jacob watch
on his wrist, which almost blinded me. The scent of his Curve
cologne, cast adrift by the wave of his arm, still hung in the air.
Ivan's flash and polish reminded me a lot of Ryan. I just hoped
his wouldn't tarnish.

"Just let me get my purse and we can be off," Deja said as she
whirled around and ran to her bedroom. Ivan smiled as he
watched her backside jiggle until he saw Theron looking at him.

"So, you a model, huh?" Theron had turned off the television
set and was getting to his feet. He and Ivan were around the
same age, but Theron had about two inches on Ivan. Something
he seemed to enjoy.

"Yeah, man. Something like that. Pleased to meet you." Ivan
extended his hand this time, and to my surprise, Theron behaved.

"Aight," Theron replied as he shook his hand.

"Deja tells me you're in the army."

"Yeah." Short and to the point. Ivan was going to let him get
away with that, but I wasn't.

"What do you do in the Army? What's your MOS?" I asked,
referring to his job.

"What?" Theron replied with pleasant surprise as his face lit up. "Infantry. Eleven bravo. What do *you* know about that?" Theron's chest was poking out.

"Nothing really. I dated this lieutenant once who was in the Army."

"Oh," he said, cooling off again.

"Let's go! Let's go!" Deja yelled as she shuffled out of her bedroom with her tiny bag in hand.

After Deja locked up, the four of us descended into the darkness that had recently been witness to my embarrassing scene with Theron. Ivan led the way with Deja in tow. I chose this time to apologize . . . again.

"Theron, I'm sorry about macing you. Forgive me?"

"Apology accepted. Forget it. I've been hit with stronger shit before. It pissed me off, that's all. It's kinda my fault."

"What do you mean?"

"Deja sent me downstairs to wait for you, because the light's burned out. She didn't want you down here alone in the dark. I was supposed to wait by the steps."

"So what happened?"

"Smoke break. Bad habit I've picked up. I was walking around by the other building when I saw you. I was just rushing to catch up with you so Deja wouldn't be pissed."

"When I turned around and sprayed you," I said, completing his silent thought.

"Yeah." Theron agreed with this raspy chuckle.

Ivan was parked directly across the parking lot from me. The large yellow Hummer H2 screamed out for all to see under the orange moon tonight. They looked nothing alike, but Ivan's toy made me think of a silver BMW . . . and its owner. What was Michael doing at this moment?

"Nice truck, bruh," Theron said as he nodded in approval. "I guess modeling pays."

"Not like that . . . yet. The Hummer's leased. Let's ride."

Deja seated herself; then Ivan closed her door. Looking at the two of them interact, I felt a strange feeling began sinking in. I was starting to climb into the backseat when I stood back up.

"Hey y'all. I'll meet you at Heaven. I'm going to take my car."

"Isrie, are you sure? Something the matter?"

"Yeah. I'm sure, Ivan. I just like driving my own car."

He looked at Deja, then back to me. "Suit yourself."

"Uh, I'm gonna ride with Isrie," Theron said with uncertainty. "If you don't mind the company?"

"Nah. C'mon."

The ride to the restaurant was filled with the obligatory small talk, but Theron still hadn't revealed much about himself. Not that it mattered. I was only doing Deja a favor and had no interest in Theron beyond the standard niceties. He seemed cool enough, though, if not just a tad obnoxious when he wanted to be.

As the valets took care of our cars at Heaven, I looked past the security and other restaurant goers standing around the front entrance to the place. Deja had told me about a wild photo shoot party she had attended here years ago, back when it was a club for goths with their freaky tastes. As diverse as her tastes were, things had gotten a little too weird that night. I was willing to bet that she was thinking about it just then. I didn't have any bad memories to spoil my thoughts of this spot, so I was more than ready to get my grub on.

Compared to the serious ballers I'd been around, it was obvious Ivan was midlevel in this town, but he still commanded respect from the staff. Unfortunately, Ivan's stroke had its limits. He was checking on our reservations when the gentleman in the black shirt three sizes too small looked back at the three of us. Theron was standing around with his hands in his pockets and admiring Derrick Fisher's date as they left in their Range Rover, so he hadn't noticed the frown cast in his direction.

"He can't get in," Ivan sighed as he walked toward us with his arms up in frustration.

"Huh?" Deja said in disbelief.

"What are you talking about, Ivan?"

"Theron. His jeans. The guy just told me. No jeans here. At all."

"I thought you knew the owner," Deja protested.

"I do, but he's not here."

"Shit. That's foul," I responded as my poor stomach growled.

"What's up? Why ain't we goin' inside?" Theron asked as he quit his stargazing and joined in on the conversation.

11

Deja

"I told y'all to go on without me."

"Like I was going to listen to you, bruh. I didn't really want to eat there anyway." Underneath the table, I gave Ivan a tap on his leg to ease his feelings at that remark. Being sneaky, I'd suggested Heaven to him to make Isrie happy, but that was my little secret. Isrie was starving, but still offered to let Ivan and me dine there and take Theron somewhere else. I knew it was hurting my girl to do that, so I passed on her generous offer. I really did want to spend time with my brother. With quick thinking on Ivan's part, we drove over to Harold & Belle's for some Creole food and were lucky to get in. I was content with either place, but Theron was still feeling bad over the whole ordeal.

"I could see if I was wearin' some raggedy jeans, but this is the good shit. *Stuck-up-ass place*," he complained. I knew he was happier with the food here anyway, but had to get that out.

"Hey, don't sweat it, man. I should've checked the dress code," said Ivan as he took a sip of his drink. He probably wanted something stronger seeing all the trouble he was being put through for what was supposed to be a simple date. Under the table, I discreetly opened my legs to allow a little airflow downtown. My dress was form fitting and reminded me why I liked to wear loose clothing.

"So, how long have you and my sister known each other?"

Theron asked Ivan as he leaned back in his seat across the table from us. The hand Isrie had been using to shovel gumbo into her mouth slowed in response to Theron's question.

"It's been a couple of years, hasn't it Deja?" said Ivan.

"Yeah. Back when I was operating that booth on the side at Fox Hills Mall," I said.

Isrie interjected with a laugh, "I remember that! Deja used to hustle photos of couples."

"I wasn't hustling. Just working on start-up capital."

"Okay. I'll cut you some slack there, girl," said Isrie.

"Yeah," Ivan continued, "well, me and one of my coworkers were hanging out and I noticed some of your sister's work. I gave her my card and put her in touch with some people and we've been working together off and on ever since." It was big forehead Sophia that Ivan was referring to, but he chose wisely to leave that out. From what I'd heard, the two of them were still sleeping together, but it never seemed to be more than casual. Besides, this was just a date as friends, I kept telling myself as I basked in sitting beside Ivan and sharing personal space with him. I opened my legs again under the table to cool the rising temperature.

"My sister's legit with this camera stuff, huh?"

"Trust me. She's better than *legit*," Ivan said as his eyes peered my way. Under the table, I felt his finger tip slide up my leg to my knee where he gave it a playful squeeze. Why, oh why. Right at that moment, I desperately wanted his hand to continue farther, but I wasn't going to share that wish with him. He would have to find out on his own, if he was ever lucky enough.

"Maybe you'll let me take some pictures, Deja. Y'know, strut my stuff. Might have a future in it." Theron pulled a piece of fried chicken off the bone and gulped it down.

"I think I can do that," I said in between bites of my catfish. "You could have been coming to work with me this whole time. I just thought you wouldn't be interested. You still never told me how long you're staying."

"Oh, I got a while," my brother replied with a wink.

"Had a lot of leave saved up from the Army?" Isrie had slowed her roll with the meal and had decided to join in the conversation. Gawd, I wished I had her metabolism. She could really put food away, but always kept her shape. Of course, I kept my shape too—that was my problem.

"Yeah," was all he said to Isrie without making eye contact. There my brother went with the short answers. Something was up, as was usually the case with him, but I wanted to enjoy what was left of our dinner, so I wasn't going there.

We finished off dinner and stayed almost to closing time. Ivan kept us entertained with some jokes I didn't know he had, and Theron finally came around, conversing with Isrie off and on. She was the kind of girl he would normally be interested in, being as cute as a button and older, but he was hiding it well.

Soon Ivan suggested taking in some jazz over in Los Feliz, just past West Hollywood. I excused myself to the restroom before leaving and dragged Isrie along with me. Girl talk, y'know.

"You got a fine motherfucker out there. Watch him tonight. I almost slipped in the drool from the girls at the table behind us," Isrie casually replied from over the wall of my stall.

"Isrie, I ain't gotta watch shit. Mr. Dempsey is used to that sort of stuff and he's not my man."

"Sure seems like he wants to be."

"Ivan's always playing around like that," I said as if half believing myself. "Shit. He's tapping *at least* one model that I'm aware of. He's been a good friend, though, so I ain't mad at him."

"If you say so, girl. I'm just glad you're having a good time."

"And how about you? I know you really didn't want to come tonight," I said as I left the stall and went to the mirror to check my makeup.

"I'm fine," Isrie said as she joined me. "It's been upbeat after goofing up with your brother and having to leave Heaven."

"I know you really wanted to eat there."

"Nothin' but a thang. This food was just as good, if not better. I could certainly use a drink, though."

"You'll be able to do that at the jazz spot. Trust me."

12

Isrie

"I'm glad you've started talking."

"Well, my eyes finally stopped stinging."

"Boy, I said I'm sorry. I think I've apologized enough times for that."

"You think, huh?"

"Are you always such a smart-ass?"

"Only with the people I like."

I was enjoying the man on the trumpet doing his best Chris Botti and, surprisingly, Theron's company. Ivan had ordered us a round of drinks and Deja's Long Island Iced Tea was already bottomed out. She was fanning herself with her hand while giggling with Ivan as they stood up and swayed to the music together. Definitely the music of lovers. It was a little bit warm in Jazz on Tap, but it was probably the alcohol . . . and that Ivan had Deja's coffeepot percolating tonight. I politely tapped my fingers on our table and closed my eyes while my head swayed. The older, balding brother on the piano had joined in with the frantic trumpet playing and was bringing the number to a boil.

"You like jazz, huh?" Theron asked as I opened my eyes, embarrassed to see him enjoying my moment.

"*Good* jazz. There is a difference," I said with one finger extended for emphasis.

"I hear jazz is the music of lovers."

"Damn straight," I replied with exaggerated confidence.

"Perhaps you can help me appreciate it then."

I intentionally ignored Theron's flirtatious entrance and replied, "So what type of music do you like? Hip-hop? Rap?"

"Damn straight."

"I hate the stuff." I lied. Actually, I hated that it reminded me of Ryan.

"Aww!" Theron jumped from his seat as if having a fit. "You've *got* to be kidding! You're not *that* old."

"Excuse you?"

He sat back down and resumed talking in a civilized manner. "I meant nothing by that. It's hard to believe that someone as fine . . . and intelligent as you wouldn't appreciate hip-hop or rap at all. Even if you don't find it uplifting or stimulating, I find it hard to believe that you wouldn't like to get out on the floor and at least shake your ass every now and then. C'mon now!" Theron was sputtering, but at least he was trying to make an effort at being charming.

"Okay. I'll admit it," I said with a sly smile. "Jazz and R&B is my thing, but I do like some hip-hop and rap. Some. Your sister and me went on this cruise to Puerto Vallarta once. There was this club on the boat that played some good shit."

There went that chuckle of his again. "Let me guess. Sumthin' like Will Smith?"

"No. No Will Smith. And what's wrong with Will Smith anyway? I'd be his Jada any day of the week."

"I'm just teasing. He's a good actor."

"But—"

"—I'll leave it alone," he answered sarcastically as he turned up his bottle of Shiner Bock.

"Uh huh. I don't see you trying to rap, but you're quick to hate on another brother."

"I'm not hatin'. Never said I could rap anyway. I got other skills."

"This is supposed to be the part where I ask *like what*?"

"*Fergit ya*, girl."

"Forget me? You can't do that. I'm infectious . . . like good jazz."

"Probably more like an STD."

I shot Theron the bird on that one, but had to laugh with him. I had begun looking at him with different eyes, but remembered he was my best friend's brother . . . and *baby* brother at that. He was still sort of attractive with his droopy eyes and cocky demeanor, but not what I was looking for. No more hardheads for me, even reformed ones, I told myself reassuringly. He probably was good in the sack, though. Lanky, bowlegged motherfuckers like him usually were.

I decided to be generous and paid for the next round of drinks over Theron's and Ivan's protests. Their egos didn't take it very well, so I obliged them on the following two. Deja felt herself getting a little giddy and went back to her water with lemon for the rest of the night.

"Thanks for coming out with us, girl," Deja said as she resumed sitting in the chair to my left.

"I'm having a good time. Your brother's pretty nice once he warms up."

"Watch him, Isrie. He's got game," she said loud enough for her brother to hear over the quartet's latest number. He jokingly popped his collar and resumed ignoring us.

"Yeah. He tried already. Enough for me to put his young ass across my lap and give him a spanking."

"Girl, don't be doing my brother any favors like that. *Yawn.*"

"Getting sleepy, D-Square?"

"Yeah. A little bit," she said with tired eyes that were starting to blink. "All those long hours at work are wearing on me. What time is it anyway?"

"Twelve thirty," I said as I tilted my watch to the light. "Stop by the spa next week. I'll hook you up with a massage."

"Alright, girl. I think I'm gonna see if Ivan can take me home."

"Need me to hold up a few hours here with your brother before bringing him home?"

"I know what you're getting at, Isrie. Stop it. I already said nothing's going on."

"Keep telling yourself that. Just give me details in the morning, alright?"

Deja got the attention of Ivan, who was chatting it up with some other beautiful people he knew, and told him she was ready to leave. Deja, trying to prove her point, asked Theron if he wanted to ride back with them.

"Nah," he replied. "I haven't been in town in a while. I'm just gettin' started tonight. If that's okay with you, Isrie?"

"Huh? I—I mean, sure. Yeah. Sure. I'll bring you home. Go on, Deja."

Deja paused for a second, as if sizing up the situation, then moved on with Ivan, who led her out with his jacket on his arm. Ivan stopped to give Theron one of those *nice to meet you, bruh* handshake/hugs. I had another name for it tonight—*Thanks for not cockblocking on a brother with your sister, bruh.* I don't think it was Theron's intent to do something nice for Ivan's sake, though.

"I thought you weren't that big a fan of jazz, Theron," I said as I sat back down to have another cosmopolitan and enjoy the music.

"It's okay, but I didn't say anything about staying here."

"Say what?"

13

Deja

No words were exchanged between us as Ivan drove me home from Jazz on Tap. He put on a CD and I hummed along with Jill Scott, as I didn't know any of the songs on her new album yet. I sat there contently, holding his hand as the warm feeling carried over from before.

Outside the club, Ivan and I shared our first kiss. It was a rather innocent way to end what had turned out to be an enjoyable evening. As he unlocked my car door, he held my hand firmly in his. I went to get in, but he pulled me back up by the hand. I returned his smile with one of my own as he pulled my fingers up to his lips and kissed the tops of them. Gently, one finger at a time, his lips brushed against each ringed knuckle, causing me to let out a cooing sound. Once he stopped, I started to let out one of my nervous giggles, but went with the urge instead and took the plunge. The kiss was soft and curious at first as Ivan's tongue tried to find its rhythm with mine. The kissing became firmer and more intense as we worked into a groove with each other, but was cut short when a group of people leaving the club interrupted our session. I was caught enjoying myself with a poster boy for most women's wet dreams, and I felt strangely awkward about it.

I slowly pulled my hand away from Ivan as we neared my apartment.

"What's wrong?" he asked, while turning the stereo down, as if sensing my attack of nerves.

"Nothing."

"C'mon now. Who do you think you're talking to? You haven't been yourself since—"

"Yeah. I know. I'm just a little nervous."

"It's just me. You know me, girl," he said as he took my chin between his fingers and turned my head to face him.

"Damn, not like this," I replied as I turned away to look out the window.

As Ivan's headlights hit it, my dark porch stairway was temporarily bathed in light, sending a cat scurrying. He parked in the vacant space next to my van.

"Thank you for the wonderful night, Ivan," I said as we both exited his car.

"You mean it?"

"I say what I mean, boy."

"Now, *there's* the Deja I know."

I grinned at Ivan, feeling comfortable once again. The date was over and we were back to the status quo. All that was left was to take that walk up the dark, lonely stairs.

"I want another date," he said.

"Now you are trippin'." Step one. It creaked slightly as I placed my foot on it.

"You didn't answer me. So do I get another one?" he continued from behind me.

"What do you want? I'm not exactly up to the standards you're probably used to." Step two.

"I don't know what you're talking about. You are a beautiful black queen, Deja. You're also intelligent and have personality for days. So what if you're not a stick? Is that what you're getting at? You know me. I'm not about all that stuff. Shit. You are *fine*."

"What about Sophia?" Step three.

"You know how that goes with her. No papers. She may be out now for all I care."

"Like that, huh?" Step four.

"Yep."

"You sound like my brother." Step five.

"It wasn't my intention."

"Relax. I'm just being defensive. I really like you." Step six.

"I know. We're doing this again? Soon?"

I didn't respond as we reached my door. I turned around and dug for my keys out of my bag.

"No answer, huh?" He whispered in my ear as he put his hands on my waist.

"No. No answer. I just want to kiss you again right now."

I let it go and finally went with the feeling. My key was left in the door as I whipped around to find Ivan's perfect features already rushing toward mine. This was good and only getting better. I threw my arms up around him and plunged my tongue with reckless abandon into his willing mouth and had my moment of enjoyment. We bumped around in the dark for several minutes, still playing it somewhat safe, until our hands began their eventual wander.

"Yes," I accidentally moaned as Ivan's head plunged down into my cleavage and began kissing that sensitive spot right between my breasts. My sounds encouraged him as his hands massaged, stroked, and teased my two pals lurking under my dress. I gave in more and more as I felt one pop free of its cup under Ivan's coaxing. I was in total disbelief that this was going down outside my door, but it was in total darkness late at night, and I hadn't had any in a while.

"Mmm. You smell good. Sweet," he mumbled as he kneeled down before me and began kissing my legs. *Hmph.* And Isrie wanted to tease me about where I sprayed.

"Uh . . . um. Ivan. You might want to stop that. Ivan?" I was getting weak in the knees as his kisses and tongue worked their way up to my thighs. My dress was sliding up with the assistance of his hands.

"You really want me to stop?" He looked up with a confident smile I could see in the darkness.

I bit my lip and took a quick look across the parking lot for any car lights or signs of late-night life before smiling back and quietly replying, "No."

It wasn't long before I was on my back and wondering why in the fuck I had passed up this date for so long. My dress was hiked up to my waist and was probably torn. I reached back and pounded my fist on the floorboards behind my head as Ivan's tongue moved sensually, methodically between my legs. It was taking all of my control to keep from screaming out into the LA night as Ivan had my pussy under his complete control. I could feel myself erupting and subsiding and erupting again as he played me like a young Stevie Wonder with a new harmonica.

I was getting tired of banging my head and begged for Ivan to let up after I lost count of my orgasms.

"You're not enjoying it?" Ivan said, finally taking a break from the frantic pace he had been at. I loved a working man.

"Yes—I mean no. I mean—it's good. Hell, it's great," I gasped as I caught my breath and he helped me to my feet.

There was an awkward silence between us as we both wiped sweat and other stuff off. Ivan's clothes were still intact on that sculpted body of his, but I was sure I was looking like a jacked-up streetwalker right about now.

"You okay?"

"Boy, I think I'm more than *okay* right now." Ivan let out a laugh as he folded his arms and tried to look suave again with my love flow on his face.

"Well, I guess you want to go in now."

"Yeah. It's late and my key has been hanging there for a couple of seconds."

"*Seconds?*"

"Yeah. Seconds."

"The cramp in my neck doesn't feel like *seconds*."

"Want to come in . . . and wash your face? It's the least I could do."

"Sure," he said while stroking his face with an embarrassed blush.

"Ivan?"

"Yeah, baby."

"You have any condoms on you?"

"No. I didn't want you to think that's what this date was all about."

"Oh," I said as I turned the key and opened my apartment door. "Y'know. I kinda went to Ralph's yesterday to shop . . . and picked up some condoms too. Just in case."

14

Isrie

"I told you I didn't like hip-hop."

"Will you at least try to enjoy yourself?" Theron asked while dancing across from me. Well, he wasn't really dancing, more like rocking back and forth and trying to look hard.

"What is this song?"

" 'Let Me In.' "

"Let you in where?"

" 'Let Me In,' " he sighed. "That's the name of the song. Young Buck made it. He's with 50 Cent and them."

"G-Unit, right?"

"Yeah. So you do know a little bit."

"I'm not a total idiot with this stuff."

"You don't dance bad either," he said while moving closer so he didn't have to shout over the crowd as the chorus was chanted: "I know you gonna let me shine 'n get mine. I know you gonna let me in wit this nine."

"You're not too bad yourself," I answered, deciding to be kind.

"They try to say Buck's supposed to be the next Pac." He laughed. "They said the same thing about 50 when he came on the scene. Everybody wants to be the next Pac, but that'll never happen."

I nodded. "Yep. Only one Tupac."

Theron smiled. "Uh huh. So you are down for a little thug life, huh? I knew it."

"Just like you said, that'll never happen."

Theron frowned, and when it looked like he had nothing else to say, he spoke again. "Y'know, I met G-Unit once in Manhattan."

"Is that supposed to impress me?"

"No. Just makin' conversation."

"What were you doing in New York?"

"That's where I was—where I'm stationed at. Upstate New York actually."

He was finally revealing something about himself, so I kept it going. "I thought your base was around here."

"Nah. I *wish* I was at Fort Irwin. It's just too fuckin' cold at Fort Drum."

"Maybe you can transfer closer to home. Deja would like that. That's my girl, but I'm sure she'd love having some real family around."

"Yeah. I might check into that when I go back."

"When do you go back?"

"I got some time still," he said sharply before resuming his recital of the song's chorus with everyone else on the dance floor. I knew when to push and when to back off. This was one of those times for the latter.

Although my coworkers always talked about it, I'd never been to Infiniti until tonight. I only knew that a lot of celebrities liked to frequent the place. After Deja and her stud boy left us at Jazz on Tap, Theron had begged me to go to a club with more upbeat music. I gave in and was going to take him to Club Drama, but we found out that it was closed for remodeling. It was going to reopen with a new name too in a few weeks. Such was the life of a club in this town.

Two songs later I finally had a song I recognized and decided to let it go under encouragement from Theron and some other guy dancing next to us, who I later realized used to play Braxton on the *Jamie Foxx Show*. I was beginning to match the crowd's enthusiasm as the bass pumped and the latest Lil Jon & the East-side Boyz rump shaker whipped us into a frenzy. Then I caught a glimpse of the couple near the mirror. The guy was wearing a loose fitting black suit and the woman, a sister with long reddish-brown curls, wore a backless red body hugger. Shit.

The guy's back was turned to me. His date frantically shook her ass against him, but I could see his face in the reflection . . . and those green eyes. I realized I was staring when I saw him break his concentration to look at himself in the mirror and caught a glimpse of me in the background.

I was startled and quickly turned my back on Ryan. Theron took that move wrong and came up behind me, dancing closer. I opened my mouth to tell him to back up, but passed. Theron was a nice guy and wasn't bothering me. Besides, I was sure Theron's body blocked any view Ryan could have of me. I got in one sexy grind session with Theron behind me, which I'm sure he didn't mind, before stealing a peek over his shoulder in Ryan's general direction. They were gone. Good.

"Let's head back to the main room," I arched back and said to a happy, smiling Theron.

"Huh? Okay."

Theron led me by the hand off the crowded dance floor and over to the bar area, which had an older, calmer flow. I couldn't get my mind off Ryan and that bitch in the red dress who was probably my prank caller. What bothered me more than anything was that I had a face and a body to go with the sounds I'd heard that night while I listened like some sick, twisted voyeur.

I stopped beating myself up when Theron found a spot for us to sit near the main bar. He had some sweat forming on his forehead, so I got up and walked over to the bar to get a napkin for him.

"Thanks," he said as I patted down his forehead for him.

"You had a good time tonight, I hope."

"Hell, yeah. Up in the club with someone like you? What more could a nigga ask for?" Theron said as he tried to give me his best bedroom eyes.

"Don't ask, 'cause that's out of the question."

"Yeah. I know. You're doing my sister a favor."

"I didn't say that."

"Shit. You don't have to. I may be a little younger, but I ain't no fool. It don't matter, though. I'm still having a good time."

"Good. So am I. For real," I said while looking at some of the crowd beginning to mill past. "But I think it's time for us to go."

"Can I ask you something then? Before we go?"

"Of course, Theron."

"I'm not your type, huh?"

"I . . . well, I . . . no. You're not my type."

"Do you always get this nervous when somebody's blunt with you?" He leaned back in his seat, laughing.

"No. It's just that I've had a hard time figuring you out since we've met. I've also been walking on eggshells since spraying you in the face."

"Okay. So, what kind of man is your type?" he pressed.

"That's hard to say. Many different things appeal to me."

"Like?"

"Well, like—"

"I thought that was you!" came a voice from the crowd that was exiting past our table. I let out a tiny groan as a couple walked up from out of the shadows and came up behind Theron.

"Hello, Ryan," I said to the pair of green eyes as Theron turned around to see whom I was addressing.

"Isrie, what are *you* doing here?" Ryan asked with a look of surprise and subtle disgust on his face. He had undone the first few buttons of his black shirt and the girl he was dancing with earlier was in tow. Her curls were no longer neatly in place and she moved them aside to get a better look at me. Her mouth was curled up in a tight smile as if she were holding back a laugh. I could hear her voice again. *Get that shit, Daddy.*

"Just out having a good time," I answered in a nonchalant manner as I stared into his eyes and tried not to think about what was probably going to go down between him and his "friend" while I went back to an empty apartment. The bit of jealousy I was feeling in the pit of my stomach was unsettling.

"Here?"

"Yeah. I come here sometimes. The music's good and so is the company," I said while motioning toward Theron. "Theron Douglas, this is Ryan Wilkerson. Ryan, meet Theron."

" 'Sup, man?" Theron said as he acknowledged Ryan with a pound on his fist and a casual glance before looking away toward me again. Behind Theron's eyes, the gears were turning in his head.

"I thought you hated coming to these types of places with me."

"I did back then. Only because of things like *this* on your arm. I no longer have to worry about that," I replied as Theron let out a snicker.

"Yeah. *I can see*," Ryan responded while looking at Theron with disdain. He was lucky Theron had his back turned and didn't see the look. Ryan's friend, who he wasn't even considerate enough to introduce, seemed content to remain anonymous behind him while smacking her lips.

"Did you meet this one on TV too?" Ryan followed up, referring to Theron as if he weren't even there. "Or did you find him working at Foot Locker?"

"Say what?" Theron uttered as he lurched from his seat. I jumped up first to cut him off before teeth started flying.

"Let me talk with you a second," I said to Ryan, not giving him an option as I yanked him away from our table. His date looked like she wanted to get ig'nant but I ignored her the same way Ryan had ignored Theron. Theron eased back down while the hoochie stood there with arms folded, talking smack to the air.

I led Ryan to the other side of the bar just as the closing time announcement came over the club speakers.

"Damn. Your standards fell off quick."

"Fuck you, Ryan! I could say the same about that thing you're with."

"No. You couldn't," he said with a glint in his eye. "Camile's prettier than you, finer than you, and *much* better in bed."

I slapped my hand across Ryan's face to the sounds of *oooh*s and *aaah*s from the few people who witnessed what had just happened. I had just done something I swore never to do— make a fool of myself in public.

"The truth hurts, huh?" he responded with a sick chuckle while holding his face. "Face it. You were awful. A stuck-up little princess who just laid there like a fish. You're lucky you called it off before I did."

"I never heard you complaining, you son of a bitch. If I was that bad, then why'd you call me tonight?" I flared back while trying to hold the hurt and tears at bay. I tried to ease the pain by telling myself he was just lashing out at me in revenge.

"I'm a man. Pussy will get fucked. You never heard me shouting from the rooftops either. Yours was just a hole I was filling to pass the time."

"But you still can't get over the fact that I dumped your sorry ass."

"Like I said, I would have called it off when I found something better," he said as he stared over the top of my head. "So who's that kid you're with anyway?"

"He's not a kid. More man than you by far. He's a friend in town from New York. He's an associate of 50 Cent and them. I figured I'd show him a good time tonight." I let that last part linger in the air, making it as ambiguous as possible.

"Yeah. Oh, okay," Ryan replied with smile and a look of disbelief until he saw that my facial expression hadn't changed. He then cut a look back across the bar at a seated Theron, but more seriously this time—the music producer in him wanting to make that contact, but his pride refusing to do it after all he'd said. "Well, I gotta run. I would say it was nice seeing you, but—"

"Go to hell."

I trailed behind Ryan, who made it to our table and was apol-

ogizing to Theron while suddenly jocking him. I rolled my eyes
as he left with his wench in tow for a night of *good* sex.

"Sorry about that," I said to Theron as he got up for us to de-
part also.

"We'll talk. Now let's just get out of here."

Ryan and his girl were almost out the door ahead of us when
I saw him turn and steal a look our way. Out of hurt, I turned
and brought my lips against Theron's. Theron resisted for a second, but went along for the ride, slipping me some tongue as he
let his hands wander down to my ass for a cheap feel. For someone I considered *just* my best friend's brother, the kiss wasn't
bad. The squeeze was another matter. I broke it off as the line
moved along, knowing Ryan was now gone. Theron didn't say
anything just then, but waited until we were back at my car.

"Give me the keys," he said while reaching out to stop me.

"I can drive. I'm okay."

"I know, but I'll feel safer. C'mon. Hand 'em over."

I had been driving all over town the entire night. I was beat,
so I didn't protest. I placed the keys in his outstretched hand.

"Don't mess up my car."

"Looks like you already took care of that," Theron said as he
laughed and pointed at the back of the tiny Scion. I had gone
most of the night without thinking of Michael. Oh, how I wished
he would have been with me in the club tonight. There I went,
going all googly over some man I barely knew. This was the same
kind of behavior that had gotten me into the predicament with
Ryan in the first place.

As Theron shifted gears awkwardly, I didn't complain as I
normally would have. I just closed my eyes and tried to purge
my mind of the pain.

"You asleep?"

"No," I said without opening my eyes. I could tell we were
slowing for a red light.

"Don't play me like that again."

"I'm sorry."

"Quit all the apologizing and start thinking instead."

"You sound like my dad."

"Bet you never listen to him either." Ther car jerked as the light turned green and Theron shifted again. The car groaned as he missed a gear.

"Sometimes."

"That punk-ass back there dump you?"

"No. Actually I dumped him."

"Coulda fooled me."

"I know. I wasn't expecting to see him out tonight."

"Uh huh. Or with the woman on his arm."

"Maybe that too," I said as I sighed and rubbed my eyes.

"Why'd he tell me to say hi to 50 Cent for him when he left?"

"I dunno. Being stupid, I guess."

"Yeah. He's stupid all right. He's lucky I didn't stomp him into the ground back there. *Foot Locker*. And what was that shit about meeting me on TV about?"

"Long story and I'm tired. Can we drop the subject?"

"Yeah, I'm tired too. I can't wait to hit my sister's couch."

Theron got us back to Deja's place in the early morning hours rather quickly. I looked forward to running in for a sec and sharing my Ryan troubles at the Infiniti Club with Deja, but that idea fell by the wayside when I saw Ivan's Hummer still there. She still had company, and my best friend, whose shoulder I took for granted too much, was actually better off than I was tonight. Ryan was having his fun tonight, Deja was too, and all I could do was go home alone.

"So, you gonna give me a good-night kiss?" Theron asked, taking another jab at me for the kiss back at the club. He took my car out of gear after stopping it in back of Deja's van.

"Bye, boy."

"You'll call me boy . . . until you see my toy. Then you'll call me Mister."

"The sick ones are always in the military." I laughed aloud as Theron got out.

"Good night, Theron. Thanks," I said as I walked around to the driver's side of my car.

"For what?" he asked as he stopped his run up the stairs.

"For putting up with me tonight."

"Aww. It wasn't that bad. A little immature, but not bad." Theron then left me with my mouth open before I could say something. I saw him knocking on the front door when I started backing up to drive away.

I stopped at the corner to put in my Amel Larrieux CD. She was always good at times like this. The first track was about to start as I put my car into gear and started rolling. I was reaching up to crack my sunroof when Theron ran in front of my car. I screamed for dear life and slammed on the brakes. Once I realized who it was, I composed myself and rolled down my window.

"Boy, what the fuck is your *main* problem?"

"I know. I know," he said as he caught his breath, resting his hands on the hood of my car. "Don't mace me again. Big favor to ask you."

"What?"

"Can I crash at your place? Nobody's answering the door."

"Okay. Get in," I said as I sighed and unlocked the door.

15

Deja

I remembered. As I moaned and panted with delight, I remembered. I had joked with Ivan about breaking him in half if we ever did the do. Contrary to my previous remarks, Ivan didn't break or snap like a twig. He stayed. Hell, he more than stayed.

"Oh, shit! Oh, damn! Oh, shit," I burst out as he found my whoo spot, sending me flailing about on my water bed. The mattress moved with wave after wave as our bodies rocked in tune. I had been celibate for a year, not counting those late-night dates with my vibrator, but I didn't tell you that.

Ivan rose up onto his knees in the bed while still in me and raised my hips up to pull me into him farther. I took that time to finish pulling my dress over my head in the flickering light of the candle next to my bed.

"What?" I asked, suddenly feeling self-conscious and inadequate as I looked up at Ivan's perfection. He had slowed his pull to look down at me—his abs and chest defined even more by the shadows that flickered across them.

"I'm just looking at you. I love making you happy, Deja."

"Oh," I replied, feeling reassured by his words. I unsnapped my bra, exposing my bare breasts for the first time to Ivan, just before he pulled me up off my back.

I rose up to meet Ivan, causing the mattress to shift under our weight and sending us wobbling before tipping over to the side, and onto the floor.

Ivan hit the floor with a thud, just in time to welcome me. I heard the air rush out of him as our tangled mess crashed into the candle stand, sending it tipping over.

I scrambled over Ivan to put out the scented candle before my carpet caught on fire and burned my place down. I righted the candle just as I heard Ivan, who was still under me, laughing. Holding the warm lavender candle in my hand, I laughed along with him.

"Wait," I said, stopping my laughter for a second. "Did you hear that?"

"Unh uh," Ivan answered. "What did you hear?"

"I thought I heard somebody knocking. Theron might be back."

The two of us stayed quiet a few tense minutes longer, but heard nothing.

"I guess it was just my imagination. He and Isrie must be having a good time."

"Yeah. Lucky for me," Ivan said as he placed his hands on the sides of my hips. He hadn't lost his hard-on and I felt his condom-covered hardness slowly rising back up inside me. Yeah, he had some *serious* staying power. I was already moist, but felt a fresh eruption in anticipation of the continued lovemaking.

We decided to stay right there on the side of my bed and not risk another fall. As I felt Ivan's pelvis rising up off the floor to meet me, I began riding up and down on him. I went slowly at first as we eased toward the sensation, but began losing it when he grasped my waist, forcing me down ever harder with each stroke. I took deep breaths and closed my eyes as I rode harder and harder, feeling indescribable ecstasy each time Ivan bottomed out inside me. The room became filled with the sounds of sheer animal lust as everything began running on automatic. If anybody had been knocking now, we wouldn't have heard it. As our bodies slammed harder and harder together, I began caressing and squeezing my breasts. Ivan's hands were busy gripping my ass anyway and he didn't seem to mind as the sight of me stimulating myself worked him into a frenzy.

"Oh. Oh. Don't stop. Don't," I screamed as I fell over onto Ivan, knowing I really couldn't take anymore.

Ivan, sensing what I really meant, dove headlong into his orgasm as I felt the sudden rush of warmth through his condom. He wrapped his arms around my waist, holding me in place as my final eruption came about a second later. We both convulsed as our sweaty bodies went limp. We were too tired to move, so I stayed on top of Ivan with him still in me.

"Girl," Ivan whispered in my ear a minute later, "whatcha got in there?"

"*Whoo*. What's left of you. I think you need to go ahead and remove it before the rubber comes off."

"Yeah. Good idea."

"Sure is. I'm not about to let some of the best sex I've had in years be ruined by an unexpected present for the rest of my life."

"C'mon. You mean you wouldn't want a baby, Deja?"

"I'm not thinking about a kid yet. And not like this *especially*." That comment brought me back to memories of the mother who I never really knew. It was something I tried to keep locked up in the recesses of my mind. To me, my grandma was my true mother, and not the confused and troubled young woman who would come by every Christmas to give a single present to Theron and myself. The only present I truly wanted was a mother's love, something she couldn't provide, or at least some sort of explanation. As the years went on, the visits dropped off, and by the seventh grade they had ended altogether.

I came back from my brief mental vacation, suddenly feeling uneasy with my body's appearance again.

"What's wrong?" Ivan asked, noting the change in my demeanor. He had stood up and was taking a quick assessment to make sure everything was still in its rightful place on his splendid frame.

"Nothing," I answered while covering my breasts with my hands. My eyes had watered up. "I'm going to wash up."

I rudely closed the bathroom door on Ivan and waited for the water to heat up before pulling the curtain back and entering the shower. I liked my showers hot, and the steamy splashes on my face and sore body helped break me out of my momentary funk. I was letting the makeup and sweat wash off my face when Ivan pulled the curtain back and joined me.

"Something I did?"

"No," I said with a smile. "You did everything right."

"Need anything?"

"Yeah. Just be my friend and hold me."

16

Isrie

"**H**ell nah."

"*What?*"

"On the floor. That's a new sofa. No one sleeps on there. Not even me."

"The hard-ass floor? How about your bed? It looks plush."

"Boy . . . you're lucky I'm letting you stay the night. I've got mace, remember?"

"Yeah. You the baddest bitch," said Theron with a yawn. He then pulled his tan Rocawear top over his head, giving me a peek at his tight, young frame. Push-ups had been doing this young thang some good in the Army. He balled his top up into a bundle and let it fall onto the floor with a quiet plop.

"Do you want to use the bath or shower or anything?" I asked, kicking my shoes off.

"Nah. I don't have any clothes here. I'm cool. A blanket or something to put on the floor would be nice."

"I have a sleeping bag."

"Cool."

I walked across the floor to one of my closets and pulled a pillow and my plaid sleeping bag down from the top shelf. I had bought it for some overnight camping up in northern Cal, but had used it only once as I wasn't really the outdoors type. I handed it to Theron, who had it unrolled and on the floor in the front of the sofa all in one move.

Since I lived alone in a studio apartment, I was used to undressing wherever. I began unbuttoning the front of my blazer as I walked across the room near the door to my balcony, which was my designated bedroom area. I slipped one arm out, exposing my camisole underneath. The arm went right back in as I smacked my lips, remembering that Theron could see.

Looking through my sleepwear, I grabbed an old T-shirt, but put it back in favor of a blue satin pajama set. I took the pajama set and walked past Theron on my way to the bathroom to change.

"Don't go in the bathroom on my account," he said laughingly as he made himself a nest on my floor while I walked by.

"Y'know, why don't you give your sister a call? I'm sure she's missing you."

"Damn. Now you're kicking me out."

"I thought you were tired."

I closed and locked the bathroom door behind me. I kept an upholstered stool in there that allowed me to sit down after undressing, so I could apply my Lancôme. As I ran the cool, white cream into my skin with upward swirls, I saw the lights under the door go out. Theron was certainly making himself at home. I reflected on the stinging hurt from Ryan earlier and fantasized that it was Michael who was waiting for me on the other side of the bathroom door. I imagined him taking the hurt away—candles lit, incense burning, and a soft piano playing. I was thinking too much about that man. Maybe I was just horny. I shrugged at my clown-faced twin in the mirror before retreating to my shower.

When I emerged from the bathroom in my PJs, feeling fresh but still drained, I noticed Theron wasn't where I had last seen him. As my eyes adjusted to the darkness, I saw the sleeping bag covering him like a cocoon . . . on my sofa. I frowned, but homey was snoring so loud that I decided to let him slide with his mortal sin this once.

By my bed, Theron's late night symphony was barely audible. I pulled back the fluffy white down comforter and slid under the covers. As I got myself comfortable, I ran my cold feet back and forth to warm them up. I hated sleeping with cold feet and preferred to have a nice, hairy leg to take care of that.

My clock flashed 4:00 before I dropped my eyelids. I slept restlessly for what seemed to be hours until opening my eyes again. This time, 4:20 greeted me. I guess I was still steaming over my confrontation with Ryan.

"Shit," I remarked to the laughing clock before pulling the comforter over my head.

I hated these kinds of nights. I didn't want to disturb Theron, who was probably sweating on my nice sofa, so I just lay there as quiet as a mouse.

I eventually drifted off, but was disturbed by the sounds of movement. My guest was up and stumbling around for the bathroom. I was about to open my mouth to scream out where the light switch was, but the bathroom light came on. I heard Theron bang into my stool, stumble, then catch himself, cursing all the while.

"Put the toilet seat back down," I snarled just as the bathroom light went out. Theron dragged himself back in there and intentionally let it slam.

"You asleep?" he asked as I watched his silhouette sit back on the sofa.

"I was."

"I woke you up?"

"Yeah."

"Sorry."

"It's okay. I've been having trouble sleeping tonight anyway."

"That's no surprise."

"Oh well. Good night."

"Night."

"Theron?" I asked, breaking the deadening silence

"What?"

"You feel like talking?"

"No, but you do and you're not going to let me go back to sleep. Are you?"

"You weren't supposed to be sleeping on my sofa anyway."

Theron sighed. "What time is it?"

"Um. Five."

"Damn, girl. You wanna scream across the room at each other or what?"

"Nah. You can come over here," I answered, sitting up in the dark.

"To your *sacred space*? Whoa!"

"I don't deserve this shit."

I crawled atop the covers and made room for Theron to have a seat. The lengths I was going to these days to get a man into my bed. My mom would be shaking her head.

"What do you wanna talk about?"

"I dunno. I just can't sleep."

"You're used to talking to my sister at times like this, I'll bet."

"How'd you know?" I asked, reaching to turn the lamp switch on.

"It's not hard to figure out. You'd probably be on the phone doing that *girl talk* thing, huh? Except things are different. She's occupied for once and you're not used to that."

"Got me all figured out, huh?"

"No offense, but you are a little predictable."

"One night and I'm an open book. Is that it?"

"Yep."

"What am I thinking about right at this moment?"

"What an asshole I am."

"You *are* good."

"And that you wish someone else was here with you instead. In this bed," he continued. The muscles in his bare chest flexed as he repositioned himself on the bed.

"I didn't say that." I wasn't about to admit or say anything about Michael—not to *him*.

"Maybe that punk from the club, Ryan?" he continued, ignoring my protests. "No, No. Not him. You did say that *you* broke up with him," Theron said with a sadistic smile.

"I did break up with him," I said as my nostrils flared. I poked my finger into his chest for added emphasis.

"Okay. Relax. I'm just messing with you, Isrie. It's what I do."

"Why?"

"Like I said before. I only do it with the people I like."

"I don't like it."

"Alright. What else you wanna talk about then?"

"Let's play twenty questions."

Theron pulled away and seemed to be in deep thought before saying, "Okay. Go."

"At what age did you lose your virginity?"

"Oh, snap! Trying to make me uncomfortable now, huh? Thirteen."

"Thirteen?"

"Yep," he replied with a gush of pride. "And you?"

"Sixteen. My parents would kill me if they knew. It was our neighbor at the time."

"My turn. Ever been with a woman?"

"No!" I answered with a disgusted laugh. "What do I look like?"

"Right now? You look like someone who's hurting over something . . . and a sexy someone at that. I've been messing with you, but I'm dying for a peek under those PJs. I know that kiss in the club was for show, but I'm feelin' you and would like to try that again," he said, shifting from jackass to smooth operator at the drop of a dime. He reached out and caressed my hand that was resting near him. Maybe it was the time of night—oops, morning—but I was actually finding some sincerity in his words.

"Don't. Don't say that. You're my—"

"Best friend's brother. I know. I heard ya before."

"Thanks for the compliments, though, I guess. My self esteem has suffered quite a bit tonight."

"Damn. Exactly what'd he do when y'all two walked off?" Theron asked

"Forget about it. I think I want to go back to sleep now." The hurt of Ryan's words was coming back, choking me up.

"Suit yourself."

Theron had shifted back to his nonchalant mode and walked back to his makeshift bed while I turned my lamp off. I saw the movement of my sleeping bag, but he had put it on the floor this time and was crawling into it. I saw him kick his jeans off, just before settling in. I crawled back under the covers and turned away to face the glass balcony door.

A flurry of emotions, all of them confused, washed over me. I tried to force myself to sleep, but wasn't successful. My next move was one based on emotion and far from logical as I left the security and solitude of my bed. My bare feet carried me in a straight line across the floor to the sleeping bag. I didn't notice the tears until I tasted the salt on my lips.

Theron didn't sense me at first, but opened his eyes when he heard my sobbing. He didn't say anything, but waited for me to speak.

"He said I was no good. No good in bed."

"Uh, you sure you want to talk about this?"

"He called me a stuck-up princess and that I just laid there like a fish," I wept, finally getting out what had shocked and hurt me. "I always enjoyed the sex with him. That was never the problem . . . I thought. I had . . . n-no idea he felt like that."

I kneeled down beside Theron, who was now sitting up in the sleeping bag. He instinctively pulled me into him and began shushing me to try to ease my obvious hurt. Here I was, a grown-ass woman behaving like a silly teen. I got sillier when I let him kiss me.

He probably did it to shut me up at first and because he didn't know what to say. I think I wanted him to kiss me just then. It was like I was getting back at Ryan on some level by doing this. It was *take that* with each kiss as our bodies got closer. I felt Theron's hands running through my hair and scalp as he began kissing me down my neck. I tilted my head back as I bit my bottom lip and allowed his hand to find its way to the buttons on my top. Before I knew it, we were both on top of the sleeping bag. I started digging my nails into his shoulders and back as I felt my top slip off, revealing my breasts and rock-hard nipples that were begging him to taste them. I imagined Ryan looking on with envy and decided to torture him further. I straddled Theron and pulled his head up to engage in another wild, wet kiss. Theron teased me at first, then playfully sucked on my tongue. His manhood had popped out of his briefs and he pushed it up against my pajama bottoms between my legs. The satin material was very thin, giving me a rush of sensations. I was aroused, and things were reaching the point of no return.

"Take them off," Theron demanded with lust in his voice. This fish wasn't just *lying there*.

"Sure," I said with dried tears on my face and yearning in my voice. I rolled off him and onto my back. I was smiling as I raised my rear up and pulled my bottoms and panties off. They slid down my legs until Theron grasped both them and my hands. His eyes were all business as his hands slid off mine and continued to pull my garments down past my ankles and off my feet.

I spread my legs open to reveal my awakened treasure to my houseguest. He smiled in approval and slid his briefs off before crawling between my tensed and awaiting thighs. Just then, I looked to where I imagined Ryan was looking on from, but he wasn't there. He never was. It wasn't real . . . and this shouldn't be either.

"N—no," I whispered as I began to realize the stupid, stupid mistake I was making. This wasn't right. I could feel Theron's head beginning to penetrate me.

"No. Stop," I said again. This time I was more forceful and tried to slide back. "I can't do this."

"Huh?" Theron responded, as if not hearing me correctly. He was starting to make his entry again.

"Stop it!" I screamed out emphatically as I put my hands against his chest and pushed away with all my might. I felt a nail break as Theron looked at me with a crazed look in his eyes. I had no idea what he was about to do.

17

Deja

"Hey. Pick up the phone. It's me. I'm at your friend's house. Come pick me up."

That was the message left for me on my answering machine while I was outside saying my good-byes to Ivan. It was daylight now and I had to face abandoning my brother, my blood, with my best friend all for a night of pleasure. Hell, who was I kidding? Theron would have done the same. But I at least owed Isrie an apology.

An hour later, the doorman admitted my ugly, smoking van into Isrie's upscale apartment community. My girl's place was a lovely sanctuary that was isolated, yet within walking distance to the Staples Center and the rest of downtown. I envied the lush garden courtyards, waterfalls, and the private park residents had to enjoy right at their disposal. Even if I could have swung the lease with Isrie, I wondered if I could have put up with the excess "convenience." Stores? Maids? Limousine service? Twenty-four-hour security? Other than the cost to your pocketbook, things were a little too easy here. Maybe I was just too comfortable with the struggle.

Isrie stayed on the sixth floor of her section, so I admired the downtown LA skyline and the Pasadena Freeway as I took the glass elevator up.

"Hey girl," Isrie said with a smile of part affection, part relief as she opened the door to greet me. She had on a pair of jeans and a white halter top and was wearing her hair up this morning.

"Thanks, Isrie. I owe you one, girl," I said discretely as I gave her a kiss on the cheek and entered. Theron was sitting at her table nearby and gave me a nod. He was wearing his clothes from the night before and was finishing off a bowl of Frosted Flakes.

" 'Bout damn time. I've been waitin'."

"Hey! Don't start with me, boy," I shot back at my rude brother. "No one told you to come here last night."

"I wasn't planning on it. You weren't answering the door when Isrie brought me home."

"Oh," I softly replied while looking at Isrie. Isrie gave me a smart-alecky smile and nodded in agreement with my brother.

"I guess I didn't knock loud enough," Theron said with a chomp of his cereal. He had to rub it in further. "And that pretty boy better not turn out to be one of those down-low brothers either."

"Anyway. I see y'all two got along alright last night after we left."

"I guess," my brother replied first, cutting Isrie off. I sat down on the couch and waited for Isrie to finish her remark.

"Yeah. We had an okay time. Your brother convinced me to go to the Infiniti Club last night."

"Yeah. You gotta watch my brother. I don't see him often, but I know he likes a good party. Anything else happen? *Did y'all two behave yourselves*?"

"Shit ain't even funny, sis," Theron interjected as he plopped his cereal bowl in Isrie's kitchen sink. "Your girl here's not my type and you know that. That'd be something like oil and water."

" 'Scuuuse me. Didn't mean to touch a nerve, bruh."

"He's probably tired of putting up with me actually," Isrie conceded. "There was a little bit of drama. Guess who I ran into last night."

"Who?"

"Ryan."

Isrie had taken a seat next to me to give me the dirt, leaving Theron feeling awkward.

"I know. I know. Y'all two want to talk. Is it okay for me to walk around outside? I don't want to get shot by an armed guard or sumthin' "

"You are crazy," Isrie chuckled. "It's alright. If anybody stops you, just have them call up here."

"I'll take your word, but you're gonna have to bail me out if a beatdown happens."

"Deal."

No sooner than Theron had strolled out the door, I was scooting closer to get the dirt on what had happened with Ryan.

"Talk! Talk!"

"Nothing much to say. Of all people to run into, I run into him."

"He's still upset about you dumping him?"

"Sure. Upset enough to be up in the club partying his ass off with his new ho."

"Whaaa? The one on the phone?"

"Maybe. Hell, I don't know."

"How'd she look? A dog?"

"I wish. He made sure to get in some jabs at me too. Fucked with my head big-time."

"I'll bet. Theron didn't trip, huh?"

"No. He started to kick Ryan's ass, but I defused that."

"*Whew*. Speaking of Theron—sorry to have done y'all like that last night."

"It's all good, my sister. So . . . did Ivan rock your world?"

I tried not to answer her question at first, but was already holding back a giggle.

"He did, didn't he? I'll be damned!" Isrie began clapping in her chair.

"I'm kicking myself for not going out with him sooner. The best lovin' I've ever had. Toes curled so hard they almost broke."

"That's enough. I'm getting jealous now. So, was it just one night or are you looking to go somewhere with it?"

"I don't know. It was just one night as far as I'm concerned," I said while trying to make myself believe it. "He wants to go out again. Maybe the four of us can—"

"No. No offense, but I think I'll pass, D-Square."

"Why? Did my brother do something?"

"No. I don't have a problem with him. I just didn't like being the fifth wheel last night. Do you know how long Theron's staying out here?"

"I still have no idea. My brother hasn't told me a thing. You have to understand, that's Theron's way, though. You two were talking a lot last night. He didn't open up to you?"

"Talked a lot, and at the end of the night he was still a mystery. I did find out that he's stationed in New York."

"New York. See, that's more than I knew. I really need to spend more time with him before he goes back."

Just then, Isrie got a call from downstairs. Theron had gotten lost outside and approached the concierge for Isrie's apartment number. Of course they didn't give it out and had insisted on checking things out with Isrie. She told me that she could hear Theron in the background cursing the man out. I decided to cut our chat short and get out of Dodge with my brother before he was forcibly removed. I thanked Isrie one final time for keeping Theron company and for accommodating him before I left. I had a nagging feeling that Isrie was more than a little uncomfortable around my brother, but I didn't know why and couldn't prove it. Trying to pry that info out of Theron would have been fruitless.

18

Isrie

"Stop? You've got to be fuckin' kidding." Theron had finally paused, but was gazing at me in the dark with amazement. His staff was at full salute and ready for action.

"No. I'm serious," I said softly as I slid away and composed myself. I was still trembling from the look on Theron's face.

"Shit. You are crazy. Y'know that? And why you acting all scared of me *now*? Two minutes ago you were Ms. Wide Receiver, now you buggin'. I ain't gonna do nothin' to your ass. You think I'm some sort of rapist? Girl, you credit yourself too much."

"No. I didn't think . . . What I meant was—look, I'm sorry."

"Enough with the apologies already! Damn, woman," he uttered while pulling his briefs up. "I learn quick. Believe that."

"I'm going to my bed. I'll leave you alone."

"Good. Please do. I'll just go back to sleep . . . if you don't mind. And I'm calling my sister at the first sign of daylight to come get my ass."

A few hours later, Theron was leaving his message for Deja. Things had calmed down and become civil again between the two of us by the time she arrived. I hoped that we would be able to chalk that incident up to experience and forget about it. The odd friendship that had started up was deadened by my totally mixed signals. I just hoped Deja wouldn't find out.

By the time Wednesday rolled around, I had already made

plans to have my car repaired. I normally would have called my dad to handle this sort of thing, but I wasn't going to admit what happened, especially not to him. There I went with the mistakes and secrets. I had a nasty pattern starting to develop and needed to nip it in the bud. Next year would be the year of truth in everything—that would be my resolution.

I called the repair shop to confirm things and grabbed a quick bite to eat from the corner deli before rushing back to work. I was walking up Wilshire with my brown bag in hand when I heard a familiar voice.

"Hello, Isrie." Chills shot down my neck to the top of my rump, causing goose pimples to pop up.

"Michael?" I said, half questioning myself. I had almost walked dead into him. "What are you doing here?"

"Oookay," he said uncomfortably while scratching his head. He looked as nice as ever. White shirt with a silk tie and tan slacks.

"Sorry," I said apologetically. "I didn't mean it like that. I'm just surprised to see you. *Happy*, but surprised."

"I was in the neighborhood and figured I'd stop by and check you out."

"Aww. That's sweet. How's your neck?"

"Much better. I see you got lunch already."

"Yeah. Long day today. It's getting near the holidays and everybody's got tension."

"Look . . . I was trying to catch you for lunch today. I *hope* it wouldn't be too forward to ask you to dinner maybe."

"Oh. No, dinner would be fine. I'm just surprised you remembered me."

"You're an unforgettable woman, Isrie. You'd have my attention without hitting my car."

"Added guilt, huh? Just for good measure to make sure I agree."

"A man's gotta do what a man's gotta do," he said smiling. The sides of his goatee curved.

"I can't tonight."

"How about this weekend? I'd like to see you out of that uniform." I wasn't about to go there with his comment. You can read what you want into it.

"This weekend would be good."

"Maybe a movie too?"

"We'll see," I said as I resumed walking toward the spa. Michael joined me.

"Why don't you give me your number?" *He asked! He asked! Hmph. About damn time.*

"I have a better idea. Why don't you give me *your* number?"

"Sure."

"And a real number too. Not some voice mail account."

"Okay, okay," he chuckled. He began scribbling a number on the back of a business card he pulled from his wallet. He had passed the first test.

"One final question," I said as I took the card with the phone number and eyed it.

"Shoot," he said with a grin as if amused by my interrogation.

"When did you to decide to ask me out?"

"When I was comfortable enough that you weren't involved with someone."

"It's that obvious?"

"No. I gambled."

"Still feel like you're gambling?"

"Maybe. But you agreed to dinner, so that says something."

"I've got to get back in there now," I said as I started opening the front door to the spa. The valets were watching Michael to make sure he wasn't bothering me.

"Isrie, will you call me before the weekend?"

"I think so."

"Good."

Michael flashed me an award-winning smile before turning to jog to his BMW parked across the street.

"Michael?" I called out almost as an afterthought.

"Huh?" He was just about to dart across Wilshire.

"When is her birthday?"

"Who?"

"Your wife."

"What are you talking about? I don't have a wife."

"Good answer." He'd passed the test.

I called Michael that night, and by our second talk broke down and gave him my home number. As I got to know more about him little by little, it turned out the pieces of our puzzle fit. Just like me, he'd grown up an only child raised by both parents and loved jazz music as well. Michael was in pharmaceutical sales with the mega conglomerate Pharfex-Williams, which kept him in and out the area hospitals visiting doctors. Furthermore, since he was a regional coordinator, he spent a large portion of any given week away in Nevada and Arizona. When he spoke of his job, I could sense a drive and determination, which appealed to me. I liked dedication. And the way his goatee curled when he smiled. Friday night we stayed on the phone till some time after midnight. Beat from the workweek, I had started dozing off, but he simply stayed on the phone and listened to my shallow breathing.

"Did you hear what I said?"

"Hmm?" I replied, nuzzling my face into the comforter. "What?"

Michael laughed. "It wasn't important. I just said it's late and I was going to let you go."

"No."

"No?"

"No," I replied again playfully. "Stay on the phone with me."

"Why don't you get some sleep? You can call me when you wake up."

"I don't wanna get off the phone," I mumbled in a pouty voice like a little baby. "I'm spoiled. Can't you tell?"

"Yeah. I'm learning," he chuckled. "You're also sleepy and talking out of your head, Isrie."

I rolled over to the other side of my empty bed. The sheets were cool. "So," I giggled. "If you loved me, you'd stay on the phone."

Silence.

I opened my eyes. "Michael?"

"I'm here."

"What's the matter? You don't love me?"

"I didn't say that. I just don't believe in throwing those words out there." He paused. "If I say it to you, I'll mean it."

The way he said it made me tingle. I giggled deliriously. "Not if. *When*. You'll see, boy. Imma make you love me." I closed my eyes and accepted the heat being generated by my thoughts. *Imma make you love me.* Then I fell asleep.

19

Deja

"You were serious about this camera stuff," Theron said in a monotone voice as he eyed my workplace through the lens of my favorite Nikon. He was struggling to get it into focus.

"Why would you have thought otherwise?"

" I dunno. I guess I was never really around much to see."

"You proud of your big sister?"

"Yeah. No shittin'. I've always been proud of you, though. You always handled things better than me."

"No. We just handle things differently."

"Yeah. You get lemons, Deja, you make lemonade. Me? I go down the street to another stand."

"Theron, you didn't have to run off like that all those times."

"Yeah. I did. The me that would have stuck around wouldn't have been a nice fella. Shit's serious on the streets."

My brother could be deep at times. I had finally managed to drag him along to my job Wednesday. I was still apologetic for bailing on him to get my freak on over the weekend. My photo studio wasn't much to look at, but it turned out quality product. The store below us used to be owned by an accountant and this space was where he lived. I had a nice view out the windows of the customers on Menlo Avenue walking in and out of the beauty salon across the street. On my slow days, it was all the entertainment I needed.

"Theron?"

"What?"

"You never told me how long you're back for."

"I got plenty of time. I saved up a lot of leave."

"You like it there up in New York?"

"It's not summer camp or anything. It's cold as fuck at Drum, way too much hiking, and it don't come close to the Westside, but it's a job."

"I thought it was an adventure?"

"Don't believe the commercials. Besides, that's the Navy anyway. You never know what it's like to be a slave until you're government property. Just when you forget about that something happens to let you know just what time it is." Theron seemed to be a million miles away.

"Yeah, especially now with the mess overseas. Something happen, bruh?"

"Nah. So, what's on today's schedule?"

"I've got some family portraits to do. Want to help me move the backgrounds and lighting around?"

"Sure."

With Theron's help, we had everything in place for my first appointment within fifteen minutes.

"I could really use you as my assistant."

"I don't work cheap," my brother replied as he made himself comfortable on the couch I used for waiting customers and guests.

"Y'know, you could do some modeling when you get out of the Army," I said while pointing to some of my work that was on the wall.

"I don't know about that." He glanced over at the wall. "That's a nice picture over there." Theron was pointing at a framed black-and-white nude I had shot. It was one of my best works.

"Thanks," I said with a gush of pride.

"What about this one? Whose is *this*?" He had bounced up and ran over to a color shot of a swimsuit-clad model on the wall to the left of the nude.

"Oh. That's Sophia. Nothing special." Nothing special about her other than the fact that she was sleeping with Ivan too and thought a little too highly of herself.

"I'd like to get with that. She probably only messes with pretty boys like Ivan, though, huh? Or somebody with bank?"

"Leave that alone, boy."

"Okay. Sounds like you don't like her," he said as he tried to commit Sophia's image to memory. It must have been getting tight inside my brother's jeans at the moment.

"Your hearing is perfect then."

Theron didn't get a chance to say anything else, as there was a knock at the door. The Wiggins family walked in a moment later. They knew the door was unlocked already, but were still hella polite. I had taken some pictures of their newborn last year and had photographed them several times since.

"Ms. Douglas, how are we?" Mr. Wiggins asked in his thick West Indian accent.

"Great, Mr. Wiggins. Y'all ready?"

Mr. Wiggins nodded as we both glanced toward his wife. She held their little baby Jessica and smiled, indicating she was ready for the pictures also. Mr. Wiggins' nine-year-old son, Lennox, was sheltered in his mother's shadow. I don't think Lennox felt like being here.

"Hey, Lennox. How you doin', man?"

"Fine," he said in a shy, drawn-out manner from behind his mother.

"He wanted to go to the movies today, but *someone's* grades weren't very good this time," Mr. Wiggins answered truthfully for his boy.

"Oh, I see. I know all about that. Lennox," I said as I stooped down to stare into the pouty little face, "I used to have times when I'd make some not-so-good grades too. And you know what?"

He just gave me a blank look and put his finger in his mouth.

"Her grandma did the same thing your parents are doing,"

Theron said, breaking the silence and answering my question. "And it made her get better grades and made her a better person too. Me? I was difficult and had a hard head. Still do."

Theron approached the group and knocked on his head for emphasis. Lennox let out a laugh at my brother's antics, which drove Theron to fall down at the little boy's feet as if being knocked out.

"Mr. and Mrs. Wiggins, this is my brother . . . and assistant, Theron."

"Please to meet y'all," Theron added as he opened one eye from his view of us down on the floor. "Here. Help me up, man."

My brother faked needing assistance until his newfound friend took him by the hand. I could only smile as I led my subjects to the area where I was going to take their family shots. Everyone was smiling now—including Lennox as he walked with Theron.

"You were good with him," I said to my brother as we looked out the window at the Wiggins driving up Menlo in their old minivan.

"Nothing but a thang."

"You did good today, bruh. Want to help me around here before you leave?"

"Sure. I've got the time and it beats sitting around your apartment."

"Good. Here's an extra set of keys. Since you're my *temporary* assistant, you can clean this place up while I run some photos over to the Sentinel."

20

Isrie

"Isrie, who are you going out with?"

"It's nothing . . . just dinner. The guy I was in the car wreck with is taking me out."

"I knew it! I knew it!" my bubbly friend squealed into my ear through the phone. "You've been holding out on me, trick!"

"Yeah. Just a little. I was still checking him out and hoping that he was doing the same."

I had my phone scrunched between my shoulder and ear as I finished putting my last diamond earring in. I smiled approvingly at myself in the full-length mirror as I slowly turned in a circle. I had just found my short black fitted halter dress that came out to a flare three inches above the knees. Yep, it was fitting all my curves just right. The straps were irritating my skin, but I was woman enough to ignore it for the rest of the night. I had a new bottle of perfume and had sprayed a light mist over my body earlier. Its gentle scent was still holding as I checked my wrists one last time.

"Where is he taking you?"

"Heaven," I said with a shit-eating grin.

"You cow. You were determined to get back there, huh?"

"It wasn't even my idea," I giggled. "But I'm not complaining."

"Have fun tonight. Just let your troubles fall by the wayside, Isrie."

"I will, girl. Look, the lobby is buzzing. I think he's here now. I'll call you tomorrow, okay?"

"You better."

I had the lobby let Michael up to my unit, and the knock followed shortly. I took one last glance at my place to make sure everything was in order. I wiggled my shoulder straps around one more time then opened the door to a potential future.

"Hello," I said in a soft tone.

"You look lovely tonight." Michael was clad in an olive-colored silk suit. A white V-neck shirt was visibly revealing the beginning of his smooth chest. "I like what you did with your hair also."

"What? Oh, *this*?" I said absentmindedly with a roll of my eyes. "I like to go with curls sometimes." I hadn't worn curls in over a year. The beautician across the street from Deja's office had managed to squeeze me in, but made me pay by dividing her time between me and four other women. Gawd, I hated that.

"I brought some wine. Mondavi Coastal fine?"

"Quite. Have a seat. I'll get us some glasses," I said, leading him into my lair.

"This is nice," he said as he gazed around at his surroundings.

"Thanks. You stay down in Long Beach, right?"

"Uh, yeah. Just a little apartment. Nothing special . . . or as nice as this."

"Near the beach?"

"A few blocks away from it. You're welcome anytime," he said as I handed the glass to him and seated myself, keeping my legs politely together while being careful not to let my dress slide up too much. He was a man and his eyes gave away that he approved of what was before him.

"I'll remember that," I said as I took a seductive sip from my glass.

Michael leaned back and reached inside his jacket for something.

"I didn't bring any flowers, but I thought you might like this."

"A CD?" I was curious as the generic case was placed in my hand.

"Yes. I had a friend of mine make this for me. He burns CDs for people as a side gig."

"Oh, so the brother's gettin' his hustle on?" I said in a mock street accent.

"Exactly!" Michael replied laughingly. A lot of the formalities between us evaporated just then. I felt my guard easing. "It's a mix CD with various jazz artists. I took a guess at what you might like and had him throw some wild unheard of stuff in just to keep you on your toes."

I put on my gift CD and we grooved and talked over one more glass of wine before rolling out.

"Are you okay?" Michael said with a look of concern. We were feasting on appetizers at Heaven. No dress code problems this time.

"Hunh? Oh, I'm more than okay," I said as I savored the piece of fried green tomato. As I was taking the name of the place literally, my toes were still twitching under the table.

"I do the same thing with the homemade rolls they bring out." I didn't believe him, but it was nice of Michael to go out of his way to put me at ease.

Following the appetizers, we got around to our entrees. I had the crusted salmon while Michael ate the shrimp and vegetable quesadilla. The place was filled with the usual assortment of celebrities, but I had my very own to focus on.

"Did I ever tell you how sweet you are?"

"Thanks, Isrie. I think you're a sweet person too. Sweet and lovely."

"No, I mean it, Michael. Really. How come you're still on the market? I just don't get it." I took a sip of Chardonnay to wash down my bite of fish.

"Maybe I wasn't looking for anything before. My job keeps me so busy."

"You mean to tell me there's absolutely *no one* in your life?"

"Not in a long time. Most women have trouble adjusting to my work schedule," he said as he continued to smile cordially. He then took a drink of his wine as well.

It was our first date, so I was careful not to rush things. I didn't want to come across as either a psycho or a snoop. We continued dinner as Michael asked me more about my parents and I learned more about his job. I find it troubling to admit, but I was already wondering about how he would be in bed.

I was too full to put away dessert, but found myself sharing a slice of cheesecake with him anyway. As the last piece of crust disappeared off the plate, our waiter approached the table to see if there was anything else he could do for us. Michael just asked for the check and the waiter walked off to calculate the final damage to Michael's wallet.

All this time I'd been rebelling against the type of guy my parents had in mind for me, but as I sat here sharing food and good times with Michael, I realized this might not be so bad.

"I'd like to do this again sometime," Michael said in a low, intense tone that reeked of seriousness.

"Okay," I answered without hesitation. "Just let me know."

The waiter returned, interrupting the intense gaze we were sharing. Michael took the bill off the table as our waiter disappeared once again. He reached for his wallet and began sliding a credit card out. I wasn't really staring, but had seen the top of the Visa symbol before Michael suddenly stopped.

Michael looked as if he was having a moment of confusion and I began thinking to myself, "Lord, please don't let this man be broke and about to stiff me with the bill." Maybe everything had been too perfect up to this point.

My brief moment of shaken faith dissolved. The credit card went back into its slot. Michael smiled, as if sensing my nervousness. His fingers slid across the eel skin and into the bill compartment, where a wad of cash came out. Some people preferred to use cash. I wasn't going to question that, as I already felt guilty.

"I hope you don't mind if we wrap this up early tonight, Isrie. I have to go out of town in the morning. . . . My job."

"On the weekend?" I was hoping to keep this going tonight.

"Unfortunately. My work schedule is a strange one, but I've gotten used to it. I should be back by midweek."

"Next week? Call me?"

"Would you think otherwise?"

We held hands as Michael drove me home. The ride was smooth and relaxing and I let out a yawn as I stretched.

"Sorry," I said at the unintentional noise I'd just made.

"It's okay. You look relaxed."

"I am. Thank you. Tonight was chips."

"Chips?"

"As in, 'All that and a bag of—.' I got that from my girl, Deja. You need to meet her. She's always coming up with original ways of saying things. Maybe all of us can go out sometime. She has a new boyfriend."

"Is that what I am?"

"My boyfriend? Hmm. It's too early to say," I said with a laugh as I placed my index finger on my temple. "I'm not in a rush, are you?"

"Nah, Isrie. Nice and smooth," Michael said with a little flare of confidence. He adjusted his grip on the steering wheel and drove on.

The BMW rolled into my complex and came to a stop in a vacant spot near the main lobby. The car was still running when I unbuckled my seat belt.

"What are you doing? I'm going to walk you up."

"No, you're not. I had a wonderful night, and to tell you the truth . . . I don't know if I would let you leave. I'm just being honest. You've got packing to do and it's too early for what I'm thinking right now."

"You're right," he agreed without making any kind of fuss. That kind of put me off guard. I would have liked if he had protested just a little. Maybe Michael was a little too nice. I didn't bother flirting with him as I was through with mixed signals after what accidentally happened with Theron.

"Good night, Michael."

"Good night, Isrie." There went those chills again.

I was still feeling the goose bumps when Michael leaned over the armrest and kissed me. His mouth tasted like an Altoid mixed with the cheesecake we shared earlier. I just focused on living in the moment as I gripped his hand tightly and offered up my lips and tongue to him. Five minutes later and I'd learned it was as good as I thought it would be and then some. I began leaning over the armrest, urging him to take this to the next level.

"Good night," Michael whispered as he played with my tongue that was darting about across his lips. The vibration from his voice tickled but brought me back from my bliss. I composed myself and gave a final smile before making my exit. Michael waited until I was safely inside the lobby and honked as he drove off.

"Nice night, Ms. Walker?" the concierge inquired as I strolled by. I didn't answer. I was rushing for a cold shower. Maybe Deja's vibrator idea wasn't so bad after all.

Inside my apartment, I shut the door as if someone were waiting on me. But the only thing waiting on me was the silence of an empty place. I backed against the door and took a deep breath. Why did Michael have this effect on me? I knew I couldn't make it through the night feeling like this.

My purse fell to the floor. I laughed nervously at myself, but that didn't stop me. I closed my eyes. I was alone, but Michael was in here. I needed him to touch me now.

I stroked my thighs as I imagined he would. Strong yet tender hands massaged them, moving across my entire body, caressing me, feeling me. Slowly caressing my hips, then across my stomach and up to my chest, I let my mind guide me, imagining the sensation of his kisses on my skin. I undid my straps and lowered the front of my dress slowly. I let the fabric linger against my nipples, teasingly, before leaving my bare breasts exposed. I played with my babies, knowing what gets me hot. I pushed harder against the door, legs tensing as I slid my hand between them. Slowly, I massaged my clitoris through my thong at first, letting the sensation of the fabric stimulate me. I moaned as the moist heat built below. My pussy was heading toward overload. Sweat was beginning to form on my chest, my breath shallow. My feet slid out beneath me until I was resting on my ass, back to the door. I moved the damp thong aside, sliding my fingers inside my throbbing, steamy cave, one finger at first, then three. Michael's dick should feel like this. I was gushing and couldn't take it anymore. I stroked faster and faster and came until I was left a panting heap on the floor. Now I was ready for that shower.

21

Deja

I didn't know what I was doing jogging, but it was my idea. Isrie looked worried.

"Are you sure you don't want to stop?" she asked as she slowed for me to catch up.

"Absolutely not," I gasped as I jogged up to her at a snail's pace. "No pain, no gain."

I had worked up the nerve to try to relieve some stress (and weight) by jogging. My girl Isrie's place had a nice path that wound through the private park on her grounds, so I stopped by with a change of clothes after work. Theron was still helping me at the studio. He even went a step further and cleared a back room for himself over there that he used from time to time to give me my space at home. I still couldn't figure out why he hadn't looked up any of his old friends. I mean, most of them were no good, but some had to be okay. If I didn't know better, I would have sworn he was hiding from something or somebody.

"What have we done? A mile?"

"Half a mile," Isrie answered as she slowed her trot to a quick walk.

"Oh."

"D-Square," Isrie said as she followed beside me with her hands on her hips, "what made you decide to go jogging with me?"

"You want the truth or a lie?"

"Your choice, girlfriend."

"Ivan."

"Why? Did he say something about your—"

"Body? Nah. We've *closed the deal* once more since that night, but I still feel self-conscious around him, y'know? He's so damn perfect."

"He's not perfect. You've been all up in his face, you haven't noticed how his top lip hangs a little?"

I laughed. "Girl, stop. You know what I'm saying."

"And what I'm saying is that if you're going to do something, you need to do it for yourself and not for some man."

Isrie saw that my breathing had come under control again, so we started jogging at a faster pace. She still looked untouched in her navy blue jogging suit, but my white T-shirt and gray, baggy sweats were stained with sweat.

"This *is* something I need to do for me," I told her.

Isrie cut her eyes at me in disbelief. "Your brother still in town?" she asked, choosing to change the subject.

"Yeah. He's at my studio now. Looks like Theron's grown up and learned some responsibility. He's been a big help. I even let him crash at the studio sometimes."

"Oh," was all Isrie said as she checked our time on her watch.

"You've been kinda quiet about your scene," I said. "What's up with you? How was your date last week?"

"Just wonderful. Everything went perfect. You know I'm a little leery, though."

"Yeah? What does he do anyway?"

"He's in pharmaceutical sales. Travels a lot."

"Any baggage?"

"Nope. I'm not into that Zen shit you be yakkin' about, but he seems at peace with himself."

"I wish you the best with your new man, girl."

"Yeah. Ditto. Both you and I deserve it."

"You never told me if y'all *closed the deal*."

"Nope. No rushing," Isrie said with a giggle. "I wanted to, though. I ain't even much gonna lie. Something about the way his mouth curves and the way he says my name. The man can kiss too."

"Do tell. Chips?"

"Chips!"

The chiming of a missed call interrupted our laughter. I stopped jogging and checked the number. It was a call from my work phone, so I figured it was Theron. Maybe somebody had showed up unannounced for some photos. I dialed my studio and walked under a nearby tree to talk.

My phone rang twice before someone picked it up. I still couldn't hear a voice, though.

"Hello? Hello?" I said with the phone to one ear and my finger in the other one.

"That was quick," my brother said on the other end as his voice finally broke through the silence.

"Something wrong over there?"

"Nah. Why would you think that? I toldja I got it straight."

"Then what's up, bruh?"

"Your boy called for ya. That's all."

"Ivan? What'd he say?"

"He said that he can't live without you and that he was going to throw himself off a cliff if you didn't call him back."

"For real? He said that?"

"Hell nah. He just said to tell you he called."

"You're going to get your ass kicked, bruh."

"Love you too, sis." *Click.*

My crazy brother left me muttering to myself before dialing Ivan's cell phone number, which I had recently memorized. I motioned to Isrie that I wouldn't be much longer. Ivan's phone rang once, then again, before someone picked up. A woman's laughter was the first thing I heard.

"Hello?" the woman said as she continued laughing with whoever was with her.

I thought I may have dialed a digit wrong and hung up. Isrie saw the disturbed look on my face.

"Everything okay?" Isrie asked as she walked up.

"Yeah." I scrolled through the cell phone menu to pull up the last number I had dialed. I hadn't messed up. I felt a lump forming in my throat. I pushed the REDIAL button.

"Hello?" It was a man's voice this time. He picked up the phone on the first ring. I smiled, but felt something other than happiness inside.

"Hey," I said matter-of-factly. "Did you call for me?"

"Yeah. *Did you just call here?*"

"Yeah. Did I disturb you?" I meant for my remark to be stinging.

"No, not at all. Why'd you hang up, boo?" Go ahead and play that game.

"I thought I had the wrong number."

"That's just Sophia," Ivan said. Like I couldn't figure that shit out.

"Uh huh. What do you want?"

"I was calling to see what you've been up to. You want to do something this weekend? Skiing?"

"I'll see. I've got a lot of work to do. And you know I can't ski," I said as coldly as possible without Isrie figuring out what was on my mind. I continued to smile as she looked on.

"I don't care about the skiing, boo. I just want to have you alone up in the mountains in a hot tub."

"Oh," was all I had to offer.

"Deja, what's wrong?" Ivan asked. I thought I heard Sophia mouth off in the background.

"Nothing. Look, I gotta go. I'm doing something with my girl, Isrie, right now."

"Sorry. Call me later?"

"Yeah. Sure." *Click.*

"Ready to finish the mile?" Isrie asked as I clicked my phone shut.

"More than ready. I'm starting to get cold. Let's do two miles, though."

"You sure about that, girl?" Isrie said as she broke stride.

"Hella sure," I replied as I shot past her.

PART II

Coming into Focus
(Where We're Going)

22

Isrie

With the time change, darkness came early. I was always sure to have my keys handy when leaving the spa. I was tense and in need of a massage myself, but ready to settle for a nice glass of wine when I got home. My coworker Kendra was talking about going to a martini bar to unwind as we walked out.

"Excuse me, miss." I didn't recognize the voice so I simply kept walking. Kendra, her usual curiosity piqued, slowed.

"Girl, I think he's talking to you," she said.

I stopped to take notice of what had her attention. A white limo was parked on the shoulder, its driver looking dead at us. Limos were so common out here, I tended to tune them out. Its driver, an overly muscular, gap-toothed brother with a courteous smile, motioned me toward him.

"I've never seen this guy before in my life. Stick around for a sec."

"Alright," said Kendra.

"Can I help you?" I asked as I cautiously approached the limo driver.

"Are you Isrie Walker?"

"Who are you?" I asked, answering his question with a question.

"A Mr. Michael Ross sent me to pick you up."

"Is he in the car?" I inquired of the driver. I couldn't see through the tint, but I still strained my eyes trying to.

"No ma'am, but he's waiting for you." Waiting for me. The driver's words gave me a fluttery feeling all over.

"You still need me?" Kendra asked impatiently. I had forgotten that she was still shadowing me.

"No. You can go, Kendra. Thanks."

"Shit. I envy you, girl" was all she said before jaywalking across Wilshire to her car. I still didn't know what to expect next. I wasn't going to leave my car here.

The limo driver, as if sensing my hesitation, reached into the car and pulled out a cell phone. With a quick dial, he had someone on the other end. He said a few words into it while nodding.

"Mr. Ross said for me to follow you to your place to drop off your car."

"I'd like to talk to him for a second," I said while extending my hand. I hadn't heard from Michael since he left town and I wanted to make sure this wasn't some sick joke. My heart was telling me it wasn't, though.

"I missed you," was the first thing out of Michael's mouth on the phone.

"What are you doing? Where are you?"

"No answers. Now go home and park your car."

"Michael, this is so sudden. I've got work in the morning—"

"So hurry up then," he responded laughingly. "You don't need to change out of that uniform either." Michael hadn't known me that long but still had me down to a tee. The driver was looking at his watch while pretending not to listen.

I let out a sigh and decided to give in. I gave the burly driver directions in case he got lost behind me in traffic. Contrary to what I thought, the limousine stayed right on my tail up until I turned into my complex on South Bixel. I wrestled seriously with running up to my apartment and freshening up, but decided to follow Michael's instructions. I had no idea what was planned, but gave in nonetheless. My driver, whose name I learned was Darrell, was happy that I was no longer putting up a fight.

Inside the limo, I adjusted my linens as I sunk into the soft leather seats. I didn't know where we were heading, but took my tennis shoes off when I saw us merging onto the Harbor Freeway. Michael said he lived in Long Beach so I assumed that was our destination. I took a peek at the stock of liquor with a smile, but left it alone. I sat back and looked out the tinted windows at the speck that was the sun as it was doing its final fade somewhere by Hawaii. Hawaii—what I would give to be there right now.

"Darrell, can they see me in here?" I asked my driver. He had dropped the privacy window moments earlier to tell me how to operate the radio if I chose.

"Not at all, Ms. Walker."

"Still not telling me where we're going? Do you know what the surprise is?"

"Mum's the word, ma'am."

"See if you get a tip."

I was trying to find some jazz on the radio and accidentally turned it to that Young Buck song from the Infiniti Club. I let out a laugh as I mumbled the chorus, remembering Theron's facial expressions, and left the radio on that station. Darrell the driver turned his head and looked back to make sure everything was okay, but then put his eyes back on the road. When the limo swerved right onto the San Diego Freeway ramp, I was sure we were headed to Long Beach or somewhere near it. Shortly after that, we were on East Pacific Coast Highway. Michael said he lived near here so when I saw the three-story white apartments with blue tiled roofs, I knew he was waiting for me inside one of them. The street sign read TERMINO AVENUE. I began fumbling to put my shoes back on as the car slowed. Why'd I let this man talk me into coming down here in my work clothes?

"Here we are, ma'am."

"I can see that, Darrell. So where's my surprise?"

"Third floor. Number 323. Over there," he said efficiently while pointing toward my destination.

"Here goes nothing," I said to myself. As I stepped out the door Darrell held open for me, the cool breeze off San Pedro Bay caressed my face.

"How do I look?" I playfully asked my driver, looking back at my tore-up reflection in the tinted window.

"Like a million bucks."

"I'll bet you say that to all the ladies," I teased.

"Actually I don't, ma'am. I'm gay."

"Oh."

23

Deja

"What's wrong with you, boo?" asked Ivan.

"Why does something have to be wrong?" I said.

"Because you never called me back yesterday."

"I told you I was busy when I talked to you on the phone, didn't I?" I snarled in a rare show of negative vibes. Breathe, girl, breathe. This was one night I wished Theron were working with me, but he actually had plans of his own. I was working late and had avoided answering my phones. I was just about to close when Ivan came up the stairs. As I walked by it, I snatched my brother's favorite photo of Sophia, which was mocking me, off the wall.

"So *that's* what this shit's about," Ivan muttered, losing his composure now. "I knew it."

"Good! I'm glad you figured things out, Ivan. Now leave."

"Girl, you *knew* about me and Sophia already!" Ivan's arm swatted at the air causing the sleeve on his denim jacket to draw up his forearm. His Dodgers baseball cap, perched atop his do-rag-covered head, threatened to fall off.

"Yeah. I did. And my stupid ass thought I could ignore it. Well, I can't, dammit!"

"And I understand. That's why I wanted you to call me back last night." Ivan's hand came to rest on my shoulder. "Things are over between me and her."

"Please," I said as I walked out from under his hand. "What

do you think this is? One of them romance novels? Like I'm supposed to believe that shit."

"No. No fiction, Deja. Just fact. I was breaking things down to her when you called. It was never anything serious and you know that. Please."

"I want to believe you."

"Then why don't you? Haven't I always been straight up with you?"

"Yes, but—"

"Unh uh. No buts," he said as he caught up with me.

Ivan's lips caressed the back of my neck, sending electricity through my hairs back there. I felt that familiar rush of reckless abandon I had in his presence coming back. As I felt the blood rushing into my bosom beneath my blouse and other unmentionable places, I knew. I was putty again and wanting Ivan to mold me as he saw fit.

"Boy, don't be shittin' me, okay?"

"Never," he smoothly replied. Both of his hands had slipped around my waist. His fingers smoothly slid into my pants, down past my elastic band. With the skill of a surgeon, he rubbed my mound with tiny, upward strokes.

"G-go lock the door. . . . And close the blinds." I gasped, losing all sense of reason and forgetting the arguments I'd just made. It was like I was addicted to him.

While strutting to the front door, Ivan threw his jacket and cap down. I watched as he pulled his T-shirt over his head, revealing rippled back muscles. The snapping sound of the latch eased my fear of Theron or somebody else walking in on us. As Ivan lowered the blinds, I peered toward the area my brother had cleared out as his sometimes bedroom. Hey, he had violated my space before, so it was only fair. Besides, I owned this stuff.

Ivan stalked toward me with that look in his eyes. I smiled while trying to concentrate on the shirt buttons I was fumbling with. My bare-chested boy toy grabbed me by the wrists and pulled my hands away from their task. Slowly, he guided my right hand to his belt buckle to undo it, which I obliged. He took my left hand and inserted my first two fingers into his mouth where he sucked the tips. As my eye lids involuntarily flickered and toes curled, Ivan grasped the front of my blouse with his free hand . . . and yanked.

Plastic buttons danced and skittered across the floor. I fought back the urge to quibble over the price of my top with him, knowing that was suddenly low on my priority list. Ivan guided my moistened fingers to his chest where I ran them over his granite curves. I hurried up, pulling his zipper down. He saw where my eyes went as his jeans fell around his ankles, but he had other ideas. I had a chaise lounge, which I used as a prop, situated in front of my background. Ivan looked dead at it.

"You're a bad boy."

"You ain't seen nothin' yet," he replied, leading me by the hand.

Ivan removed the rest of my clothes and had me lay across the lounge. I was waiting for him to remove his white Calvin Kleins and join me, but he just stood there. Ivan surveyed the dimly lit surroundings. He glanced toward my automatic camera that was mounted in front of us, then toward my boom box.

"What are you looking for? Everything's right here," I said in a low, sex-kittenish tone. I could smell my sweet, sticky syrup as it began to boil.

"You'll see."

First, Ivan pushed PLAY on my boom box. Soft, hypnotic sounds came from the speakers. I assumed he was finished. Next, he located the ON switch to a nearby strobe light and flicked off the overheads. The whole room erupted into a wild light show.

"You are hella wild, Mr. Dempsey."

"The only way to be with you," he replied. "I'm trying to keep up."

"Then come here 'cause I'm getting cold." I brushed my hair aside and patted a spot on the lounge next to me.

"Not yet," he replied as he walked behind the camera that was aimed dead at me.

"No! Leave that alone!" I shrieked with part shock, part embarrassment.

"Relax, girl. Y'know, I did a little photography when I was in college."

The strobes were still going as I squinted to see Ivan set the Olympus on automatic and focus it.

"This is just too freaky," I said as he rejoined me at the foot of the lounge.

Ivan pulled off his briefs, revealing his stallion that was rearing up.

"There's nothing freaky about *that* though," I giggled, admiring the view. I reached for him, wanting to take it in my mouth and suck the shit out of it.

Ivan pulled away from my grasp, pausing for a moment before saying, "You know what's missing?"

"Not a damn thing," I said as I tried to reach for him again.

"Hang on."

I curiously watched him gather up his jeans. He fished around before reaching into one of the pockets. He palmed a small plastic bottle, then held it up. In my business, I had seen enough of the pills inside it.

"Want some?" he asked nonchalantly.

"No, Ivan. I don't do that shit . . . and didn't know you did."

"Relax, relax," he said in an even tone. "It's just a little something to spice things up."

"To each his own, but I don't do Ecstasy. Now please put that away."

Ivan looked indignant but then changed his expression. He opened the bottle anyway, emptying two pills onto his hand, which he quickly swallowed. "Alright, boo. You'll never see it again. Like I said, it was just a little something to spice things up."

"What else are you doing that I don't know about?" He could see a look of seriousness was creeping onto my face.

"That's it. Just a little X. I've only used it a few times, nothing stronger. I hope you don't think any less of me."

"No, I don't. We've all done crazy things in our lives," I said, pointing to the strobe light. Part of me was screaming inside my head to not let this issue slide, but another part was rationalizing things by saying I was making a mountain out of a molehill. I looked into his eyes and went with the latter. "Just promise me you won't do it again."

"Done. Now . . . will you let me love you?"

In a low whisper, I said, "Yes."

Ivan had nothing more to say as he pushed me onto my back and began working on warming me up again. The flickering, slowed-down images caused by the strobe aroused me as Ivan's tongue blazed a trail across my body from head to toe. His warm breath across my belly and breasts had a sister catching seizures 'n shit. When he finally had me begging, Ivan took care of business and slid up inside me. I could feel him swelling, expanding even more as I flowed, like trying to plug a dam with his dick. Damn, I was loving me some Ivan. Over the music and the high notes of my own I was suddenly reaching, I paid no attention to the whirring and clicking as the camera committed its sensual subjects to film.

24

Isrie

Darrell the driver offered to escort me up to the apartment, but I passed. It was dark now, but the place looked safe enough. For a second, my only thought was that my parents would never forgive me if I misjudged Michael and he turned out to be a serial killer. The odds of that were low. I mean, who ever heard of a black serial killer? Especially a *good-looking* black serial killer. Think about it.

The door to 323 was already open. I knew the limo driver must have called Michael when we arrived. Fresh-cut flowers and jasmine were inside, as I could tell from the way my nose was twitching. My first visit to what I presumed was Michael's place and he was going to extra lengths to impress a sister. *Hella tight*, as Deja would say.

"Come in, come in," Michael said as he saw me drifting in the door. He was clad in a white wife-beater and linen pants. I noticed his shirt thrown over a chair as he bounded back and forth between the kitchen on my immediate right and the dining area on my left. He was just finishing preparations for the dinner he'd made. Places for two were set on the table. I could see a tossed garden salad in the bowl and fried green tomatoes cooling on a napkin-lined plate. My boy was just adding to his resume.

"Michael, this—this is wonderful," I said as I blushed and took everything in. I was regretting not changing clothes.

"Close the door, Isrie. I don't want anybody else smelling this food I'm burning." He had done something to his hair. It was edged as always, but it had grown out some. Curlier too. It had been almost a week since I last saw him, but I held his image close to me, as well as our kiss that night.

"I look awful and probably smell as bad," I said as I walked into the kitchen behind him.

"There you go. I wouldn't believe that for a second," Michael said just before giving me a quick kiss on the lips. I wanted more but I wasn't about to disturb a man trying to cook for me. "If you want to freshen up, though, the bathroom's just around the corner."

"That would be nice. Thanks."

"You're quite welcome. Hurry up, though. Dinner's almost done. You like overcooked lasagna?"

"Boy, you know you didn't overcook it."

"True. But I have to lower your expectations. That way you'll be more impressed with my handiwork." Michael chuckled. There went the goatee curling.

"You just don't know how impressed I am with you."

I left Michael alone to absorb the compliment and excused myself to freshen up. I took notice of the large living room on my way to the bathroom. It was very tidy, but kind of empty—a large flat-screen TV with two African statuettes on each side, plush gray carpet, the typical stereo system with mismatched components in the corner, and a gray sectional sofa. No pictures were on the walls or lying around. I could still smell the flowers and jasmine, but they must have been in the bedroom. I smiled to myself at the thought.

In Michael's bathroom, everything was trimmed in silver. The black towels were neatly arranged on the racks and looked brand new. I guessed that what he said about being on the road a lot was true. There was another door to the bathroom—presumably an entrance from the bedroom. Out of habit, I turned the lock on that door as well to feel more private. The nice man even had the toilet seat down. He was just too good. God must have seen what I'd gone through with Ryan and took care of me.

After applying a little bit of makeup in the bathroom, I rejoined Michael. By then, he had the table completely set and was just waiting on me.

"Sorry about making you wait."

"You're worth it."

"Enough with the clichés, Michael. You already got me over here."

Michael let out a deep laugh. "Okay. I'll stop. The only thing is, these clichés are true."

I sat down across the dining table from him. "How come you didn't call me?"

"While I was out of town?"

"Yes."

"I was very busy."

"Too busy to call," I pushed.

"Most of that time? Yes. Of course, after the way things ended after our night out last week . . . I was afraid that if I called you I wouldn't be able to finish my work. I've already been thinking about you *twenty-four/seven.*"

"That's why you had me kidnapped tonight?"

"Yep," he answered as he raised his wineglass in a toast. I raised mine back, but wasn't drinking more than one glass. I had to be to work in the morning.

"I like your apartment. You keep it so neat."

"Thanks. Remind me to give you the grand tour when we finish."

"I'm still mad at you for not letting me change."

"Feeling out of place?"

"Yes! You're looking all good 'n shit and I'm looking like a refugee intern."

Michael stroked his goatee while he laughed. He was thinking up something. He sat up from the table and excused himself. I was wondering what was up when he returned wearing a T-shirt, shorts, and a pair of socks. My mouth dropped while he continued smiling at me.

"Get your plate," he said.

"Huh?"

"Get your plate. We're going to do this casual. C'mon."

Michael pulled out my chair for me, then led me by the hand to the living room where he set his plate on the floor.

"We can't do this . . . your carpet. What if we stain it?"

"Then I'll just clean it. Sit down, girl."

"You're sure?"

"Sit!"

Both of us laughed as I set my plate down, then went back for our wineglasses. We sat on the floor next to one of the African statuettes.

"So, what's the story behind this one?" I asked as I pointed to the brown carved figure.

"That statue is from Ghana. It's supposed to be an ancient fertility god."

"For real?"

"Nah, I just made that shit up."

"Smart-ass. You remind me of my best friend's brother."

"Is that good or bad?"

"No comment," I said as I kicked off one of my shoes and started stretching my toes. I was dying to get out of my work clothes as well.

"Y'know, you can make yourself more comfortable, Isrie. It won't offend me."

"Do you have something I can change into?"

"I might. It may be too forward, but I'm hoping you spend the night."

"Maybe. Maybe not," I smiled. "Is that why it smells so good by your bedroom?"

"Oh, you noticed. You didn't sneak a peek, did you?"

"No. That would have been nosy of me. You might have a surprise in there for someone else."

"No. No plans for anyone but you. I'll let you see when we finish eating . . . if you want to."

"Alright."

An hour later, after my food had digested and I'd had more than my one glass of wine, Michael led me to the master bedroom. We had just come inside from his deck, where we had conversed and kissed like a couple of horny teenagers. I was still barefoot and the carpet felt cool to the touch between my toes.

"Oh, my God," I said as I was caught off guard when the bedroom door opened.

"Surprise," he said as he held me by the shoulders. "I hope you like it."

The pleasant scents should have prepared me, but they didn't. Michael's bedroom was filled with bouquets of fresh flowers. Rose petals were sprinkled across his king-size bed and candles flickered inside the glass globes that were positioned around the room.

"Michael, *oooh*," I moaned. "Why couldn't you wait 'til the weekend to do this?"

"Because you need this kind of treatment now and because I didn't think I could wait any longer," he answered in one of those deep, manly tones that make a woman's clothes fly off.

My clothes didn't fly off, but Michael did assist me in removing my top once I raised my arms above my head. He held my shirt as he admired me standing before him in my bra. I watched his eyes as I slowly pulled my pants down, revealing the other half of my black Prada underwear set. Michael said nothing, but continued to smile, slowly looking me over admiringly.

"Are you joining me?" I asked my silent host. He hadn't removed any of his clothing.

"Yes, but not now. I still have other plans."

"Oh. Okay," I said, feeling uncertainty now about what was going to happen.

"Lie down on the bed. I want to make this memorable for you."

I complied and sat down on the large bed before inching myself back while facing him. His penetrating gaze was making me wet, and I'm sure he could see my nipples popping up through the spaces in the lace fabric of my bra. I reached back with both hands and released the clasp on the bra. The straps slid down my arms, giving Michael a full view of what I was offering to him.

Michael nodded in appreciation of the show he was getting, then put on the face that said he was deep in thought. I was puzzled too as he waltzed over to the side of the bed and picked up something resting on the nightstand behind one of the bouquets.

"Told you I had other plans," he said while he waved a tube of massage oil from . . . my spa.

"That's from my place!" I screamed out.

"Yep. I bought it that day I asked you out. When you were at lunch. I'm not certified like you, but I'm not too bad my damn self. You did such a great job on me, I figured I'd return the favor one day. You don't mind, do you?"

"What? Do I mind your putting your hands on me? *Do I look like I mind*?" I asked facetiously while gesturing at my seminude self in his bed. "Bring it on, man."

Michael joined me in the bed to begin rubbing me down. I was ready to get the knots worked out of my back, but wanted another kiss from those lips first to tide me over. Before I let him put me on my stomach, I pulled myself next to him and ran my hands across his firm chest as I slid my tongue into his mouth. His T-shirt was still on and had to go. I pulled it out of his shorts and over his head before throwing it on the side of the bed. As we kissed, the sensation of our bare chests against each other was about to send me into overload.

"Come do this massage before I tackle you."

"Alright, Isrie," he said calmly. "Let's do this."

I spread out on the bed and waited patiently. Well . . . kinda patiently while I listened to Michael's hands rubbing back and forth, warming the oil he had applied to them. I knew the scent very well. It was called Freesia Dreams.

I moaned as soon as I felt the pressure from his fingertips. They slid and glided across my back muscles at first, spreading out from my spine and toward my shoulder blades. As he moved his strong hands, he kneaded my skin like he was handling dough. The man worked over my back and neck, then moved down to my lower body, stopping only to apply fresh oil. When he did the unthinkable and began massaging my ass, I really felt that this was someone I needed to be married to. I still didn't know enough about Michael, but I liked the way I felt in his presence. Safe. Safe and wanted, was a good way to put it.

"Oooh. You're hired," I giggled. Michael had moved to the arches of my feet that were naturally ticklish.

"But we never discussed salary . . . or vacation," he replied with a laugh.

"Boy, this *is* your vacation."

"So when do I go to work?"

"Whenever you feel like," I replied.

I said nothing after that, but waited for Michael to do with me what he wished. I closed my eyes and thought about what I craved just then as if he could read my mind. He could. I heard the rustling of fabric as Michael removed his shorts and whatever else. His hands gripped both my ankles before flipping my oil-stained backside onto his petal-covered comforter. I finally had the full view I had been longing for since I first touched that scar on his back.

"You are so beautiful," he said.

"Thanks," I bashfully replied. I was busy checking out his package and got caught.

I imagined Barry White music playing as Michael slowly stalked me across his bed. There wasn't much stalking involved as I was his willing prey and just waited for him. He crawled up between my legs and smiled at me as his face came to rest just below my bikini line.

"N-no. I've been sweating . . . at work," I apologized. I wasn't going to admit that I had done a little clean up job *down there* earlier while in his bathroom, but my kitty still wasn't as fresh as if I had recently showered.

"So?" he responded. "I want you, Isrie. Sweat and all." My chills came over me on cue. Well, come on down then and make yourself at home, I thought.

Michael was dedicated as he probed me with his mouth, sending me quivering every which way but loose. I was one of those sisters that didn't need it, but when a man was good, and knew what he was doing with his tongue and *where* to do it—hey. When I couldn't take his oral manipulation any longer, I found myself trying to move back. His firm hands on my thighs wouldn't let me escape, though. If I didn't know any better, I would have sworn that he was enjoying this more than me.

When I was on the verge of tears and begging for him to stop, he took one last dart at my sweet spot with his tongue that flicked in and out like a snake's.

"Do you have condoms?" I asked breathlessly.

Michael answered, "Yeah. Hang on."

While he regrouped and walked to the bathroom, I watched the candlelit shadows on the walls and caught my breath. In less than a minute, he was back with his magic wand wrapped in a ribbed condom. *Now* we were ready.

I felt a sharp pain as Michael's wrapped goodness entered me. Sensing my brief discomfort, he eased his thrusts and began working it slowly to bring on another climax inside me. I had thoughts that he might be a little too large for me, but I wasn't about to admit it.

"Are you okay?"

"I'll be fine," I replied as I looked into his eyes. "Kiss me."

He went right to work, kissing my lips briefly before going over to my ear and down my neck. His hands moved across my breasts, then up my arms where our hands interlocked.

"Shit," I said as things got comfortable and very good. It wouldn't be the last time I uttered that. I brought my legs up and wrapped them around his waist, nudging him on to go deeper. Mmm, he felt so good inside me. As I came again and again, I relished having someone that was meant for me in every way and prayed that nothing stupid would happen to fuck it up.

"Do you love me, Michael?" I asked as I sensed his intensity increasing. I knew he was about to climax. I really didn't intend on asking that, but it just seemed natural. Like something from a dream I'd had.

"Y-yes, *yessss*," he hissed as he looked into my eyes with sharp clarity.

"Say it. Tell me."

"I love you, Isrie," he said in a low tone as he huffed. I still got chills at the sound of my name on his lips.

"Don't hurt me."

"I won't. I promise."

At hearing the assurance from him, I joined in sending him hurtling toward his inevitable explosion. Michael was drenched in sweat now as I threw myself up to meet his long, penetrating thrusts.

"That's it. Love me, baby. Give it to me, daddy," I purred seductively.

Michael howled as he shot past the point of no return. I came with him as he erupted before crumpling in a trembling heap inside me. I held him tightly in my arms as we recovered from our release, neither of us able to speak. Once his energy returned, he rolled over to the side where he lay motionless for a long time.

We slept nude by candlelight most of the night. I knew I would need to be up in time to go home, change, and get to work in the morning, but time was on our side. Before daylight, I would have to have some more of him, though. I let Michael sleep a few more hours, heading to the bathroom for another condom before climbing on top of him for another go-round. He had no objections as I rode him as if my life depended on it. He was a keeper.

25

Isrie

At the crack of dawn, I forced my eyelids open. My body was spent and Michael was still sound asleep. I admired the peaceful, content look that draped his face as he lightly snored. He didn't know how much I wanted to rejoin him, but I reeked of sweat, sex, and Freesia Dreams and had to be to work in just a few hours.

The shower crackled to life and I stepped in once it warmed up. All that was available to me was a single bar of deodorant soap. Michael was a serious bachelor, with the the bare minimum in his crib. I hadn't looked inside his extra bedroom but figured that it was where he kept his extra junk.

Mr. Right was stirring when I returned. In the bathroom, I had found his terrycloth robe hanging on the door and put it on. It was soft and very comfortable, but a lot smaller than I thought it would be. I wondered how he wore it.

"How do you squeeze into this?" I asked while briefly flashing him. He was still groggy but his eyes flared at the sight. The ends of my hair were damp so I pulled them out of the collar.

"Huh? Oh. I don't use that. It was a gift that was too small. Why are you up?"

"Because you need to bring me home," I reminded him. "I've got a normal work schedule, *unlike some people I know,* and need to change and stuff."

"Can't you just call in?"

"Yes, but I like my paycheck."

"I can't hold you hostage?" *Damn, he was fine.*

"Ha ha. Nope. You already kidnapped me yesterday. Get up, boy."

Michael yawned once before stretching and rising up from his bed. Rose petals were all over the floor and were sticking to the bottoms of my damp feet.

"Do you want me to clean some of this up?"

"Nah. I have someone come in and do housecleaning."

"You don't care about what they're going to think?" I smiled while pointing at the petals, evidence of our night of passion.

"Nope," he said as he stopped his walk to the bathroom to look back. "I've got nothing to be ashamed of."

"You certainly don't!" I laughed as I ran up and gave him a slap on his firm buns. "Michael?"

"Yeah?"

"How'd you get that scar?"

"The one on my back?" he grunted. "I was in the navy and young and stupid. This crazy girl I was messing with cut me."

"You were doing her wrong?"

"Like I said. I was young and stupid then."

"Yeah. I see. Stupid enough to turn your back on her."

"Once. You want to join me in the shower?"

"No. I'm finished and I need you to hurry up."

"Okay, okay." He chuckled. "Feel free to help yourself to some breakfast or something while you wait."

While he showered, I found both pieces of my uniform and put them on. I balled up my bra and panties and carried them into the living room, where my purse, socks, and shoes were waiting.

I cleaned up last night's mess in the kitchen and put our dishes in the dishwasher. I wasn't really hungry, but found a granola bar in the cabinet and poured myself a glass of milk. I turned on 100.3 The Beat to catch the *Steve Harvey Morning Show* and took a seat at the table. Steve was cracking on J-Lo's love life and the newest celebrity court case. I could hear Michael as he left the bathroom and went back into his room. A knock at his front door startled me in the middle of a laugh. He had mentioned a housekeeper, so I assumed it was her at the door. I checked my clothes and placed my granola bar on the napkin.

I opened the door to a surprise.

"Who the fuck are you?" came from the mouth of the angry ebony visitor before I had a chance to say anything. She was a beautiful, dark-skinned girl slightly younger than me in a black Guess T-shirt and gray denims. The sister's long black locks hung down her back from under the gray sequined scarf on her head and were blowing in the morning wind. My anger started flaring up as I realized I was being played as well.

"Who in the fuck are *you?*" I shot back, getting in her face.

"Bitch, step off before I hurt you," she said as she took a step back. "So my boy's fuckin' with *you* now? Where's that no good motherfucker at?" She was really too pretty to have a mouth like that, but I guess a situation like this brings out the worst in anyone. I've been known to be unladylike when pissed off as well.

I heard someone running up behind me and turned to see Michael. He was looking shocked as he held the fluffy towel around his waist. Disappointment and rage came out in my fist that struck him dead in his eye. I wasn't putting up with getting played . . . or being hurt.

"Ow!" he screamed as he let the towel drop to reach up to his face. "What the hell was that for??!!"

I didn't say anything as he stood there nude. I simply moved to the side for him to see his visitor in the doorway. What happened next was unexpected as well.

"T, what the fuck's going on! Who is this bitch in the hospital scrubs? Where's my boy at? Is Lloyd in there?"

"T? Who's *T?*" I turned to ask Michael. "And who in the hell is Lloyd?"

"Uh. Hold on. One at a time," he said as he stooped down and snatched his towel back up. He was blinking his sore eye.

"First off, Lloyd's not here, Charletta. He's at his cousin's. I wanted some quiet time with my friend here."

"Oh" was all that came from an embarrassed Charletta. Her claws had gone back in. "Sorry about this, T. But you know how thangs been with Lloyd and me. I thought *she* was up in here with him."

"Yeah. It's cool."

"Cool? You still didn't answer my question, Michael," I shouted, still not accepting everything as cool. "Why is she calling you T?"

"That's my nickname, Isrie. Lloyd's my roommate. He stays here too since I'm gone so often. The other bedroom is his."

"Oh." It was my turn to imitate Charletta.

"Look, Imma let y'all go handle y'all's business," Charletta interrupted. "Tell Lloyd I stopped by."

"Alright," Michael or T answered. "I'll do that."

I didn't know what to say, but decided to just walk past Michael. I headed straight to my tennis shoes in the living room and plopped down on the carpet to put them on. The front door slammed shut.

"So, that's how much you trust me?" he said.

"Sorry about your eye." I continued putting on my right shoe.

"Forget my eye. It's not what's hurting." He was sitting on the sectional behind me and I was too ashamed to look at him.

"I know. Look, just give me a ride home and I'll be out of your hair. Last night was wonderful."

"So that's it?"

"Why do they call you T?" I asked choosing to ignore his question.

"That's my middle name. Thomas."

"Oh. I guess you can tell I've got some issues."

"Yeah," he chuckled. "But that doesn't mean I don't want this to continue."

"I dunno. I need to think. Why don't you get dressed and take me home?"

"Stay, Isrie. Just a little while longer. I enjoy being with you."

I didn't answer. I was still sitting on the carpet with my back to him. He still had just a towel on and I was afraid to look and turn to jelly. I closed my eyes and controlled a sniffle.

I felt Michael move off the sofa and onto the floor behind me but I didn't move.

"Please. Stay," he whispered as he slowly creeped up. His arms began wrapping around me, but I flinched and got onto my knees to crawl away from him.

Michael followed me across the floor. From beneath his towel, I could feel his manhood pushing from behind as he caught up with me. I was aroused and caught off guard by a mini orgasm, which made me stop fleeing for a second. He sensed my body's reaction and his towel slipped off as he pulled me back into him. I knew I didn't really want to leave, but my mind had been in control up until then. Now my mind was following my body's lead.

My resistance fell as I felt kisses on my neck. Michael was on top of me and I liked it. His hands slid my bottoms off with ease, revealing my bare ass to him. I let out a moan as the hand reached around between my legs and gently stroked me, making me purr like a kitten. My wetness surprised me this time. As he did this, I slowly backed onto what was awaiting me and spread my hips. This was stupid of me as there was no condom, but I was on the pill and was feeling guilty over not trusting him minutes earlier. Who am I kidding? I did it because the dick felt so good.

I gasped as he slammed me back onto him with a yank. My eyes rolled back in my head and I let out a scream of passion.

"Told you I wouldn't hurt you," he panted.

"Yes, yes, yes. I know. Don't stop."

Michael was now crouched on his knees with me riding in his lap. His hands were free to roam now and were both under my top, squeezing my breasts and pinching my nipples. With each squeeze, I came more and more until I was screaming obscenities at the ceiling. I rode him as if to break his dick, but it only went deeper.

I began crying and pleading for him to stop when I couldn't take it anymore, but he would have none of it. I was almost hyperventilating when I felt Michael release all he had into me. His hands finally let go and I fell onto my face into the carpet while he lifelessly tipped over onto his side.

Nothing was said. Nothing needed to be said. In addition to the deep physical attraction between us there were also deep emotions. Michael made my soul soar.

"So . . . besides being called T and your having a roommate, is there anything else I need to know about you?"

"No. Not that I can think of. Can you think of anything?"

". . . No."

26

Deja

I had become a favorite of Ivan's modeling agency these days, which meant I was getting more steady work and more steady pay. It also meant that I got to see Ivan more often too. Definitely a plus. The part that was distasteful was that Sophia had the same agency. On this shoot downtown in Little Tokyo, I had to deal with her.

Vibe magazine had a shoot for its fashion section. The theme we had decided upon was futuristic-techno-anime Japanese. This had already been beat into the ground, but I had to give the people what they wanted and this was a great opportunity for me—my name would be in print in the credits. When the issue dropped, I was going to run out and buy about twenty copies. I was still trying to decide how I wanted credit. I was thinking about using D-Square, Isrie's nickname for me.

"That's her!" my brother screamed as he saw Sophia step out from makeup.

"Calm down, Theron. Keep your mouth shut too. She's nothing but trouble, so just do what I tell you to."

"Need I remind you that I'm doing this for free, sis?"

"No. But I'm letting you stay with me for free too. Speaking of that . . ."

"You're asking me about when I'm leaving *again?*"

"Yeah. I worry about you. Promise me you're not in any trouble."

"I told you before. I'm just on leave. I saved up a lot of time out there and deserve it too. Give it a rest. You act like you tryin' to shove a brother out the door."

"You know better than that, bruh."

"Do I? If I'm cramping you and pretty boy's style, just let me know."

"You're not. That remark hurt, though," I replied as I checked the settings on my camera. It was a little cloudier than I expected so I had to make some adjustments to compensate. If I wanted to keep getting well-paying jobs, I needed to keep my product high quality.

"Deja, when are we starting?" It was Sophia, looking all impatient.

Even with her hair up in those silly spikes, she still was stunning. Theron didn't even crack a joke about the red leather swimsuit and heels she was in. Hell, it probably was a fantasy of his.

"Soon, I guess. Is everyone else ready?"

"I don't know and really don't care," she said. There was a small Japanese symbol freshly painted under her left eye. I wondered if it said BITCH. It was red also—her favorite color, as I had learned while doing shoots with her over the past year.

"Hello," said Theron.

No. My brother wasn't trying to deepen his voice. I could have kicked him in his ass . . . or dead in his nuts.

"Hi," Sophia answered him with a smile that was a mix of curiosity and amusement.

"I'm Theron, Deja's assistant. I don't think we've met."

"No, I would have remembered you. I'm Sophia. Sophia Williams. Deja, I didn't know you could afford help."

I replied, "I guess there's a lot you don't know about me, Sophia. Can you go check with your people to see if we can get this started? I don't want your spikes drooping."

"Sure."

Theron watched her turn and walk away. He didn't take his eyes off her bony little rear as it swished back and forth.

"I don't care what you say. . . . That bitch is *tight!*"

"Behave. You want to get me fired?"

"You're doing a fine job of that yourself. Pissing off the models ain't good."

"I'm a photographer. We're known to be temperamental. You don't have an excuse, bruh."

"Yeah, but you're sleeping with a model. I'm just trying to be like my big sis." Proud of himself, he let out one of his throaty laughs.

"We're only clear for another hour and a half, so let's take these pictures and get out of here."

"You're the boss."

The security had done a good job of keeping the downtown onlookers back this afternoon while we shot in the middle of the intersection. We wanted some traffic coming though to give the spread the right look. We used heaters that Theron gladly helped set up for the women. The men that were freezing their Johnsons off were grateful for the warmth too. I was glad I had my windbreaker on because it was too cold for swimsuits today.

"That was a great shot with Malcolm, Sophia," I said as I was putting away my equipment later on. She was wrapped up in a robe and sipping an espresso from a Styrofoam cup. I really meant what I said. That particular pose was going to jump off the page when someone was reading *Vibe*.

"Thank you, Deja." She smirked. "It would have been better with Ivan. The two of us usually turn it up for the camera. Don't you think?"

"Yeah. The two of you know how to work it." I was doing my best to maintain my professionalism. Lord knows, I wanted to curse the bitch out. I shouldn't have felt that way, though. I had no reason to be hostile. I was the one with Ivan now.

"In more ways than one," she sighed. Maybe I did have a reason to be hostile.

"Excuse you?"

"Oh, nothing. I was just reminiscing. How's Mr. Dempsey

doing lately? I haven't seen or heard from him since that day you called and hung up."

"He was doing fine last night when I saw him." Pow.

"Good, good. So you two really are—"

"Yes." I popped my lens cap on to add emphasis.

"Oh . . . I see. Well, it's time for me to go. I could just stay in this robe all the way home. It's so warm."

"Bye, Sophia."

"Before I forget—I'm doing a big shoot for Ebony Emotions Books soon. I'm their new cover model, so I'm going to be touring a little too. Anyway, they asked if I had a preference of photographers. Would you be interested?"

"Me?" I asked, assuming she was high on some shit. EEB was one of the new black imprints dominating the bestseller lists with their own brand of books about urban relationships. On any given month, you could find at least four of their books in magazines like *Essence* or *Upscale*.

"Yes. Personal feelings aside, you're a better photogragher than most of the pretenders in this town. It could set you up. Besides, we sisters need to look out for each other."

"Um . . . sure. Thank you."

"Don't thank me yet," she shot back as she sauntered away. "No promises, so keep it under wraps. Understand?"

"Gotcha."

I was dumbfounded that Sophia took everything about Ivan and me in stride then went a step further and offered me a job. As the set was being disassembled and put away, she passed Theron, who was lending a hand to the workers. Theron, true to form, tried to strike up a conversation with her on the pass by. Sophia was all smiles as she turned on her fake charm and listened to whatever my brother was saying. As I zipped up my equipment bag, I tried to ignore them but kept glancing over. There she was laughing and brushing her hand against his arm. Even with her weird niceness, I still didn't trust her. As they finished their conversation, Sophia whispered something in his ear, catching him off guard. Theron blinked once, then looked in my direction before ending his chat and coming to join me.

"What was she talking about?" I asked.

"Nothing. Just making conversation. I was focused on trying to look down her robe. Think they real?"

"Boy, you are sick."

"Nah, I ain't sick at all. Ready to go?"

"Yeah. If you would be so kind as to carry this bag." I held it out to him.

"Sure, sis." He took it and pulled the strap over his shoulder.

"Now, what were y'all two *really* carrying on about?"

"Shit, girl," Theron snarled. He then let my equipment bag fall on the pavement with a clank. "You don't know when to stop. Ivan's got you all twisted, huh?"

"No! But why'd you bring him up? What did Sophia say to you?"

"Look at you. Wake up, girl! Damn. Don't ask me nothin'. I'm tired of this shit. No more questions. Stay out of my shit and I'll stay clear of yours until I'm gone."

"Sorry, bruh."

"Whatever. Can you drop me at your studio? I'll spend the night there."

"Okay."

Until I got wrapped up in Ivan, I was always the carefree one. Now I was wound tight like I was on my period twenty-four/seven. But I was happy, right?

27

Deja

"This is going to be fun."

"Yep, can't wait," I replied, looking out my window so he couldn't see my grimace.

I'd taken Thursday off to be with Ivan. We decided to Rollerblade on his side of town, Santa Monica, since the weather was being kind to us. I lied to him and told him that I'd been doing this for years, even though this was only my third time trying it and was expecting to break my neck. Theron got a laugh out of me busting my fat ass on the parking lot of my complex earlier in the week, but didn't say anything to Ivan when he came to pick me up. I rewarded my brother by leaving him the keys to my van so he could get around town if he felt like it.

"Don't wreck it, okay?"

"It's already a wreck," Theron laughed as he closed my door and sent us on our way.

Ivan lowered the windows on the Hummer and turned up the music for me to hear over the rushing wind. His muscular arm flexed as he reached to switch stations.

"You look good today."

"Huh?" he replied, still concentrating on finding a song he liked. "Thanks, Deja. You look good too."

"Liar. I'm dressed like a bum." I was wearing a pair of purple sweats and an oversize tee. My hair was bunched up beneath my backward-turned Lakers cap.

"Me too," he said.

"Alright," I chuckled, "but your bum style is different than mine." Ivan wore an old Boston Celtics jersey, long khaki shorts that ended just past his knees, and Adidas tennis shoes. He was missing the designer watch that usually adorned his wrist. For a second, I thought he'd noticed my staring at his bare wrist. The sun was reflecting off his sunglasses so I couldn't get a good look at his eyes. Maybe he's afraid of falling and breaking it, I thought dismissively.

For an hour, we Rollerbladed up and down the pier. Ivan tried to show off, racing ahead through the crowd as I screamed for him to wait up. I got my revenge when he wiped out doing some sort of spin. I eased back on my heel to brake as I caught up. I was laughing when Ivan pulled me down by my shirt. He was kind enough to use his body to cushion my fall.

"Relax," he chuckled, taking me in his arms. "I wasn't going to let you get all bruised up."

"Whoo! I . . . I'm a little winded." The dark spots I was seeing stopped me in the middle of my laughter.

"Deja, you okay?"

"Yeah," I said as I touched my forehead. "I just need to eat something."

"Sure. Let's put these blades up in the car. Give me your hand."

I knew what was wrong. I had started taking these diet pills someone had told me about. They gave me a boost of energy and were supposed to suppress my appetite, but they didn't agree with me. I had dizzy spells whenever I took them, but they would go away if I ate a little. Ivan didn't know, but I was also running over a mile every night. I had him now and was committed to keeping him.

Instead of walking, we drove over to the Third Street Promenade and found a seafood bar. Ivan was hungrier than he thought and had some crab legs. I had only a small salad and my usual glass of water with lemon in it.

"Feeling better?" Ivan asked with a look of honest concern on his flawless face.

"Much. I don't know what happened back there."

"You're not pregnant, are you?"

"Hell, no. If I was, though, would you be happy?"

Ivan blushed. "Now's not a good time. Not with my career and things."

"Relax, boy. I'm not ready to bring a child into this troubled world yet either. Besides, you wouldn't be my choice anyway."

"Oh?" he remarked as his flushed look gave way and his color returned.

"Nope. You know I'm just using you for the wild, raw sex. I'm kicking you to the curb in a couple of weeks," I giggled.

"Try it with a straight face next time," he laughed back. "Speaking of wild, raw sex . . ."

"What imaginative new technique is your sick mind dreaming up, Ivan?"

"None. I rented this movie *Motives* the other night."

"That movie with Vivica and Shemar, *the only man I consider prettier than you?* And you watched it without me?"

"Yeah, it was late. You and your brother were on that *Vibe* shoot earlier, so I didn't want to disturb y'all."

"You should've. That's a sexy MF."

"Whatever. I don't know about Shemar being sexy, but the movie was wild."

"So did they really have a ménage à trois?"

"Oooh yeah," he said in one of those dirty-old-man tones as he smiled. "Vivica wasn't a participant, though. Hmph. Must've been in her contract."

"Freak. I'll bet you wouldn't mind something like that."

"Like what? A threesome? Why? Have you thought about it?"

"*Hell No!* I'm not down for that shit. Ivan, you've been having me bent over and twisted every which way and then some, but this sister don't share."

"Relax, relax." Ivan laughed as he held his hands up. "A brother can't joke with you?"

"Ha. Ha. Speaking of bent over and twisted . . . guess who I saw at the downtown shoot."

"The Alonzo brothers?" The Alonzo brothers were these twins from Rowland Heights that Ivan considered to be his competition.

"No. Sophia."

"Oh, no."

"Nah. She wasn't bad, though." I didn't know what to make of her extending the hand of friendship to me in the form of a job offer, so I chose to keep quiet. "Have you seen her lately?"

"Nope. Don't care to. Are you trying to ruin my appetite? How many times do I have to tell you it's over? Shit." Ivan pulled some crab meat out with his fork.

"Sorry." I decided to put the Sophia issue to rest from now on.

As Ivan finished his meal, I drank my water and did some people watching. I saw a beautiful black dress that caught my eye in the window of Tiffany's Boutique across the way and imagined myself fitting in it one day. I was still more Ashley Stewart than Tiffany's Boutique right now.

As I still liked my independence, I offered to pay for our meal. Ivan wouldn't have it and made me put my credit card away. After we figured out the tip, I took care of that and we were off.

"I had fun, Ivan. Sorry about getting dizzy on you."

"As long as you feel better, it doesn't matter." He put the key in the ignition, starting his big toy truck.

"Have I ever told you how much I love this?" I said as I patted the seat.

"You really like it?"

"Yep. Feels like you could drive through a wall in this thing. It's chips."

Ivan simply laughed, not acknowledging whether he understood me or not.

"Want it?"

"Huh?"

"The Hummer. Not to keep. Just to use when you want."

"This is too much," I chuckled nervously.

"I know you have problems with your ride, so take mine. Seriously. You deserve it."

"Boy, please. What are you going to drive?"

"I've got my old car still. Tell you what. I need to pick up some groceries real quick. Let's go to the store. Then you can drop me back at my place. Go ahead. Take her for the day and let me know what you think."

We took Lincoln Boulevard past the Santa Monica Freeway and drove to Bob's Market on Ocean Park Boulevard. A small, single-engine plane coming in for a landing at Santa Monica airport up the street flew overhead as we parked. I hadn't agreed to Ivan's suggestion, but was wearing a smile as big as the bill for Janet showing her nipple.

"I'll be right out," Ivan said as he left his truck running. "You just rest your pretty self. You need anything inside?"

"No. I'm straight," I answered. Ivan leaned over and gave me one of his tender kisses before running inside the store. The phone that never left his side was clutched in his right hand.

I reclined the seat back and admired the sky through the sunroof. The clouds drifted by slowly and I looked for familiar shapes in them to pass the time. A little, familiar cramp interrupted my fun 'n games. Realizing what day it was, I cursed to myself. There went my weekend. *That* time of the month had slipped up on me. Knowing my body, I estimated that I had until morning before my period came . . . and I wasn't going to be in the mood to pick up some tampons just after waking up.

I could have easily gone in the store and bought what I needed, but Ivan was already inside . . . and why not test his love? A sign of a good man is how they deal with the uncomfortable situations, not just the easy stuff. I grabbed my cell phone from my bag in the backseat.

"Hmm," I thought aloud as I lowered the volume on the radio and waited for him to answer his phone. I hung up as the voice mail automatically kicked in. I raised my seat to its upright position and sighed. If this woman wanted something done, she was going to have to do it herself. I took my baseball cap off and played with my curls in the visor mirror.

The store wasn't crowded, so I expected to see Ivan being rung up in line when I came in through the automatic doors. Nope, wasn't there. I found the small box of Tampax in aisle four, then went looking for Ivan. I came up empty on the first few aisles, then noticed something.

Two middle-aged women of color were huddled together by the canned peas on the end of aisle nine. They were talking in hushed tones while smiling at something that was getting their panties in a wad. I had seen this countless times before. I had just found Ivan. He'd probably given them his autograph.

"He looks good, huh?" I asked the middle-aged groupies as I excused myself past their shopping carts. They didn't take it very well when they realized I was with him and went about their shopping again.

Ivan was oblivious to all of us. His back was turned. A loaf of his darned oat bran bread was in one hand and his cell phone, which he was using, in the other. Not wanting to eavesdrop, I cleared my throat once. He kept on talking.

". . . I told you. Now. Yes, now!" he growled into the tiny mouthpiece.

"Ivan?"

"Deja . . ."

"I had to come in for . . . *this*," I said, waving my box of goodies, "since you wouldn't answer your phone."

"Oh. Hang on." He smiled while putting me on verbal hold to end his frantic phone conversation. I stared on impatiently while his demeanor changed with whoever was on the other end of the phone. He'd become more cordial and businesslike.

I decided not to listen in and began walking toward the

checkout counter. I heard the click of the phone as Ivan shut it. I kept walking, making him overtake me if he wanted to discuss anything.

"You don't want to know what that was about?" he asked as we reached the cashier.

"Nope. Oh. Here's your car key." I held it out to him.

I had the lady put my tampons in a paper bag and waited for Ivan by the front door. I really wanted to know who he was talking to. I had my suspicions, but had promised to leave the jealous girlfriend routine behind me. Ivan hadn't done anything to betray my trust and I was acting very out of character. He said nothing as he carried his loaf of bread in a plastic bag past me. I followed through the automatic door.

"You thought it was Sophia, huh?" he asked as we slowly drove toward his apartment on Ocean Front Walk, right next to the pier. I didn't answer. "Do you want to know what that was about?"

"It's up to you."

"I guess I have to if I want my sweet, wonderful baby named Deja to come back."

"Go on."

"I was going to surprise you, but I guess I'll let it out. It did have something to do with Sophia in a roundabout way."

"*What?*" I was about to ask to be let out.

"Not like that. The *only* way it has to do with Sophia is that we're with the same agency."

"I'm lost."

"A party. The agency is having its annual Christmas cruise and party at sea in a few weeks. We're going down to Mazatlán this year. I wanted to invite you as my guest, but planned to spring it on you later. Like maybe when you didn't have tampons in your hand." Ivan smiled.

"Shit ain't funny. Maybe I should shove one of these up your ass."

"Nah. I'll pass," he laughed, playfully pushing me away as

he drove. "So do you want to take my whip . . . or are you still mad at me?"

"I wasn't mad."

"Alright. Well, we're here. Take the keys."

"You're not inviting me up?"

"Sure. I just thought you wanted to get your drive on. You weren't feeling too well just a little while ago."

"You're right," I replied as I looked around for a sign of Sophia's red convertible Lexus in the parking garage. Her car was hard to hide, just like her forehead. I got out and walked around to Ivan's side. "You sure you want me to take it?" I asked as I handed him his bread.

"Yes." I felt Ivan's lips press against mine as the loaf of bread smushed between us. I was back in that warm spot he took me to.

Ivan took his ruined loaf and headed to his apartment lobby, his khaki shorts now bulging in front. I blew him a kiss as he entered the lobby, then carefully exited his parking garage. I had never driven anything this big, or expensive, and didn't want to do anything to ruin the experience.

I was a little off from the diet pills, but giggled as I pushed down on the gas pedal. The big toy smoothly rocketed down the street, Outkast's song "Roses" now playing. I had planned to go home and rest, but my girl Isrie's job wasn't that far out of the way.

28

Isrie

"I should have come here earlier," my two o'clock appointment mumbled. She was an attractive Filipino woman a few years older than me. The questionnaire she'd filled out said her lower back had been flaring up for years.

"If you don't mind my asking, how did you first hurt your back?"

"I had a bad fall during a fight with my husband."

"Oh . . . sorry." Way more information than I needed. I shut up and focused on the massage. Her back was pretty sensitive in that area, so I was sure to be careful.

She waited to say anything else for several minutes, as if she were debating things in her head and choosing her words carefully.

"It's okay," she said after I had put the conversation out of my head. "We've had a stormy history."

"You mean it's not over?" She left the subject open so I figured it was okay to jump back in. That was a major no-no at the job, but I always felt it was good to establish a rapport with my customers.

"No. It's not over. That's why I'm in town now."

"You're not from LA?"

"I—we live in Rialto. We used to live here though, before moving farther out."

"I drive by Rialto all the time. My parents moved to San

Bernardino. But, you were saying, you're here now because of your husband?"

"I'm embarrassed to say it, but I'm out here looking for him. He's supposed to be working in the LA area, but I don't trust him. I hired an investigator to tail him, but he slips away sometimes. One of my girlfriends gave me a gift certificate to your spa last year, so I figured I'd use it and get some pleasure out of this trip. There's been too much misery."

"So your husband's a dog?"

"I think so. That's a good word for him. It wouldn't be the first time he's disappeared like this. There'll be hell to pay if I catch him cheating on me again."

"Why don't you just dump him?"

She turned over to look at me.

"Kids?"

"Yes, one daughter . . . Malia. But I love him too."

"Oh," was my reply. I didn't understand why a woman would put up with that sort of shit. Here she was scouring the area for her man like she was desperate or something. If she was single, she would have to beat the men away. Her black hair, which was longer than mine, had two gray strands in it. Her no-good husband probably caused those. Even with a kid in the picture, I would have bounced.

I began daydreaming again, wondering how different my relationship with Michael would be if we were married. I had already called my mom and told her about him. He was really inside my head . . . and heart.

I hadn't realized that my client's time had expired until Kendra tapped on the door and peeked in. Kendra had a note in her hand, which she politely slipped on the counter. I finished up my manipulation of my client's muscle tissue and left her alone to change.

"Thank you," said my customer as she pulled her towel up around her.

"Don't mention it, Mrs. Michaels. Glad to help you out

some kind of way. Hope the rest of your trip goes without any problems."

"Thank you for allowing me to vent," she said as she placed a twenty-dollar bill in my hand. "And call me Maria."

"Sure. Maria. Good luck with your husband. I mean it. Be careful."

"I'll be fine. It's my husband that needs to be careful," she said with a wink. She had a smile on her petite face but her eyes were jet-black and cold. I felt sorry for her husband if Maria did catch him dippin' his spoon.

On my way out, I snagged Kendra's note off the counter. In the hallway, I read it. Deja was waiting for me outside. We had been busy with our men lately, so it would be good to catch up with her.

"Okay. What are you doing, girl?" I asked as I approached her. Deja was propped against the front fender of Ivan's Hummer, which was parked front and center. I'd interrupted her conversation with Armando the valet, which she was definitely enjoying.

"Hey, girl! You like my wheels?" My crazy friend copped a pose like she was on *The Price Is Right* or something.

"Whoo. *Someone's getting serious*," I sang.

"Maybe," she said bashfully in front of Armando, who excused himself and went back to work. He picked up a set of keys from storage and ran across the street to retrieve someone's car.

"Aww, sookie-sookie now!" I said.

"I've missed you, Isrie," she said as she gave me a big hug and kiss on the cheek.

"Ditto, girlfriend. You look different."

"What? These raggedy workout clothes?" she replied while adjusted her favorite Lakers cap.

"No. You've lost weight."

"Maybe," she giggled as if hiding something.

"Go 'head, go 'head. You off from work today?"

"Yeah, I just dropped Ivan off at his place. We went Rollerblading this afternoon."

"Since when do *you* Rollerblade?"

"Trying new things all the time. Hella fun."

"Scared of you."

"Don't be skurred!"

I was laughing along with Deja when my client Maria walked out. She was now dressed like some exotic movie star in her bright yellow dress.

Noticing me, she gave a brief *thank you* smile before focusing on her Volvo wagon as Armando drove it over. Deja had the space in front of the door partially blocked, and the valet had to squeeze Maria's wagon past the Hummer. She and Deja locked eyes as she dropped a serious frown on my girl, the woman's eyes suddenly becoming cold and black again. Armando apologized as he held the door open for her and received a tip for his trouble.

"Um . . . you're going to have to move your car," Armando requested of Deja as he pushed his tip down into his front pocket. Deja nodded and smiled, stopping to cut a scowl at the station wagon as it drove off. I think she was hoping Maria was looking in the rearview mirror at her.

"That was one of my customers."

"What a crab."

"Nah. Cut her some slack. She's got some things on her mind right now." I wasn't married, but I empathized with her hurt. "Damn. I forgot to give her one of my business cards. She's not going to know my name if she comes back."

"I know her from somewhere," said Deja.

"You took some pictures of her before?"

"Maybe. Probably. Her look is unique. I forget names, but faces stay with me. I'll remember later."

"So when are we getting together and doing something, girl-friend? I've got stuff to tell you and I *know* you've got some dirt."

Deja giggled. "I might have a little bit. Call me. Maybe this weekend? Just us girls?"

"Bet. Michael's usually gone on weekends."

"Good. I'll talk to you later, girl. I'm going home and get me some rest."

29

Deja

I saw the image of the black uniform in my mirror as it got closer and closer, not stopping until it filled my view completely.

"Ma'am, please keep your hands on the dash." I remembered what happened to Tyisha Miller. I wasn't even going to breathe hard.

I was almost home and couldn't think of why I had been pulled over. I may have done something wrong, but right now I was only feeling my color. DWB: driving while black. It had happened to people I knew, but I was lucky with my old, noisy van. Today, I was in a screaming yellow billboard. As I clenched the steering wheel, I looked out. Less than a mile away was the safety of my apartment.

"License and registration please," he said as he bent down and put his face next to mine.

"Officer, what did I do?"

"License, registration, and insurance please." I wanted to raise the window up on his neck.

"Here." Ivan kept his paperwork right next to his owner's manual. The redhead lowered his sunglasses and compared the name on my license to the name on the paperwork. I let out a deep breath to voice my disgust.

"I need you to step out of the car while I run this through."

The asshole further degraded me by making me place my hands on the hot roof of the car while he sat all comfy in his cruiser and mumbled into his radio. I could see his bushy moustache wiggling with every syllable.

"C'mon, c'mon," I cursed to myself. As I began sweating, I saw my van over the top of the police lights. As it got closer, I heard the familiar rumble of my muffler. It was Theron heading down La Brea. I let out a laugh and smiled at Officer Friendly. He gave me a confused look, not knowing my backup was driving up behind him.

I started to wave my hands to get Theron's attention, but decided it was best to keep them put. Besides, Theron couldn't miss me or Ivan's Hummer. My brother applied the brakes. He frowned as he took in what was going on. As quickly as my cheer came, it ended. The police officer exited his car, catching Theron's attention. My brother flinched when he saw him. Instead of stopping, my muffler growled and I watched my van resume speed and continue down La Brea. My little brother had bailed on me.

"Here you go, Ms. Douglas."

"Huh?" I had temporarily forgotten my oppressor of the minute. I slid my hands off the roof and took my license and paperwork away from him.

"Drive safely."

"I could have told you it wasn't stolen," I yelled in the direction of the officer as he walked away. He didn't answer, but instead gave me a goofy smile. He turned his flashing lights off and drove away in search of another "criminal." My lights were still flashing . . . red.

The Hummer made a screeching sound as I came to a stop. I was already hauling tail up the stairs when I pushed the remote button to lock it up.

"Give me one reason not to throw your ass out onto the street!" I screamed as I slammed my apartment door shut. My brother, whose back was to me, jumped at the sound. He placed the sandwich he'd bought down on the kitchen table and stood.

"I didn't do nothin', girl!" Theron hollered raising his hand to blow me off

"That's just it! You left me hanging out there, little brother! I could be on my way to jail or shot by now! And you just drove on by like you didn't know me. And in my shit no less!'

"It wasn't like that—"

"The hell it wasn't!"

"Look, calm down," he said, placing his hands on my shoulders. I shrugged them off and got up in his face.

"No! I won't, dammit! I would have never done that shit to you out there. I—"

"I'm AWOL."

"Whaa—?"

"I'm AWOL. Y'know. Absent without leave. I—I couldn't stay out there and be recognized."

"*Nooo.* Theron," I said with a gulp. "What did you do?"

"Don't worry about that. It was nothin'."

I brought my hand up and slapped his face.

My brother was shocked by my reaction, but I wasn't fucking with him. He tried to fight the tears that were welling up in his eyes from my slap, but a drop rolled down anyway.

"Boy, what the fuck kinda trouble have you gotten yourself in? And don't even think about blowing me off again."

"Okay. I owe you that at least, Deja. Lock the door . . . and I'll tell you."

Theron didn't even have a chance to sit down as I ran to the door, locked it, and was back before him in the blink of an eye.

"Damn. You really want to know, huh?"

"Talk. Now."

Theron walked over to the sofa and took a seat. "I ain't nobody's slave. I ain't cut out for that shit. That's all."

"Theron, when I said cut the bullshit, I meant it. Talk or your ass goes out that door and I call the government or Army on you myself."

"You wouldn't do that. As much as you hate them mother-fuckers in Washington?"

"Yeah, I saw *Fahrenheit 9/11*, but don't test me, boy. You'll lose."

Theron smiled as he avoided eye contact. He was squirming and trying to think up a story, but gave up with a sigh.

"Motherfuckers accused me of stealing. I wasn't staying around for the lynchin'."

"Did you do it? Were you stealing?"

"Don't matter. They had their minds made up. My black ass wasn't about to go to no Leavenworth or Iraq."

"I thought I knew you," I said with disgust. "I *knew* something wasn't right with your *leave*. So, you're on the run and came here? To my door?"

He chuckled, out of habit. "Didn't have anyone . . . or any-where else to go. You're family. My only family."

"So some men in black masks may be breaking my door down any moment now. That's nice to know. Thanks, bruh." I sat down on my sofa next to him and rested my head in my hands.

"Nah. It ain't even like that, sis. They don't know where you live or *where* I'm at. I gave them a lot of my info from Ohio when I signed up. I still gotta lay low, though."

"Three weeks."

"What?"

"Three weeks," I repeated with my hands still covering my face. "You've got three weeks. I love you and you can keep in touch, but you gotta go."

"It's like that?"

"Yeah. Just *like* that. It'll be hard, but I'll see if I can scrape up some cash for you. It's almost Christmas. Call it an early pres-ent."

"Maybe you can get some money from pretty boy. I see you're sportin' his truck already."

"Shut up. You've already done enough stupid things, don't

you think? You don't want to piss me off anymore. Leave Ivan out of this."

"Cool, cool. I was just playin' anyway."

"I'm tired," I said as I stood up to go to my bedroom. "Try not to surprise me anymore while you're here."

"I can do that, sis. Thanks."

"What did you steal?"

"I never said I stole anything."

"What do they *think* you stole?" I said as I turned around with an eyebrow raised.

"Weapons. Guns 'n shit."

As much as I wished my brother had changed, he hadn't. I shook my head and closed the bedroom door behind me. I was only *hoping* that my silent prayers to the man up above for my brother's safety were being heard.

30

Isrie

"**L**eaving me for the weekend again?" I asked.

"Yep. Unfortunately. I don't want to, though." Michael was looking up at the ceiling of my apartment. The sheet, still damp from the sweat of our bodies, had slid down to his waist. My comforter, having fallen off hours ago, lay across the floor.

"Where to this time?"

"Let's see. Umm, Tempe mainly. You want to come?"

"I'd love to, but you know I'm going out with my girl tomorrow. My parents might be coming by too. Put me down for next time?"

"I'll mark it in my PDA," Michael replied as he made a gesture in the air with his finger. He had met me at my place after work Friday so we could spend some time together before he left.

"Oooh, I love it when you talk high-tech!"

"iPods."

Kiss.

"DVD burners."

Kiss.

"Bill Gates."

Kiss. Kiss.

"Umm . . . Hard drive," I said as I took my turn. My hand, which was under the covers, had found its way to his chocolate shaft. He wasn't quite there yet, but my grip was doing what it could to bring him around again. I took my thumb and gently stroked it across his tip, making him all twitchy. I was still learning all of his spots, but then, wasn't that part of the fun in a new relationship?

"Are you sure you want to go there?" he said.

"Hey, I'm going to be missing this all weekend. You not getting tired on me, are you?"

"No."

"And you better not be sharing *this* with anyone while in Arizona." Michael now had a tiny little tent pitched under the sheets. I grabbed it for emphasis.

"Never. It's all yours. All for you."

The look in his eyes sent my soul dancing. Even with my hand gripping his manhood, he remained calm and fixated on me. There was a comfort level between us that I had never known.

"Are you for real?" I asked as the heat of passion I was feeling was replaced with a different type of warmth.

"What do you mean?" he asked, sensing the climate change in me.

"You know, Michael. Are you for real? Is *this* for real? I just don't want to wake up if it's not."

"You flatter me too much, Isrie. I will say this, though. I'm here for as long as you'll have me."

"I—"

My phone rang.

"Shit," I cursed as my train of thought was interrupted.

"You better get that. I need to get up anyway. I have to go home and pack."

The phone continued to ring softly, but it seemed as loud as a gong to me.

"Nooooo," I whined. "Okay. I know. But you need to promise me you'll stay put one of these weekends."

"Well, after Thanksgiving I should be able to do that."

As Michael left for the bathroom, I ran across the floor toward the phone. I held my breasts with one hand so they wouldn't jiggle while I made my way over. I checked the number on the caller ID.

"What's up, D-Square?" I asked

"Caller ID, huh?"

"Yep. You're lucky I picked up."

"That's why I like you, girl. You're such a good friend."

"Do tell, do tell," I said with a smile. "Did you drive that Hummer some more yesterday?"

"*Unh* . . . yesterday."

"What's that *unh* for? Something happen?"

"Yeah, you could say that. I don't feel like rehashing it on the phone, though. Want to hang out tonight? I might even hit something harder than lemon and water."

"Oooh. I would, but Michael's here and he's leaving—"

"For the weekend. Yeah, I had forgotten."

"We're still doing something tomorrow, though, right?" I asked as I looked in the mirror and found an unsightly bump on my face.

"Of course, girl. Ivan's not answering his phone and I've got some work to finish up here at the studio, so I'll be getting out of your hair."

"You know you're never a bother, D-Square. Is your brother helping you tonight?"

"No. He's at my apartment, I think. He'll be gone after Thanksgiving."

"Finally going back to New York, huh?"

"Yeah."

"No offense, but I was beginning to think your little brother was AWOL or something."

"Oh. Nah. He's a character at times, but everything's straight with him."

"Good, good," I said as I heard Michael finishing up in the shower.

"Hey, I'll talk atcha tomorrow. Go be with your man. I know I would be . . . if I could find him!"

"Bye, Deja!"

"Bye, girl."

Deja's tone had bothered me to some extent. There was something she wasn't saying, but that was her choice. Maybe she would feel more comfortable tomorrow.

Michael came out of the bathroom. He had dried off and was picking up his clothes that were scattered around my place.

"You want me to cook you something before you go, Michael?"

"You cook?" he asked with a bit of shock in his voice.

"Yes. A little," I admitted embarrassed. I had always wanted to learn from my mom, but it never quite sank in.

"You've been working all week. Let's just go to Aunt Kizzy's."

"Sounds good to me." I laughed, having been let off the hook. "I've been craving some greens."

"Well, hurry up and get dressed. I personally wouldn't mind, but I don't think their dress code will let you in with nothing on."

"You're too funny," I said as I headed to the bathroom. "You *have* to meet my girl, Deja. You're the two nicest people I know."

31

Deja

I was developing a roll of film in my darkroom when I thought I heard someone knocking. Most photographers have gone digital and I was no different, but sometimes I still liked going old school and getting my hands dirty. Getting tired of the red light, I quickly finished up. After speaking with Isrie earlier, I tried calling Ivan again to see when he wanted his car back, but had been unable to reach him. Maybe it was him at the door.

"Who is it?" I asked just as the knocking stopped. I could hear footsteps moving away.

I looked at the time. It was after my usual business hours, but I wasn't well off enough to be turning away business. I turned the keys that were dangling in the lock and peeked out the door.

"Hello?" I shouted, knowing my mind hadn't been playing tricks on me. I heard steps and stuck my head out farther. I recognized the brown curly locks and forehead as the figure was walking down the stairs.

"Sophia?"

She turned around at the sound of my voice, squinting in the light to make out who was talking to her. "Oh. Hey, Deja. I—I thought nobody was in," she said as she began walking back toward me. "Nobody answered." She was wearing an aqua-colored top with white cargo pants and sandals. For as casual as she was dressed, her makeup was flawless.

"Sorry about that. I was developing. You're not out partying tonight?" *Or out screwing my man, Ivan, since I can't reach him all of a sudden?*

"No, no. The Infiniti Club is calling me, but I'll pass tonight. I was in the neighborhood and decided to stop by."

"Well, come on in. I don't want to leave you standing out here in the hall."

"Thank you, Deja."

I locked the studio door behind my guest. I was going to invite her to have a seat or offer her something to drink, but Sophia was making herself at home already. I watched her looking at my work on display with amusement. She gave everything a superficial once-over until she came upon her photo. It was the same one of her in the bikini that Theron liked. I snickered as she admired her own beauty.

"What?" she asked. I didn't intend for her to hear me, but didn't really care.

"Nothing. Just thinking to myself. So, what do you want, Sophia?"

"Nothing much. Remember when I told you about Ebony Emotions Books the other day?"

"Yeah. How could I forget?" *It was the one time you were less of a bitch than usual.*

"They're scheduling a cover shoot for me now. You're still in? Ready to step up your game?"

"Are you sure you want me?"

"I mean what I say, Deja," she said with a steely glint in her eyes that didn't match the light, carefree look she was trying to pull off tonight. "You're looking at more pay than I *know* you're used to, and it'll be fun too."

"Okay. Count me in."

"Good, good. I'll let you know once we have definite dates. Umm, where's Theron?"

"Huh?"

"He's your assistant, isn't he?"

"He's not here," I answered coldly. *I told him to leave her alone.*

"Oh. Well, I guess I'll be going."

"Did you come here looking for my brother, Sophia?" I asked, stepping into her path.

"No, I was just asking a question. I told you what I stopped here for." She was lying. Her eyes were moving down and to the left when she answered. I'll be damned. She was fucking my brother. That explained her being in the neighborhood and her easy-to-drop-the-drawers attire. She must've known Theron had been spending some of his nights here.

"When should I hear back from you about the gig?" There was no need burning bridges to a potential payday over something that had probably already gone down. Last time I checked, my bills were still piling up on the regular.

"As soon as I hear something definite. Probably in a week or two. Relax. I'll be in touch. I already told you this is about the quality work you do."

I unlocked the door again to allow her to exit. I was torn. I was grateful to Sophia for the job, but still had issues over Ivan and now my baby brother. I just prayed my brother was using protection with the Hollywood ho.

"How long have you been fucking my brother?" I *had* to ask.

"I don't kiss and tell, Deja. Theron's a big boy and makes his own decisions. . . . Kind of like Ivan, don't you think?" I wanted to slap the taste out of her mouth as she smirked.

As Sophia walked back into the dimly lit hall, I said, "I'll tell Theron you stopped by. He's going to be leaving town soon."

With a backward glance, I left her looking surprised as I closed the door on her and locked it again. I took joy in her few seconds of confusion and fell back onto my couch like a schoolgirl who just put gum in another girl's hair. I never did that, though, mind you. I was always the one on the receiving end.

Isrie wasn't joining me, but I was going to the Neon Owl

Don't Get It Twisted

169

tonight anyway. There was an apple martini there with my name on it. It was late and I was looking a little rough, but had a few odds and ends hanging up in wardrobe. I guess it was time to play dress-up.

32

Isrie

Saturday night we started the night off by going to a comedy club. Kendra's brother, Jamal, did stand-up on weekends at Slap Happy. He'd promised that all drinks were on him, so the reason for our choice was obvious. Deja met me at my crib and Kendra was supposed to meet us later.

All eyes were on us as we sauntered to our table—or I should say, all eyes were on Deja. D-Square was on fire as she proudly proclaimed her new dress size to the world. She *had* to be down to either a size twelve or fourteen now. Her smooth, golden brown complexion was accentuated by the fresh curly weave she'd put in. Beneath her Baby Phat denim halter dress, her thick, newly shaped legs popped into view with each step, commanding attention. Carrying her reshaped figure were a pair of tan ankle-wrap sandals. I couldn't help but wonder what kind of hell my girl had been putting herself through for this sudden weight loss. If it *was* hell, she sure seemed fine . . . and looked fine to boot. She was happy, so I was happy.

Being no slouch myself, I accepted the secondhand stares and grins and moved on. I rocked a sleeveless white cotton bodysuit with white sandals. My black jacket was on my arm in case I got cold. I wore my hair parted in the middle and let it hang straight down on both sides.

Jamal was the third comedian on stage in the old, refurbished brick building that had become a recent hot spot in Inglewood.

We had a table two rows back from the stage, but could see everything including the case of nerves the last comedian had.

"Have you seen him before?" Deja asked about Jamal who was just being announced.

"Nope. I met him once, but never saw him perform. Kendra told me about his act, though."

"I hope he's better than the last one. That lady was stale as hell."

"As long as he keeps these free drinks coming, he can be mute for all I care," I whispered laughingly to my best friend.

Actually, Jamal turned out to be hilarious. He had the whole place erupting in laughter at his performance. Both Deja and I barely touched our first drinks as we giggled and high-fived each other at the true-to-life situations Jamal was touching on in his own way. Whenever he thought he was on a roll, he would flip his derby off his head and give a wink in our direction. Jamal was wearing a blue sharkskin suit along with the black derby—way too Steve Harvey. His hair was cut close to conceal his prematurely receding hairline. Deja would never admit it, but she liked him. I picked up on it from her demeanor whenever a wink came our way.

"So, how long is Ivan letting you keep his whip?" I asked Deja out of idle curiosity.

"Beats me, girlfriend," she shrugged. "I haven't been able to reach him since Thursday. I called him before I came by your place, but no answer. I left a message, though, to let him know I was out with you and to call me on my cell if he needs his truck back."

"He probably got a zit or something and had to check into therapy."

"Cute, Isrie. You want to go up on stage when Jamal's finished?"

"Nah. You know I leave that stuff to the pros," I smiled. "By the way, what was wrong when you called me yesterday?"

"I just had some issues going on and needed to vent. Y'know I got pulled over after I left your job the other day?"

"DWB?"

"Straight up."

"Damn, Deja. You alright?"

"I'm fine. Typical bullshit. He let me go once he found out I didn't have any warrants and that the Hummer wasn't stolen."

"Are you going to file a complaint?"

"For what? I just don't have the time or energy to go through that. Besides, I don't need to be on anyone's long memory list. What's worse was that Theron . . ."

"Yeah? What about Theron?" I asked, trying to egg my friend on to finish her sentence.

"He wasn't even supportive. That's all. Typical brother of mine."

"Oh." That was odd. I didn't know Theron that well, but I would have thought him to be the type to run down to the station if somebody messed with his sister.

"But enough of that stuff. Guess who came by the studio after I got off the phone with you."

"Michael Ealy?"

"No!"

"Damn, *I love me some Pretty Ricky*. Then I don't want to hear about it," I teased before giving in. "Okay, okay. I'll bite. Who?"

"Sophia Williams."

"That model you can't stand? The one you say got a big forehead?"

"Yeah, *guuuurl*. Anyway, I got a job. Well, actually, she got me a job. I'm gonna be doing shots for Ebony Emotions Books!"

"Naaah!"

"For true!" she squealed in her exaggerated slavery-time Cicely Tyson voice. "Sophia's their new cover model and she recommended a sistah. I knew about it a while back but couldn't say anything until Sophia confirmed things."

"So y'all two are *best buds* now? Wasn't she humping your man?" I asked while simulating spanking the table.

"Yes, but he wasn't *my man* then. I still don't trust the wench, but this is business."

"Watch that, D-Square."

"I'll be watching alright. *Allll* the *waaaaay* to the bank." Deja held her glass of melted ice up in a toast.

"Need a new drink, I see," came from the tall brother in the suit with Michael Jordan eyes and a receding hairline. His derby was held in his left hand. "Ladies, no need getting up on my account," he said jokingly as he approached. He gave a nod to the other customers who were sitting near us as they muttered compliments in his direction.

"You were funny up there," Deja said as she turned in his direction. Jamal borrowed an empty chair from the next table over and smoothly slid up next to her.

"Then how come you two ladies didn't applaud just now when I wrapped up on stage? Y'all two hurt my feelings. *For real, though*. Everybody was clapping up in here and I look toward the two of you for a little *approval* and y'all two are deep in *convo-sation*."

"Sorry, Jamal," I replied to his silliness. "We *were* paying attention and loved you, bro. We just had something we got caught up talking about at the end. *For real though*."

"She's not lying," Deja added with a smile.

"Okay, okay. I'll lay off . . . but you have to tell me your name. I've met your friend in white over there," he said, pointing in my direction as if having no interest in me.

"Hi, I'm Deja." *No, she did not just bat her eyelashes.*

"So, Miss Deja, do you think I need to be headlining here?"

"I don't know. I would need to see more of the competition."

"Okay, okay. An honest answer. I like that in a woman. I'll have to arrange for you to come here again."

"Stop trying to pick her up, Jamal," Kendra said as she hurriedly rushed to join us. My coworker, who had the same smooth chocolate complexion as her brother, was wearing a tangerine minidress with ruffles just above her knees. Her oiled, natural-styled hair was worn back with small twists on the ends. Between her and Deja, I felt left out being the only one not showing leg tonight.

"You missed my act," Jamal said as he stood up from his seat to greet his sister with a kiss on the cheek.

"Please. You've rehearsed your act in front of me too many times, Jamal," she replied with amusement. She snagged the other vacant chair and slid it over to our table. "Sorry I'm running late, y'all. How's your night been so far?"

"I'm used to you running late at the spa, Kendra. Somehow you keep your job there."

"Girl, you know nobody gives a rub like me," she laughed. "I got the stroke over there, y'know? Jamal, why don't you get me a drink? And while you're at it, take care of my girls again. Shit, all I see is water in their glasses." From watching the two of them interact, you could tell they shared the same sense of humor.

Jamal, whose attention was solely on Deja, listened to his twin sister and went in search of fresh drinks for the three of us. Someone else had taken the stage, but we had girl talk on the agenda while Jamal was away.

Kendra made sure her brother was gone before she exclaimed, "*Whew*. I had to sneak out tonight, Isrie. I broke my man off, then jetted after he fell asleep."

"So, what are you going to tell him when you come back?" I asked.

"I'll think of something," she said with a smile.

"I don't get it," Deja jumped in. "You're just out with your girls. Your boyfriend's one of those possessive ones?"

"No, no. It's not the girls he's worried about. He's worried about me gettin' with fine motherfuckers like that nigga over there. *Hmph*. He should be worried."

"Damn. That's harsh," Deja's distaste was evident in her eyes.

"Girl, you don't know what I've been through with my man," Kendra huffed. "We all don't have men picking us up in limos like Isrie. Some of us have dogs . . . and I've been played one too many times by my German shepherd. I've learned the game the hard way and I'm not going to be anybody's second string anymore."

"Second string?" I had to ask.

"Yeah. I'm not sittin' on the bench while my man has some-one else starting for him. Sorry. Sports talk. I used to play a lot of sports growing up with Jamal."

"Is that right?" I said, trying to move on to a less touchy subject.

"Don't get me wrong." Kendra continued anyway, as she had to school us. "My man is good, but he's still a man and has his times when he does his dirt all by his lonely. He's now all para-noid 'n shit from it, though."

"Oh," came from Deja's mouth first. I knew she was thinking about Ivan and Sophia just from her tone. Kendra had me think-ing about Michael for a second too, but I had already made a fool out of myself over my trust issues.

"Hey, Jamal's back with our drinks," I said, trying to quash Kendra's *foul reflections* moment again. This time it worked. I don't think Jamal knew about Kendra's issues, because her voice lost the hint of bitterness as soon as he rejoined us.

33

Deja

Whew! Kendra's got issues in her life, I thought to myself as Jamal came back. Her issues didn't bother me as much as Isrie thought. I noticed my girl trying to change the subject for my benefit. I think she didn't want me developing an opinion of Kendra before I'd gotten to know her, but I wasn't in any position to be judging someone. I had my own share of emotional complications over Ivan's past with Sophia, and Kendra's talk made me reflect on them.

"Excuse me for a second," I said to the table as I scooted my chair back.

"I'm not chasing you off with my breath, am I?" Jamal asked.

"No," I laughed. "I just need to check on something." He was funny—and cute—but I had a man.

I snagged the black minibag, which held my ID and cell phone, off the table and exchanged glances with Isrie. She gave me a *hurry up and come back because I can't handle these two by myself* look. I nodded to confirm I'd be right back. I made my way past the tables to the restroom area at the rear of the building. There was a small line formed outside the ladies room, but I wasn't planning on using it anyway.

I had already pushed the MEMORY button on my phone. It was ringing as I put it to my ear. I took a deep breath and waited, not expecting to have someone answer.

"Hello?" Ivan picked up on the third ring. I was comforted by the sound of his voice.

"Hey, it's me," I replied.

"Where you at, baby?"

"Slap Happy in Inglewood."

"Yeah, I know where that's at. Who're you out with?"

"Isrie and this girl Kendra from her job." It didn't pay to mention Jamal.

"Oh. I've missed you."

"I've missed you too. That's why I called."

"You want to come by?"

"Where have you been?" I asked, sidestepping his request. "I've been calling since yesterday."

"Taking care of some business, that's all."

"You went out of town?"

"Yeah. Trying to close some deals. Taking care of our future."

"Any deals I know about?"

"Maybe," he laughed. "I'll let you know about it later. So, are you coming by tonight?"

"Maybe later. I'm having fun with my friend for now. Okay?"

"Ooookay," he huffed. "Just don't have too much fun."

"If I do, I'll fill you in on all the details. When do you want your truck back? I left it at Isrie's tonight."

"Whenever. I'm not going anywhere tonight. Just enjoy yourself, girl."

"I love you, Ivan," I chuckled, letting it casually slip out.

"How could you not?"

"Whatever."

"Before I forget—your girl, Isrie, is with you, right?"

"Yeah. She's at the table," I said, looking back. From where we were seated, I could make out Jamal peering in my direction. He couldn't see me, but I could see his ever-present smile.

"I found out that I can bring more guests on the upcoming

cruise to Mexico. You think she and a friend might want to come along?"

"That's sounds great! I'll ask her, but I already know what her answer is."

"Good, good. Go have fun, babe."

"Bye."

When I returned to the table, Isrie and Kendra were laughing about something while sipping on their drinks. Jamal was the first one to notice me as I stowed my phone back inside my minibag.

"Calling your man, huh?" Jamal asked with his smile unchanged.

"Yes," I admitted.

"Damn. There goes my night," he said with exaggerated frustration. "And I liked you too."

"You can still like me," I said, sitting beside him. "Just as a friend though."

"Oh! That damned F-word. You kill me, girl. You're a little small for my tastes, but I thought we had a chance."

"Small?" I was caught off guard by his comment and didn't know what to make of it. I had never been accused of being small in my life.

"Yeah. *Small,*" he snorted. "I like my women a little thicker. No offense to my sister and your friend here, but I get tired of seeing these silicone-enhanced celery sticks day in and day out. A brother needs something more to work with and appreciate."

Kendra took offense to her brother's offhanded remark and replied, *"Celery stick?* Jamal, I *know* you're not trying to talk about somebody with your barren scalp."

A chorus of laughter rang out from all of us at the table, drowning out the comedian who was on the stage. We looked around and everybody in the joint was looking rudely at us.

"I think it's time for us to move on," Isrie said, pointing in the direction of the front door.

"Yeah. Y'all need to get outta here before I'm out of a job and begging for time at the Improv," Jamal said in a hushed tone. I couldn't tell if he was serious or joking, but we weren't going to take the chance after the free drinks.

"Where to?" I asked.

Jamal recommended a little hot spot that was within walking distance so we wouldn't have to drive . . . and so he could tag along. I didn't mind his company, though. He was silly and I liked that.

"You like him, huh?" Isrie asked teasingly. The two of us were walking a few steps behind Jamal and Kendra, as they knew where we were going.

"Don't start, Isrie," I laughed. "You of all people know Ivan has all of this on lock."

"I know, I know. I'm just saying that Jamal wouldn't mind jiggling his key around in that lock."

"You're too nasty, girl. You must have your man on your mind."

"Yeah. I'm thinking about him. I'm happy for both of us to be in stable relationships for a change."

"Amen to that. I've got some other good news for you," I said with a smile.

"What?"

"I spoke with Ivan and he said to invite the two of you on the agency cruise with us."

"I'm sure Michael would love that. Thank you."

"*De nada.*"

"When?"

"I think in about two or three weeks. I know it's after Thanksgiving."

"Good. Michael promised a weekend for us after Thanksgiving anyway. That would be perfect. Is it going out to Catalina or something?"

"It goes down to Mexico."

"We'll be there!"

"Y'all, this is the spot," Jamal said, getting our attention as we came upon the strip mall shopping center on the corner. Most of the stores were closed, but the small parking lot was starting to fill with the cars of club goers and the less serious who were slowly driving through to check out the scene. My eyes moved across the Korean Laundromat and dry cleaners first, then the pawnshop with burglar bars on the windows and doors. The next doorway was open with a man checking IDs at the door. If I was lucky, he would think mine was fake. The neon sign with the name of the nightclub was something scribbled in cursive that I couldn't make out. Jamal had left his hat back at the comedy club and removed his tie to fit in with the crowd. He let us ladies go first as the large gentleman with the metal detector was going to take more time with him anyway.

Isrie put on her careful smile and brushed her hair out of her face as she surveyed the club. I was at her side as my eyes became accustomed to the dim lights. The crowd seemed to run from the early twenties to mid-thirties for the ladies, but was all over the board for the men. There weren't many available seats, but I did see a few barstools on the end of the bar near the dance floor. Most of the seats were taken because the dance floor was empty. The deejay was sitting back and letting the club make its money on drink orders. I was finished drinking for the night and just wanted to hang and maybe sneak in a dance or two.

Jamal walked behind the three of us as we headed to the open seats at the bar. There were only two left, so Isrie and Kendra claimed them so they could order from the bar. Jamal stood near us and was scoping out the ladies. It was time for me to take a powder room break and I began walking off.

Suddenly "Breathe" by Blu Cantrell started playing up in the joint. The sistah's strong voice mixed with Sean Paul's dance hall riddims and the thumping beat drove waves of couples onto the floor and had the people at the bar wigglin' in their seats.

"C'mon," I said as I grabbed Jamal's hand.

"I thought you had to go to the restroom."

"It'll wait. I like this song."

With the hard (and I do mean hard) work I had put into losing some of my weight, I was feeling a little feisty as I whirled around with Jamal. He, being the comedian he was, still had to clown. Halfway through the song, Kendra had found a tall, athletic stud to get out on the floor with. She cast her spell, twisting and sensually working her derriere in front of his eyes, giving him a sample of her womanhood in all its splendor. Isrie was at the bar guarding our purses and snapping her fingers as she cheered me on from afar.

"Your man doesn't know what he's missing," Jamal said over the music as I juked past him.

"Uh huh."

"What's his name?"

"Ivan." I closed my eyes and thought of him as I hummed. Jamal's conversation ended as he realized I was focused on the music. It was best for him to save his energy this evening for someone single with no strings attached. We finished our dance and another good song was following on the heels of the last one. Two steps into it, my bladder called time-out. Jamal understood the look on my face and let me by.

Two gentlemen parted to let me enter the restroom they had been blocking. They were hawking every woman in the place, but were nice enough to let me by with only some not-so-subtle smiles. One had a toothpick in his mouth as if he thought it made him look like P. Diddy. I could hear the mumble of their conversation through the locked door as I relieved myself. It wasn't until I exited the restroom that I realized what they were talking about . . . or should I say *whom* they were talking about. I pretended not to pay attention as I got them to part for me again. They had been talking about their friend who was dancing with Kendra, and were placing lewd bets on whether or not he would be hitting that tonight. Of course, their language left nothing to the imagination.

As a slow jam came on, I intended to talk to Kendra when she was finished pressing up against her partner on the floor. I found my way over to the bar and took a seat by Isrie.

"Where'd you go?" she asked.

"Bathroom."

"Oh," Isrie said as she smiled. "I thought you and Jamal were up to no good, but he's . . ."

Occupied. Jamal was occupied. It was none of my business, but Jamal had moved on. I'd be lying if I said I felt nothing as I scanned the back of Jamal's head at a nearby table. The attention I'd received felt good, as I wasn't used to getting it from anyone except Ivan. Jamal was all cozy with two ladies now, though. One was a redheaded white chick sipping a margarita and the other, a sister with a fro like Adina Howard, medium complexion, wearing a black top and black low-rise jeans. Jamal was eased up next to the sister kind of like he had been with me at the comedy club. Her body language as she chatted with him told me they had been together. There's a look we women have that speaks volumes to other women, especially in settings like this.

"Why don't you go dance, Isrie? I'll watch our stuff."

"No. I don't slow drag."

"*Since when?*"

"Since I got a man. I don't want him to do it, so I ain't either."

"I hear ya. I guess we'll just have to watch Kendra out there."

"Yep. She's having fun. You want something to drink?"

"Nah, Isrie. Just a lemon and water. I had enough at the comedy club."

"Suit yourself," she said as she motioned the bartender over.

"You might want to watch your girl."

"Who? Kendra?"

"Yeah. I had almost forgot. Ole boy's friends were talking about her by the bathroom."

"Alright. Sometimes I can't tell if she's all talk. We haven't been out together much."

"She's acting like she doesn't get out much," I said disapprovingly.

"Damn. Now you're sounding like somebody's mom. Chill out and have some fun."

The music picked up again and Isrie went to dance to Terror Squad's "Lean Back." Some guy who recognized her from TV—again—had asked her dance. He was cute and she was itching to get on the floor, so it didn't matter this time. Jamal finally pried himself from the two ladies he had been seated with. Before leaving, he gave his lady friend a kiss on the cheek and slipped her a wad of money, which I thought was odd. I was alone at the bar as he approached me with that infectious smile of his.

"Want to dance, Deja?"

"Umm, could you watch our stuff, Jamal? Thanks!" I left Jamal hanging with our purses and latched onto the nearest single male. Luckily, the guy put up with me grabbing him by the arm. I giggled to myself at the stunt I had just pulled.

From the look on his face, Jamal seemed amused. We exchanged silly glances periodically while I danced. Isrie, Kendra, and I got our dance on for what seemed like the whole night.

When we were ready to leave, Isrie sauntered across the packed dance floor to inform Kendra. That left me to stroll back through the crowd to a waiting Jamal at the bar.

"Save any more of those moves for me, sweetie?" he said with a smug look and his arms folded.

"No . . . no." I smiled. "We're about to go."

"Will I see you again?"

"I'm sure we'll run into each other around town. Maybe I'll stop in and check out your act again."

"You're serious about leaving me in here . . . alone?"

"Please. You're not alone. You got your sister and your friends at the table over there. You lied, though."

"Huh? About what?"

"You said you like your women thick. She definitely ain't thick."

"You saw that, huh?" he said with a sheepish grin.

"Of course . . . but it's none of my business."

"She's the mother of my child. We keep things . . . cordial."

"Gotcha."

"No, you don't. And neither does she. I wouldn't mind your having me, though."

"It was nice meeting you, Jamal. You're a good comedian." I held my hand out for him to shake it as I grabbed our purses. Isrie was coming our way.

"What do you do?" he asked, softly shaking my hand.

"Pictures. I'm a photographer." There was a pause between us before he finally let go of my hand. I handed Isrie her purse as she said good-bye to Jamal and we were off. I could feel his eyes at my back as we walked away.

"Kendra decided to stay, huh?" I asked as we walked down the street to Isrie's car. The temperature had dropped in the short time we were inside. I was wishing I had brought a jacket like Isrie. I rubbed my arms to keep warm.

"Yeah," was all Isrie said. I could tell she had some reservations about Kendra's decision, but she kept them to herself.

I heard someone running behind us and thought that it might have been Kendra. It was Jamal.

"Ladies, ladies," he huffed, half out of breath. "It was rude of me to let y'all two walk out here alone."

"We're fine. Go have a good time."

"You're cold, aren't you?" he asked, intentionally ignoring my dismissal. Isrie said nothing, knowing this conversation didn't involve her. She just continued walking.

"What are you doing?" I screamed as Jamal began unbuttoning his shirt in front of me.

"Chill. I'm not stripping. I only do that at nursing homes these days. They're great tippers."

Jamal took off his warm shirt and placed it over me. I could still smell the Issey Miyake cologne on it and inhaled deeply. Jamal's undershirt was clinging to him. His ebony chocolate bod underneath was almost as chiseled as Ivan's.

A few minutes later, we were at Isrie's car. Jamal had spent the walk trying to make me laugh, but I kept a straight face. I took his shirt from around me and handed it back.

"Here," he said, reaching into his wallet. "My card. Call me sometimes if you need anything . . . or if your man messes up. It's got my e-mail address on there too."

I deliberated over whether to take the business card, then decided to be polite. "Thank you," I said.

Isrie turned the key and started her car on cue.

"Can I at least get a hug?"

"Sure." I smiled, giving in to the nice, fine young man. *Did I say he was fine?* No extra squeezes, though. I felt the pressure relieved off my back as Jamal's arms constricted and picked me up off my feet. I closed my eyes and let out a moan from the good feeling of my back cracking. As I moaned, I felt his mouth meet mine . . . and lost my composure for a second. The kiss was short but nice. I still had my eyes closed and my mouth open when Jamal pulled back, leaving me hanging.

"Didn't want to offend you," he whispered. "I just couldn't resist finding out what those lips felt like. Sorry." Jamal slowly lowered me back to earth. I felt embarrassed by what had just happened, so I was quiet. As I opened the car door and got in, I wiped my mouth and gave a confused wave to Jamal. He simply smiled and jogged back across the street.

As we drove to Isrie's apartment, where my—oops—*Ivan's* truck was waiting, I couldn't stop thinking about how aroused I was. I guess flirting with danger can have different effects on different people. Some people might be rarin' to go for a roll in the hay with a stranger. I was in that other category. After that kiss from Jamal, I was rarin' for a roll with my man now.

Isrie at least pretended like she hadn't seen a thing and made idle small talk. Back at her place, we gave each other a hug and promised to get together as couples soon after Thanksgiving.

As I drove down the Santa Monica Freeway later toward Ivan's place, I couldn't wait to have him all over me and feel our bodies pressed together. I didn't have the radio on, but music played in my head. I still had Jamal's card on me and read over the information once with a smile. He was nice, but it was the wrong time and wrong place. Never taking my eyes off the road, I lowered the window and let the wind carry the business card out of my hand. I was going to be with my lover. It was going to be good tonight.

34

Isrie

I decided not to embarrass my girl on the drive back to my place. Deja had a model letting her push his whip and now had a comedian chasing her. Deja was far richer than that, though. My girl had a natural glow and kindness within her that no man and all his gifts could compete with. At times, I wondered if she was aware of this.

I was wearily dragging myself through the front lobby with thoughts of sleep when the concierge startled me.

"Ms. Walker?"

"Oh! Hi, Webster." Webster was the one concierge I knew by name. The cute young blonde, for all his polish, appeared to be more surfer punk than concierge. I imagined him daydreaming about waves along the coast.

"I didn't mean to scare you."

"That's alright," I answered with a blush. "Long night."

"I wouldn't bother you, but you have an item here," he said, reaching under the counter, "It was left earlier tonight and I thought it would be safer down here."

"Whoa," was all I said when the two items—a jewelry case and a bottle of champagne—were set in front of me. Webster eagerly watched my reaction as I slowly opened the jewelry case and was surprised by the glare. I blinked once and Webster blinked twice as I raised the platinum and diamond baguette bracelet up to the light.

"Oh . . . my . . . lord," I gasped. "This is too much."

"Whoa," was all Webster said, sharing my thoughts.

"Is there a note? Or something?" I pleaded with Webster as I frantically looked inside the case and on the champagne bottle in vain.

"Oh, here it is," he said, looking behind the counter. "It must have fallen off." He placed the envelope in my hand.

"Thanks, Webster." I gathered everything and scurried off to my apartment. It took all my control not to read the note in the elevator, but I wanted to be sitting in the privacy of my home. I arrived on the sixth floor of my building and ran down the hall, keys in hand. I kicked my sandals off, freeing my sore feet, as I disarmed the alarm.

I seated myself comfortably and read the note, imagining his voice.

> *Isrie, I love you and you know that. Even though I couldn't be with you right now, I just wanted you to know you're never out of my mind. Hope you don't mind the gifts. I know what you said about receiving gifts and jewelry, but a man has to be hard-headed, otherwise he wouldn't be a man (insert laugh here). Hope you like the bracelet, as it is just a small token of my affection for you. Don't touch the champagne. It's for us when I get back. I'm out entertaining clients, so you probably won't be able to reach me. I'll call you.*
>
> *—Michael*

I was overcome with emotion and got a little choked up after reading Michael's words. God was kind enough to bless me with someone such as him. It was already Sunday, but I was going to put forth the effort to attend morning services at Calvary Baptist in Bellflower.

On my way home from service, I had a craving for donuts. I drove into the parking lot of the Dunkin' Donuts but decided to call Michael first. I hit the MEMORY button on my cell.

"Hello?" Michael's voice bellowed through on the fourth ring.

"I didn't think you were going to answer."

"Yep. You almost got my voice mail. I'm a little busy."

"On a Sunday?"

"Clients. They enjoy free stuff . . . especially on weekends. Golfing today."

"Oh. I got your gifts last night. Thank you."

"You don't have to thank me. Did you like the bracelet?"

"Of course," I said with a blush. I had parked and was digging for money in my purse. "When are you coming back?"

"Either late tomorrow or early Tuesday. Miss me?"

"Always. Do you need me to do anything? Need anything at your apartment?"

"No. My roommate, Lloyd, is probably there holdin' it down."

"You sound funny when you use slang."

"You just see too much of my professional side. I'll have to break it down for you when I get back," he laughed. "Had a good time last night?"

"Yes. It would have been better if you were there, but it was nice to have a ladies night. We've been invited somewhere."

"Where?"

"Deja's boyfriend invited us on a cruise. Something to do with his modeling agency."

"Sounds like a winner."

"I've got somewhere else I want you to go before that though."

"Oh? Where?"

"My parents. Thanksgiving dinner."

"Hmm. I've been wanting to meet the parents of such a wonderful woman. I should be able to take off for the holidays to do that."

"Good. You better. It'll be here before you know it."

Just then I heard a noise in the background that Michael appeared to react to. Things were noisy in the Dunkin' Donuts and my phone was crackling, so I wasn't sure what I heard.

"What was that?"

"What?"

"That noise in the background."

"What? The TV?"

"I guess."

"I had changed channels with the remote just now and it was loud."

"Oh."

"Look, I need to run, Isrie. I've got clients waiting for me in the clubhouse and need to get a move on."

"Alright. Love you."

"Ditto. Bye."

"Bye."

As I moved up one spot in line, I couldn't help but think I had heard the sound of a small child in the background. I wrote it off as just me being silly. Today's sermon taught a good lesson about trust, and I was going to strive to stay in the moment.

"Three glazed donuts, please," I said as I placed my order.

35

Deja

"You sure you don't want to come up for a spell?" I asked Ivan as I stared at my apartment from the car window.

"I'm sure," he said tapping the key against the steering wheel. "I have some jobs out of town this week and it's late."

"Oh. I guess I'll go face my brother then."

"Something wrong?"

"What do you mean?"

"Something wrong with you and Theron?" Ivan asked, the concern etched across his brow. We had spent most of Sunday together at his place and playing around on the beach while having an impromptu picnic. I didn't want it to end.

I chose my words carefully. I trusted Ivan, but still didn't know how he'd react to an AWOL brother in my family. "No, no real problems," I said. "Theron's always difficult. I simply curse him out and move on."

"Well, I guess I should go. Give me a kiss, baby."

We kissed for a little while as I leaned over into his arms. Ivan had pushed me to keep his truck longer, but I just didn't feel right about it and had asked him to drive me home.

"You love me, right?"

"Baby, you know I do."

"I need to come clean with you then. I don't want any secrets or surprises between us. You can't tell anyone, though. Okay?"

"Okay. What's on your mind?" Ivan was about to put the key back in the ignition. He stopped.

"My brother's in some trouble. It's been kinda wearing on my nerves."

"The po-pos?"

"No. Army. Well, maybe the cops too. Shit, I don't know."

"What'd he do?" he asked. Ivan was listening intensely. I didn't know he'd care this much.

"He claims he did nothing." I sighed. "Some stuff was stolen back where he was stationed."

"Are you harboring him or something?"

"Yes, but promise me you won't tell *anyone*." I grasped Ivan's hand and held firmly.

"I promise. I just don't want you in any danger . . . or trouble."

"I'm fine. Thanks for your concern, but Theron's going to be leaving soon."

"Good. The sooner the better," he chuckled before catching himself. "Sorry."

"I'll talk to you later."

Ivan watched me walk up to my apartment before driving off. I wasn't sure if what I had done was right. Hell, I hadn't even told Isrie . . . and *she* was my best friend. I heard movement inside my apartment and hoped Theron was by himself inside.

"Say, bruh," I said, walking in. I was in some sweats I had left at Ivan's. My dress from last night was tucked under my arm. Theron was sitting on my sofa in his draws and watching *Soul Train*.

"Hey," was all he said as he put the TV on mute. My bedroom door was ajar and I got curious all of a sudden.

"Do you have company?"

"Nah, girl. Just me and the *Soooooooooooooul Train*."

I closed the door behind me and let out a yawn. I wanted to go straight to my bed, but plunked down beside my brother.

"Everything okay?" I asked, wanting to really bond with Theron instead of arguing.

"Yeah, things are straight," he said, looking me in the eye. "I'm still here . . . layin' low."

"You know where you're going to go next?"

"I've got some ideas, but I really don't want to leave. LA is my home."

"We already talked about that. You sure you can't just explain things to the people in charge at Fort Drum?"

There went that laugh of his. "That's cute. I ain't going back, girl."

"When are you going to tell me what happened? I think you owe *that much* to me."

"Deja, I don't want to drag you into this. The less you know, the better off you are."

"Fuck you. I am getting sick of the mystery games. I'm going to take a nap, but we're going to talk about this before you go—whether you want to or not." I left Theron to his *Soul Train*. He began raising the volume on the television.

"Sis, I got a message for you too," he said in a low tone.

"From who? Isrie called while I was out?"

"No. Sophia said to tell you she'd be in touch later this week. Something about a big job."

I stopped dead in my tracks and looked through the crack in my bedroom door at the darkness. "Did she call?" I asked.

"No."

"Where'd you talk to her at? The studio? I know you've been seeing her over there."

"She was here," he said barely over the volume of the TV. "Last night."

I let my bedroom door swing open and turned the light on. I quickly scanned everything before turning back around to face Theron who was still seated. "Tell me that bitch wasn't in my bedroom. Please tell me that." I was trembling with disgust.

"No, no! Don't be going all psycho. Nothing went down here like that. I remember how you tripped last time. I'm not gonna lie and say I never hit it—*heh*—or that it wasn't any good, but nothin' has gone down here . . . ever."

"Keep it that way. I don't want her coming to my house ever again. Understand?"

"Shit, Deja. You breakin' my balls over her, but I bet you're gonna be callin' her for that big job. Ain'tcha? You *that* jealous over her?"

I ran up on my brother and gave him a hard shove upside his head. Theron gave me one of those crazy military stares before jumping up in my face. "Boy, you're still my baby brother. I'm going out of my way to take care of you and you've got the *nerve* to talk shit? In my home?"

"Alright! Alright! I'm talking shit now, am I? Then why don't you set me straight, huh? Why you hatin'?"

"Dammit! Sophia used to sleep with Ivan," I screamed in his face, losing it altogether. "Is that what you want me to say? Huh? Am I supposed to feel comfortable because Sophia looks like a million bucks and I have to bust my ass, run a zillion miles, take diet pills, and still look like *this*?? Am I supposed to feel good, knowing that she can just snap her fingers and most men, including fools like you, will get down on all fours and bark? Am I supposed to feel good, knowing that she's rubbing it in my face by *playing* with my brother? Huh? Am I supposed to feel wonderful, knowing I need the work sooooo bad that I have to tolerate her and swallow my pride? Am—am I supposed to feel good . . . knowing that the man I love has made love to her before me and—and probably still thinks about her when he's with me? You want me to be a hater, bruh? Alright then, I'll hate! I hate you for being an insensitive asshole of a brother!"

I ran off in tears to my bedroom and slammed the door behind me. I got into bed and yanked the covers up over my head. I could smell a perfume that wasn't mine on the sheets. Theron had lied about that. I cried myself to sleep.

My brother, choosing to wait until things quieted down, knocked on my door later, waking me up.

"Whaaaat?" I shrieked from my bed. My throat was still hurting and my eyes were swollen.

"You okay?" he asked through the door.

"Yeah. Go away."

"I have to ask you something."

"What?"

Theron slowly opened the door, expecting something to come flying at him. His droopy eyes looked unusually alert. If I hadn't been pissed at him, I would have found it funny. "I'm sorry, sis" were the first words from his mouth.

"Yeah. Whatever. What do you want?"

"I know you said I could stay a couple o' weeks longer and Thanksgiving's almost here. Can I stay around till Christmas? I really want to be with family then. With you."

The smart aleck in me really wanted me to tell him to go be a family with Sophia, but it wasn't in me. "Christmas it is. Then you gotta go. I'm not going to jail over this shit."

"Thank you, sis. I love you."

"I know. One thing, though. I don't want you messing with Sophia anymore or want her in my home or my studio."

Theron left well enough alone and nodded before closing my door again. I sighed deeply and went back asleep. A knock came again a little later.

"Whaaaat?" I shrieked again.

"I already knew she slept with pretty boy," he said through the door. "It didn't take a braniac to figure that out from the way you were actin'. I really wanted to tell him something or run him off, but I saw you were in love with him and left it alone. If you trusted him, who was I to judge? I ain't never had the best judgment anyway. I love you enough, sis, to let you make your own decisions. . . . That's all."

I smiled in the darkness of my room at my brother's mushiness. Then his muffled voice came back.

"Oh yeah . . . and another thing. You're prettier than Sophia could ever be—inside and out. And I wish you and Ivan the best. You've always been my guardian angel, sis."

I didn't answer or respond. What could I say? I just let the sleep take hold of my weary body and mind again and went on autopilot with my dreams.

36

Isrie

At my job, we all bowed heads as our director said a generic, nonoffensive, nondenominational blessing for our little Thanksgiving luncheon. She was careful not to refer to any higher power, but I was saying my own little prayer anyway. We had closed early for our luncheon party, which was catered. Our director, who usually was out rubbing elbows with the big names in Hollywood to drum up clients, had graced us with her presence to give us a pep talk and speech about what a successful year Calming Images had been having. Duh. My sore hands and forearms were telling me that.

I had seen Kendra at work off and on since our night of comedy and dancing a few weeks earlier, but we hadn't had much of a chance to just talk until now. I had noticed that she called in sick most of the week after we clubbed with her and her brother, but thought nothing of it.

"Hey, girl," I said, in line behind her to have my plate filled with carved turkey slices, gravy, stuffing, and cranberries.

"Hey, Isrie," was all Kendra spared without taking her eyes off her plate. The caterer finished serving her and she snagged a roll before shuffling off to the table. I watched Kendra, considering sitting somewhere else, but remained stubborn and pursued her.

"We haven't talked much since we went out that night. Something bothering you?"

"No. I've just been under the weather."

"Oh? I guess someone had a better time that night than the rest of us," I said slyly.

"Yeah," she said as she chewed a piece of roll. "Great time. Jamal was asking me about your friend Deja just yesterday. He's still waiting on that call from her."

"Tell your brother not to hold his breath. She and her boyfriend are serious. If I know her, she probably threw away Jamal's card that night. No offense."

"None taken. Jamal can try too hard sometimes. He's used to having to do that in his business. How's your food?"

"I never turn down a catered meal, girl," I laughed. "I can't each too much, though. Gotta save my appetite for the real Thanksgiving meal this weekend."

"Parents?"

"Oh, yes! Ella will be throwin' down as always. I would go there early to help my mom because of her knee, but Michael's supposed to be coming with me, so we're going to drive out on Thanksgiving Day."

"Any *wedding bells* in the future?" she asked sarcastically.

"I don't know, Kendra. If it ever comes to him popping the question or if that topic comes up, I'd have a hard time saying no." I beamed with emotion and pride for a moment before continuing. "Do you know he had a bottle of champagne and *this* bracelet waiting for me when I got back from the club?"

"*Hmph.* He probably thought you were out doing something—or somebody—and was just trying to make you feel guilty." Kendra let her remark fly out with all the venom she could muster before realizing how mean-spirited it came across. She made eye contact with me for the first time in weeks and her mouth appeared to be opening to utter some kind of apology.

"I don't think so," I said with a scowl across my face. "I've got a better relationship with Michael than that. Besides—"

"Isrie, I—"

"I wasn't the one up in the club throwing my ass at brothers after sneaking out on my man." I think I regretted my response as much as she regretted setting it off, but it was too late. I had issues with how she carried herself that night, but it was not my place to criticize.

"I—I," she stuttered as if trying to fix things in her head. Her next reaction caught me as well as the other employees off guard. Kendra burst into tears and ran from the conference room, sending her plate plummeting to the carpeted floor. The director and everyone else were left staring at me since I was the person talking with her when it happened. I felt some guilt as I looked at all the staring faces and wondered what they were imagining. It seemed like an eternity had passed before I was up and running after the woman who I considered my friend a few minutes earlier. A new round of office gossip had just started, but I couldn't do anything about that.

"Kendra," I called out as I ran into the hallway. She was nowhere in sight, so I decided to check the nearest employee restroom. There she was, sobbing uncontrollably with her face bent over the sink. The water was running.

"Umm . . . look, I'm sorry. I didn't mean what I said back there."

"Fuck you," she sobbed. Her hands covered her eyes and her cries became louder. I was feeling more uncomfortable as she went on.

"Do you want me to leave? I can tell everyone outside you just need some time."

"Yes. Go. Just go," she bit out between outbursts of coughing and crying. I could hear the snot in her nose wanting to come out. I was trying to think up explanations to the nosy questions that would be awaiting me, but Kendra called me back before I'd left.

"I'm *really, really* sorry about what I said," I told her.

"Oh, shut up," she said as she revealed her face to me. Her eyes were swollen and red. "It's not always about you."

"What's up?"

"I don't remember."

"You don't know why you're crying?"

"No! I don't remember what happened at the club after y'all left." She paused to blow her nose. "Nothing!"

"But you were with—oh, shit. No." If I weren't black, I would have been as white as a ghost. "Where was Jamal?"

"He—he was there. I remember him coming back inside. He left to give Claudia, his baby's momma, and her friend Treselle a ride home. I told him to go on and that I would be fine. That's the last thing I remember, Isrie."

"No, no. You have to remember something. What are you saying? The guy you were dancing with—"

"He's the last person . . . I—I saw." I had begun crying as well, taking up her slack. "I don't think I can talk about this."

"Shhh. It'll be alright. You are okay, right?"

"Isrie, I woke up in the parking lot in a Dumpster. No, I'm not okay!" she shouted, losing all composure again. "My—my panties were gone. I think I was drugged. Something m-m-must've been put in my drink."

One of the other massage therapists peeked in the bathroom door and saw me holding Kendra close to me as we both cried. There was the start of the *lesbian* rumor. Fuck 'em.

"Did . . . umm. Were you—?" I stumbled.

"Yes," she confirmed my incomplete question. "The bastard. I'd kill him if I knew who he was."

"Did you go to the police?"

"No. I can't. I don't remember anything."

"What'd your boyfriend say?"

"Nothing," she said, taking a deep breath. She started wiping her eyes in an attempt to be strong again. "I couldn't tell him. What was I going to say?"

"The truth. You can't keep something like this from him."

"Yes, I can. And I will. I've kept my mouth shut this long."

"Have you gone to a doctor at least? I mean, he could have something—"

"*Hmph*. Make me feel even better, Isrie. Maybe I'll start calling you Misery. My man has been wondering why I won't let him touch me. I can only use the period excuse for so long."

"Look, let me make an appointment for you. You need to be checked out and tested for STDs. I'll even go with you, girl."

"I—I need to think things out," she said. Fear of what might come back from an exam was evident in her eyes. Her ignorance wasn't bliss, but it was comfortable for her at the moment. "I'll let you know later. Look, I can't stay around here."

"I'll drive you home."

"No, no! People will know something's up, and my boyfriend's home right now. Look . . . just forget what I told you, okay? I need to think."

"You got my number. You don't have to go through this alone, Kendra. Maybe you should talk about it with Jamal."

"Just leave it alone. Leave it," she said with her finger in my face. She was running scared and there was nothing I could do except be there when she got tired of running. Kendra left the bathroom and went home. I went back to a conference room filled with warm whispers, cool smiles, and cold turkey and tried to sell them on Kendra having *family problems*.

37

Deja

"Yes, this is Deja. How may I help you?" I was trying to get some clothes washed before the holidays. I didn't recognize the number on my cell phone, so I answered in my professional voice. I closed the lid on the noisy washing machine with my free hand.

"I'm calling to help *you*. Are you ready?" she cackled with a hint of arrogance only I could pick up . . . or imagine. I bit my lip.

"Oh. Hey, Sophia."

"What happened to your energy and enthusiasm? If you're going to be sounding all lifeless in front of the Ebony Emotions people, I won't be able to help you."

"Yeah. Sorry. I'm in the middle of washing clothes. That's all."

"How's Theron?"

"I thought you were calling to speak to me?"

"I waaaas," she giggled. "I was just trying to make conversation and be civil. It's next week. Monday. Are you ready?"

"Monday? The Ebony Emotions shoot is this Monday?" Tomorrow was Thanksgiving, so I only had the holiday weekend to prepare and steady my nerves for my big break. Who was going to be there? What was I even going to wear?

"Yes. Problem with it?"

"No. I just thought I'd get a little more notice."

"Life's a bitch."

No, you are.

"Yeah, I guess it is. Where's the location?"

"Studio City, I think."

"You *think?*"

"Yes. *I think.* Things are running last minute. They want to throw a press conference too. I'll call you first thing Monday morning with the specifics."

"Monday? Oh, come on, now! I need to know now so I can choose my equipment."

"You think the big names in this town always have everything laid out for them? Shit happens and they still manage to get it done. I've seen that with my own eyes. Deja, if you're ready to step up with the big fish, I need to know if you can hang. I'm putting my reputation and career on the line by recommending you for this. Don't let me down. If it helps, I can tell you that everything's going to be indoors."

"That helps some. I'll have everything ready. Call me at the studio Monday."

"Oh, I will. You won't be disappointed. Trust me. Have a happy Thanksgiving, Deja."

"You too. Thanks again for this gig."

"Bye."

I finished washing clothes in the laundry room and rejoined a still-sleeping Theron, who was sprawled across my sofa. I had planned on just unwinding for Thanksgiving Day, but now I was going to have a lot of shit on my mind. Isrie had invited both my brother and me over to her parents' in San Bernardino for dinner, but she didn't know about Theron's predicament and I didn't want to cause any trouble for them. I politely declined on behalf of both of us. I wanted to spend time with my girl and her parents . . . especially with my grandma not being here. I had met Isrie's parents before and they were hella cool, but Theron was my brother and we needed to stick together.

I left Theron's clothes neatly folded in a stack on the floor beside him and went into my room to put my things away. After storing my clothes in their proper places in the dresser and closet, I took my Lakers cap off and looked at the weave I was still adjusting to. I wondered if I truly would have everything prepared for Monday.

I walked into the kitchen where I had a small chicken defrosting in the fridge. Neither one of us was going to eat a whole turkey.

"Unh. Can you keep the noise down in there?" Theron groaned, just removed from his recent slumber. I almost asked for his help with the Ebony Emotions shoot, but I was paranoid about him being ID'd and shipped back to New York. Part of me just felt uncomfortable about him seeing me swallow my pride before Sophia after my emotional outburst Saturday.

"I'm trying to get food ready for tomorrow, so you're just going to have to put up with the *noise*, bruh. Besides, you need to put those clothes up I washed for your dirty ass. My apartment is starting to look like a pigsty."

"Huh? What's a pigsty?" My brother was yawning and scratching himself as he rudely reached past me and grabbed the bottle of Sunny Delight out of the fridge.

"I don't really know. Grandma used to say it," I chuckled. "Don't be sassin' me, boy. Just clean up your mess."

He laughed. "Yes ma'am," he replied with a mock salute.

True to his word, Theron began straightening up the area around the sofa that had served as his home while I made sure everything I needed for our meal tomorrow was on hand in the kitchen. Just then I had a thought of grandma looking down on us from heaven. I wondered what she would have thought of how we turned out.

"Sis?"

"What?"

"You ever wonder where our mom is?"

"Holidays, huh?" I avoided his question with another.

"Yeah. Every year," he answered with a smile that he knew I understood.

PART III

Arrivals and Departures (Where It Hits the Fan)

38

Isrie

The drive out to my parents' was filled with silence. Michael could have been saying something, but I wasn't hearing him. I was pissed, so I just drove. We were as late as could be for our Thanksgiving dinner with my parents.

My dad used to say, "If a man does you wrong, you've got problems. If a man does you wrong in front of your family, then he's a bum." Michael wasn't a bum. He was just having bumlike tendencies in my eyes at the moment.

I was supposed to pick up Michael at his apartment in Long Beach around noon for our drive out to San Bernardino. It was a big parking lot, so I thought nothing of it when I didn't see his car.

"Yeah?" was the response I had received from my knock on Michael's door. This was my first introduction to his roommate, Lloyd. Lloyd was a short medium-brown brother with curly hair and a build that looked like he could throw a car. He was wearing a white wife-beater shirt with blue scrub bottoms similar in style to the kind I wore at work. A fraternity brand on his chest was barely visible just above the line of his shirt.

"Hi, I'm Isrie."

"Yeah?" he replied, his interest piqued. The way his eyes bore into me made me feel unclean.

"I'm here to pick up Michael. Is he in?"

"Uh . . . oooh. Nooo!" he said, his mood lightening as he realized that I was here for Michael. "He's on his way. He said for you to wait. Come on in."

"You're Lloyd?"

"Yeah. Can I get you sumthin'?" he replied, grabbing clothes off the backs of chairs as he escorted me toward the living room. Michael's roommate left a lot to be desired with his housekeeping skills. It was like night and day compared to the way the apartment looked the night the limo delivered me.

"I'll have some water, thank you."

"Alright, alright! Have a seat over there," he said, pointing to a clear spot on the familiar sectional. The fertility god statue was smiling at me, welcoming me back. Lloyd brought me my water in a clean glass with a courteous smile. He then grabbed more of the clutter and junk that was scattered on the sectional and ran off with it to Michael's room. The nerve of him, I thought. Lloyd returned after a few minutes to entertain me.

"You look familiar," he said, taking a seat on the other end. He pulled a remote control out of the crack between cushions and brought the TV blaring to life. "I know! Weren't you on TV before? That dating show? That producer dude took you to the zoo or sumthin'. Yeah . . . that's it!"

"No. Wasn't me. Sorry," I said, shrugging my shoulders and lying through my teeth.

"Oh. Sure look like you . . . legs and all. *Unh, unh, unh.*"

"So, what are your plans for today?" I figured I would change the subject before I got too uncomfortable.

"Nothin' much. I'll probably break out after y'all leave and go by my old lady's crib. Her moms throws *down* for Turkey Day."

"Charletta?"

"Yeah. That's her. How you know her?"

"We met when I was over here before. She came by looking for you."

"Yeah, yeah," he said, stroking his barely visible facial hair. "T—I mean Michael told me about that." He let out an unusual giggle as a gleam appeared in his eye. I didn't like this guy, but continued smiling and sipping my water. My legs were already crossed and I nervously pulled down on the hem of my print dress. As if sensing my discomfort, Lloyd spouted off, "I'm sure Michael will be here any minute."

Two tortuous hours later, a winded Michael barged in the door. Lloyd was the first person to meet him and they exchanged some whispers while I sat and smoldered some more. He was probably filling Michael in on how pissed I was. When I heard him finish his conversation, I got up, took my purse in hand, and faced Michael. He was looking all good as usual in a French blue Hugo Boss dress shirt and black slacks, but I didn't flinch. He even had the nerve to smile at me.

By the time we neared the end of our car ride, my face was hurting from keeping a frown affixed for so long.

"Are you listening to me, Isrie?"

"Yeah. I'm listening," I responded, my face still locked up. "I'm just thinking about what my parents are going to say. I tried to call you while I waited, but your cell phone wasn't on."

"Look, I'll apologize to your parents."

"Hell, you should be apologizing to me."

"I already did if you had been listening. I told you over an hour ago. I had business to take care of. I had some reports to complete and mail off; then I had some Hollywood Bowl tickets to drop off across town to some clients at the last minute."

"We're almost there," I said as I downshifted in the curve on the freeway. I didn't want to get into it.

A short time later my phone rang. It was my mom wondering where in the hell we were. I was pulling into the driveway of Ella Walker's house then, so I cut the conversation short. Almost on cue, my father began opening the garage door.

"I love you," Michael said assuredly, taking my hand in his and kissing it. He spoke the words without moving his mouth so my parents, who were swooping out of the garage to greet me and meet my man, couldn't read his lips. Seeing them, I put on my happy face.

"Did I ever tell you that I hate your job?" I asked, looking at Michael for the first time since our trip began. My feelings inside were beginning to mirror the happy face I was wearing on the outside.

"No, but I do too. . . . Anything that keeps me away from your lovely face. Ready to do this?"

I smiled, genuinely. Michael had weathered the storm and was still looking at me with love in his eyes. We were more than three hours late for Thanksgiving dinner, but things were going to be alright.

"You know your father had to take first shot at him. Must be a man thing. You know how protective Harold is with you. Remember how he did with Ryan?"

"I'll never forget it, Mom. I'll say this . . . the two of them are getting along well." I was helping my mother in the kitchen after we cleared the table. She had whipped out her roll of aluminum foil to cover the leftovers. My dad was giving Michael the grand tour of his castle.

"He's cute," my mom remarked. "More mature than Ryan." Michael had worked that same magic on my parents that had won me over since day one. Sure we caught some flack for being on *serious* CP time, but even that was limited to a few remarks by my dad as he said grace.

"No comparison, Mom. No comparison," I proudly proclaimed.

"He lives in LA?" my mom asked as he handed me a covered dish.

"Long Beach. I thought you might know him or know of him," I answered, clearing a space in the back of the fridge.

"Why?"

"Well, he does some pharmaceutical sales in the area. Always

wining and dining doctors and stuff—too much of it on weekends. Pharfex-Williams."

"Pharfex-Williams, huh? They do a lot of business at the hospital. I always see their people running in and out. I'm just vol-
unteering there so I don't pay them no mind. Now, I'll pay them
some mind if they come up with a cream for my aching knee
that lasts longer than an hour."

"Why don't you ask Michael, Mom? He might know of some
good stuff."

"You're right, Isrie June. He might be able to hook this old
lady up. Shit, I'm not above free samples," my mom said with
that delightful laugh of hers that was so full of life.

"Now's probably a good time to ask him, Mom. I think
Michael's in the den with Dad. I doubt he wants to hear the in-
tricacies of a good mystery novel. And . . . Mom?"

"Huh?" Ella replied with a turn of her head. She was already
darting to the den to take her crack at my man.

"Please don't call me Isrie June in front of him, okay?"

"Okay," she chuckled. "I get the feeling this is *the one*. Don't
answer, girl. I don't want to jinx anything."

I shook my fist at her and watched her run off. I could have
saved Michael from the two of them, but wasn't suffering what
the holidays were about—at least the worthwhile ones? Besides,
he had kept me waiting earlier.

I hung out around the kitchen and took the time to pour myself a glass of Mom's holiday wine. When no one came back
into the living room, I became curious and went in search of
them. From the voices carrying, I knew they were still in Dad's
den. I tiptoed across the carpet and watched them from the hallway through the crack in the door.

I don't know how long I stood there, but I watched Michael
interact with my mom and dad without them seeing me. My
dad had his latest book out and Michael seemed to be genuinely
interested. There was laughter and joking as my boyfriend
thumbed through the pages and commented on the writing. He

was really getting on my dad's good side. My mom was looking over Michael's shoulder and was saying something as she pointed to a particular page. She patted him on the back as everyone broke out in laughter. I grinned as I continued to watch. To a total stranger, the three of them would have looked like family.

"Isrie. Come on in here, baby girl," my dad called out in his hoarse voice upon noticing me, I left my hiding spot and joined the festivities.

The night rolled on and Ella's holiday wine gradually disappeared from its bottle. My mom pulled out some carrot cake for dessert to satisfy my dad's sweet tooth.

"Michael, you play spades?" my dad asked as the clock struck midnight.

"Sure do, Mr. Walker," he said, looking at his watch.

I was sitting beside him on the sofa and whispered, "Don't you have to work tomorrow?"

"I said I love you, Isrie," he said with a comforting gaze. "I guess they'll just have to do without me for one day."

It was men versus women, and when my mom and I won the first hand, we wound up playing more . . . and more. In the end, Michael and my dad won on the final hand only because my mom and I were getting sleepy. My dad surprised everyone in the room when he asked Michael if he wanted to stay the night. I was tired and knew I was in no shape to drive, but couldn't believe my dad's offer nonetheless. We agreed to stay till morning, then get on the road. My mom went make up the spare bedroom for him. The topic of where I was sleeping never came up, as my parents knew we would be in separate bedrooms. Sure, I was a grown woman, but this was *their* house. I knew the rules and would have been too embarrassed to object or try to say anything to the contrary.

It was before daylight when my bladder woke me up. Too much wine. In a few hours, my parents would be up clanking pots and talking in the kitchen over coffee. Even on a few hours' sleep,

Mom and Dad would get up like clockwork. For now, things were still calm. I had been sleeping in my underwear, but my mom had given me her robe to borrow, which I'd wrapped myself up in. I was yawning with my eyes closed when I misjudged things, running into the wall outside the bathroom door. I rubbed my head, laughed at myself, then went inside to take care of business.

Like a great shoe sale, the closed guest bedroom door down the hall beckoned to me. I had to spy on Michael before going back to sleep. It was next to my parents' room, so I knocked lightly once and turned the knob. The door came open in my hand. I peeked in first.

"Michael?" I politely asked as I came in farther. He didn't answer. He's probably knocked out, I thought to myself. In the dark, there he lay. He was sleeping atop the covers, his clothes off and neatly folded at the foot of the bed. The white briefs he wore stood out in contrast to his pretty brown skin. I watched his chest move up and down with his breathing. I imagined what it would be like looking at this sight every morning.

I couldn't resist the urge to give him one kiss before leaving. I bent over him and pressed my lips down. At first, I was going to give a quick, light smack but instead ran my lips across his gradually. He was still asleep, but his mouth opened slightly and he let out a low chuckle. I think he was aware of my presence or maybe was just having a good dream. I decided then to continue kissing him. Michael's eyes flashed to life as he awakened and I smiled, running a hand through his hair. With my other hand, I rubbed his firm chest, letting my fingers carve imaginary impressions in his flesh.

"I was wondering if you would come visit me," he said in between the long, wet kisses he was now delivering.

"I had to see you. Even if it was just to watch you sleep."

"I'm awake now." In more ways than one, from the bulge I saw in his briefs.

"My parents are in the next room," I whispered softly to remind him and to talk myself out of what I wanted to do.

"Then be quiet," he said, grinning wickedly.

We continued kissing, till I paused to let the robe drop to the floor. Michael sat up in the bed and waited for me to come to him. This was one of those moments where I should have been wearing spiked heels—better yet, clear pumps, as Chris Rock would say. I decided to be sexy and walked slowly, sensuously into his powerful arms. His kisses on my belly button caused warmth to flow out across my whole body. I gripped his shoulders as I would to give a massage while he planted teasing kisses along my waistline, grasping my hips tightly to steady me.

I moaned his name softly with my eyes closed. His fingers gripped my panties just before he yanked them down with a snap. I was so hot and feenin' for him that I almost came from the suddenness of his move. I felt his warm breath along my thighs before he pulled me down on his lap. The two of us went back to the intense kisses and I wrapped my arms around him, digging my nails into the small of his back. His tongue slid along the side of my neck, tasting of my flesh before tugging on my ear. With one finger, he slid my bra straps off my shoulders, causing my breasts to heave out before him. He grasped one and let out a grunt before plunging it into his open mouth. Oh, the joy of it all. Michael had a way of sucking while looping his tongue around in his mouth that sent cold air rushing over my nipple. Not to neglect its twin, he repeated the service he had just performed. Now I was coming freely. I turned to straddle my lover and reached back to unsnap my bra completely. Michael suddenly froze.

"What?" I asked. I thought that maybe he had heard Mom and Dad stirring in the next room.

Michael stared at me, but it was like he was a million miles away. "Nothing," he replied. "Nothing. You'll never leave me, right?"

"That's a silly question."

"No, it's not. I just want to be sure, Isrie." Michael then gently lowered me onto the bed. He reached down and removed his underwear before pulling the sheets over us. It was easier this time when he entered me. I wanted to gasp, but clenched my teeth and brought my legs up and out to accept all he had to give.

This time was different from the rest. I hadn't been with Michael *that* long and I'm sure he had many tricks left in his bag. His strokes were slowed and deliberate as he crouched between my legs like a cat. I met each stroke and we held it, bonding together. We then gradually released, only to repeat it all over again. I flexed my stuff to latch on to every inch of him as we went through our torrid lovemaking session. This was some good shit he was breakin' me off.

"Yessss, don't rush it," I said, going along with him. As we clenched and stopped again, rivers of my love came drizzling down. I could feel him throbbing inside me.

"I love you, Isrie."

"Yesssss." My eyes rolled back as my pelvis trembled uncontrollably under the spell of his snake. His chest was pressed firmly against mine as we locked in a deathlike embrace. We could feel every heartbeat and every breath the other took.

"I love you."

"Yesssss. Don't stop baby. *Please*, don't stop," I pleaded a little louder this time.

"I . . . I don't want this to end," he shuddered as he hit another gear. I began bucking on the bed, causing the frame underneath to creak in tune.

"Oooooooh!" I let out with a shriek. "Oh, oh, oh. This is gooooood. I'm coooooooming!" Right after I screamed out, I remembered where I was. I gasped and came crashing back to reality. Michael either hadn't realized how loud I just was or just didn't care. He was still as intense as ever and didn't miss a beat. It was so good that I gave in to his strokes again and just hoped my parents weren't hearing any of the racket.

"Yesss, yessss, yessssss," Michael growled deeply. He was approaching his climax. I wrapped my legs around him to pull him deeper, wanting to feel all of him inside me. I dug my nails into his ass to drive him on. I didn't want the intensity to end. Onward we went until I felt Michael lurch just before the explosion of warmth inside me. Tears streamed down my face as both of us gasped for air. Our bodies were stuck together in more ways than one.

"Ohmygawd, ohmygawd. That was—"

Knock! Knock! Knock!

"Shit!" we whispered at the same time.

"Michael. Is everything alright in there?" my mom asked through the door.

After no answer, my mom stuck her head in the door and saw a snoring Michael sound asleep with the sheet pulled up to his head. It was dark in the guest bedroom and Ella's eyes weren't what they used to be. I knew that must have kept her from noticing one of her best robes lying crumpled on the floor beside the bed . . . or from realizing that her dear daughter was hiding naked beneath Michael under the sheet. I could have gone to sleep right there, but I was being crushed and he was falling asleep for real. I waited . . . and waited, to make sure it was safe before I gave Michael a quick kiss and ran back across the hallway with my bra, panties, and robe in tow.

The light of morning came sooner than I would have liked. The pots were clanking as my mom made breakfast. I could hear my dad's coarse laughter too as he read through his *LA Times*. I would have sworn they were intentionally noisier than usual. I was quick to find my way to the shower before joining them in the clothes I'd worn yesterday. My mom's freshly squeezed orange juice and hot biscuits were already waiting. Michael came slinking out to meet and greet us just as I finished off my third biscuit with syrup. Hey, I needed to get my energy back up. Besides, I left some biscuits for him.

No mention was made of the bedroom fireworks and I was thankful for that. Michael kept his head down and claimed to be thinking about his workload. The two of us kept any visible signs of affection to a minimum. The only thing unusual was my mom smiling every time I looked at her, to which I would nervously smile back. At least my dad had no clue.

After finishing breakfast, we prepared to head back to LA. My mom made us take some leftovers with us and my dad gave Michael an autographed copy of his last novel. I was touched again watching him hug both my parents before heading to my car. My man was a true gentleman and offered to drive, which I gladly accepted. I threw my keys to him.

"Give your mom a kiss, Isrie June," my mom said.

"I love you, Mom," I said, kissing and hugging my nurturer and provider for so many years.

"Thank you for coming. You've got a good man there."

"I know. I know," I said softly as I was still embracing her.

I took a deep breath and began walking to the car. Michael had finished moving my driver's seat waaaay back so he could fit comfortably and was just turning the key.

"What? No hug for your old man? The princess is too big to honor the king?"

"No, Dad. I guess you can have one too," I laughed.

As he hugged me and chuckled, he said, "Don't ever do that shit in my house again. Disrespectin' your momma and me. You're lucky I like the boy, otherwise I would have thrown him—and you—out on your asses. You ain't too big for me to spank you. Don't ever forget." I was amazed at how he kept a smile on his face the entire time.

I was so dumbfounded that I simply smiled sheepishly and replied, "Uh huh." I began retreating to my getaway car. My mom was standing nearby and chuckling. She gave me a wink and pointed to her wedding ring. I shook my head and blushed.

"Home, Michael. And don't stop for anything." I put on my seat belt and waved bye.

39

Deja

I had a quiet, peaceful Thanksgiving with my brother. Over the weekend, I had spoken to Ivan once or twice, but would've preferred seeing him. Maybe it was for the best, as I had a lot of stuff on my mind. When Monday came around, I was psyched and nervous. I'd worn a hole in the floor of my studio waiting for the call. Hell, I'd been here since before dawn. I was beginning to question my sanity when the call finally came. I ran to the phone, but let it ring an extra time before picking up.

"It's showtime," was all Sophia said.

"Studio City still?"

"You got it. Are you ready?"

"Totally."

"Good. Things are pretty hectic around here, so take down these directions and I'll give you the details when you get here."

I arrived at the parking lot of studio 412 west. The smoke spewing from the back of my van was embarrassing, but I acted as if I didn't see it. Once I made a decent paycheck, I was dumping this piece of shit. The short notice by Sophia was still bothering me, but I had brought enough equipment to cover most situations.

The security guard that manned the little white booth proved to be my first obstacle when he couldn't find me on the visitor list. I showed him my cameras and even repeated Sophia's directions to him, but the stone-faced rent-a-cop wouldn't budge.

I didn't know how much time I had or even if I was late. I tried to reach Sophia on her cell phone but it was turned off. I began losing my composure and was almost in tears before he found my name scribbled in on the last line of page two. I thanked him for nothing before snatching my parking permit from his hand and blasting him with a fresh cloud of smoke.

"Chill, girl," I thought aloud as I searched for the studio. After I found it fairly quickly, I looked for familiar faces in the crowd as I struggled to park. I recognized a few writers and reporters as they entered the large open bay doors. I checked my makeup one last time in the mirror, then ran to join them. It was showtime.

I strutted into the large open bay, determined to look like I belonged. I had struggled with whether to dress a little conservative or to be *rawwwrr*, and had decided to keep things simple. I wanted to make a good first impression with the Ebony Emotions people. Besides, they would see my award-winning personality, and that would seal the deal. Now, all I had to do was find Sophia.

"May I help you?" A middle-aged white man with brushed-back white hair in a gray designer suit had noticed me looking around. Half the studio was being used. There was a set where I assumed the Ebony Emotions models would be doin' their thang, as well as a long covered table for panel interviews. My eyesight wasn't good enough to make out the names on the cards placed in front of each microphone on the table.

"Hello. I'm Deja Douglas, the photographer. I'm looking for a Sophia Williams."

"Yes, she mentioned you."

"*You* work for EEB?" I asked, the surprise in my voice noticeable. I felt bad the way it came out.

"Yes. You could say that. Y'see, I *am* Ebony Emotions Books—at least, here today anyway. Hal Travis at your service." He seemed amused with my discomfort.

"Oh. I thought—"

"Mr. Anderson?"

"Yes." EEB was synonymous with its owner, Rowley Anderson, a self-professed hustler from Philly who had gone from operating EEB out of his basement to making the *Black Enterprise* 100 list.

"Mr. Anderson sold the company to our group a few months back," he informed me. "The news isn't completely out yet. The press conference following our presentation and shoot will touch on a lot of that, I'm sure. I've heard a lot of good things about you, Deja."

"Thanks. I guess I need to set up. Mind if I check out things before I bring my equipment in?"

"Of course. You may want to be careful not to interfere with Murphy and them. He can be pretty territorial."

I was beginning to run off when I processed what was just said. "Murphy? *Murphy Johnston*?" I asked as I took a hard look at the set for the first time. Camera equipment complete with backdrop lighting was already positioned around the set. Murphy, one of the biggest photographers in the business, was making final adjustments and working out final details with . . . his crew. Ooooh shit.

"Yes. I thought you knew."

"Umm . . . *knew*?"

"That Murphy is the primary photographer for this project," he replied with a look that was part curiosity, part confusion. "Sophia didn't tell you?"

"I'm lost," I admitted, smiling to conceal my embarrassment and anger.

"You're *technically* not the photographer for today's shoot. As a favor to Sophia, we're going to let you observe . . . and take some photos also."

"What?"

"Don't get me wrong," he said with both hands up to calm me down, "EEB wants to see your work. We'd like to see your product from this shoot once it's over. Look . . . I'm sorry if there was some miscommunication."

"Miscommunication my a—. Is Sophia around?"

"Yes, but things are about to get under way. I guess you need to get into position, huh? Do you need any help with your equipment, Deja?" Music began playing, signaling everyone the event was about to start.

"No. I didn't bring much. I can handle it. Thanks, Hal."

Outside, I was tempted to say fuck it and just bounce. Sophia had bullshitted me, but at least there was still the potential to pick up some much needed future work. I swallowed my pride once again and grabbed my shoulder bag and a tripod out of the back of my ride. All the other gear was staying put.

Hal's energetic voice boomed over the speakers, introducing himself and welcoming the media and industry professionals. When Sophia was introduced, I gritted my teeth and got ready for her to come out on stage. What really sucked was that it paid for me to get good photos of the bitch, even with my limited access on the shoot. I hastily worked myself through the crowd as if I were one of Murphy Johnston's crew, then took up a position behind them instead. Murphy noticed my invasion of his turf almost immediately. I pretended not to notice his frown or his subtle cursing as I pulled my light meter from my bag and tried to play catch-up. Boy, this was bootleg. Then it was time to do what I do and my excuses and obstacles just didn't matter anymore.

A roar of cheers and whistles erupted from most of the men and some of the women in the crowd of invited guests and onlookers. Sophia came through a white curtain behind Hal, where her handlers and assistants had finished making her up, and began walking across the runway to the shoot set. Her introduction to the world of book covers and ad campaigns was off to a rousing start. She was all smiles, full of her typical confidence . . . and looking *hella* tight. She walked in her open-toed sandals with her usual exaggerated hip twisting, seemingly unfazed by the larger-than-normal audience. Sophia's brown hair, which she usually wore curly, was died jet-black and blow-dried straight. She wore a pink sleeveless polo, its zipper open to just above her exposed midriff, and a pair of designer denim shorts whose frayed ends barely covered her cheeks. This image being shot today would be plastered in magazine ads all across America and Canada as EEB now had its cover girl.

Sophia came to a stop directly in front of me, but I was behind the flashes coming from the crew's cameras. I had to snap my shots in between theirs, but it didn't stop me. I worked my zoom to catch Sophia's smile as she posed for a shoulder shot. Lance's people stopped shooting, leading me to think the press conference was about to begin.

Instead, Hal began speaking on the microphone again. Sophia paused from her posing and looked toward him. I figured out then that she would be joined by another model, probably a man. Women were the majority of EEB's readers, and it only made sense to give them some eye candy. I couldn't wait for days to see what hunk of chocolate fineness would be walking out from behind the curtain with no shirt on and muscles. What Mandingo had they gone out and landed?

"Allow me to introduce Ms. Williams' partner for this project, and Ebony Emotions' latest find . . . Mister Ivan Dempsey! Let's give him a hand!"

Sick. A sick, tortured feeling. That's what I felt when I heard Ivan's name and he stepped out into the applause. Sophia smiled smugly as my man walked in her direction. His upper body was oiled down, defining every line of toned muscle. He had his game face on that I had seen so many times from behind the lens. While the photo crew was flashing away tirelessly, I lowered my camera. I was too stunned to do anything except watch.

Have you ever had the feeling you were dreaming because things were just too damn weird, but you couldn't wake up?

Yep. That was my stupid ass just then. My hands clenched my camera tightly, and the closer he got to that she-devil, the tighter my grip became. Hal was still talking, but I didn't hear what was being said. The voice I heard was mine and mine alone as I cursed to myself. When I realized this was doing me no good, I sighed and tried to focus on the job again. Neither Sophia nor Ivan had told me about his involvement in this shit. Did I say shit? I meant shoot. Yeah, *whatever*.

Sophia opened her arms and embraced Ivan with the kind of hug that showed their familiarity to everyone in attendance. Hal had turned off his mic, deciding to watch with the rest of us as Murphy began barking out instructions to his subjects. Ivan took a quick stretch as the music resumed and the studio lights beyond the set dimmed, casting us into darkness. I zoomed in on Ivan's face, hoping those baby brown eyes would look my way. Murphy had Sophia stand facing us and had Ivan position himself behind her in one of those classic poses. My man's glistening arms came around Sophia's thin waist and I saw her intentionally wiggle her derriere into him.

Things started rolling as Murphy left the two of them free to be themselves. Any good photographer knew to let the natural chemistry ride. That was great for Ebony Emotions, but bad for me. Hands familiar with the layout of their partner fell into familiar patterns and I kept telling myself that this was just a job. There had to have been enough photos and enough *oooh*s and *aaah*s for things to move on to the press conference. This was torture. Slow, Chinese water torture. Sophia's pouty lips grazed Ivan's cheek as she turned in to him. Her arm came up around his neck as she dipped back. He held her steady as they looked into one another's eyes. Cameras flashed, including mine, freezing that moment in time.

This was some of the best work I had seen them do and I wasn't too jealous to admit it. Murphy knew it as well. He upped the ante and asked for the two of them to kiss and hold it. I couldn't take much more and dropped my head. I resisted looking for as long as I could and took a peek when I thought it was over. Their lips were moving. *Their fucking lips were moving.* They were kissing and enjoying it. As they pulled apart, Ivan gave one of those smiles of his to a lusty-looking Sophia. I started to hurl my camera at his head.

"Your friend Sophia is incredible." Hal had snuck up on me and was beaming admirably. I couldn't answer him. I put my camera back up to my face and pretended to be shooting. "Those two are something special, don't you think?" he asked, torturing me even more.

"Yes. Yes, they are." I gave a fake, dry smile as my throat tightened. Ivan and Sophia had moved on to another pose and she now had both of her claws on his bare chest.

"Do you know Ivan as well?"

"Yes. He's my . . . I—I've done some shoots with him before." Sophia had to be lovin' this. She had set me up. Smooth. Did Ivan know I was here? Did he even care?

The lights came back on, distracting me from my self-pity. Hal was cutting back through the crowd to get to the conference table. Ivan hesitated as he toyed around with Sophia. I noticed his hand run across her shoulder as he laughed. It was a move I was all too familiar with. I couldn't take this shit anymore. Professionalism be damned.

"Ivan!" I shouted, catching some of Murphy's crew off guard. My eyes watered and my face twisted into a scowl.

From his expression, it was clear he didn't know what to do. I was focused on him, but out of the corner of my eye I could see Sophia covering her mouth to conceal her laugh. She knew I had been in the crowd the entire time. As he stood there looking dumbfounded and guilty, I grabbed my stuff and got the fuck up out of there.

A truck was blocking me in the parking lot and I screamed at the man to move it before jumping behind the wheel of my van. He probably thought I was on something. The only thing I was on was a good case of *mad*. The inside was sweltering from sitting out in the sun. I rolled the window down and jammed the key into the ignition. There was a whirring sound, then nothing.

"C'mon. Don't do this shit to me!" I yelled as my engine tried to come to life. I turned the key again and stepped on the gas. I don't know what good screaming did, but my grandma used to do that with her old Pacer. I let out a large puff of relief as my van finally cooperated.

"Deja! Wait! Stop the car!" Ivan's arm lurched in through the window, grabbing the steering wheel. I turned to look my lover in the face. He had thrown on a T-shirt and it was sticking to the oil on his body.

"Leave me the fuck alone!" I screamed. I beat Ivan's arm back and slammed my car door into him. He stepped back, holding his sore arm. His face showed shock and disbelief at first, then turned nasty.

"What the hell is your problem? Huh? And what the fuck are you doin' here anyway?"

"My fucking job! That's what I was doing! Your little tramp in there, Sophia, set this up! And you were just too happy to be all over her on the set, huh? Maybe it was good I got to see this. Now I know what a no-good fucker you are and what a stupid idiot I've been. I guess you weren't going to tell me about this job, huh?"

"Hold up! Hold up! I don't recall you telling me about this job *either*, Deja."

"That's because Sophia told me to keep quiet."

"So, you thought that included me? Look, I'm in there trying to get my paper just like you. You got anything else you care to share that you haven't told me?" Ivan grabbed my handle and opened the door, inviting me out where he stood barefoot on the hot pavement.

"No. Don't *even* try turning this back on me, Ivan. Your ass was the one up there getting familiar with your ex again. What would have happened if I hadn't called your name out? Huh? Now move. I'm leaving and don't have time to be playing childish games. Hal and the Ebony Emotions people are probably waiting on you now."

"No." He stood there, arms folded, in my door so I couldn't close it.

"Move, Ivan."

"No. Where in the fuck do you get off screaming at me and embarrassing me in front of people?"

"I am—was your woman, boy. I don't appreciate being disrespected and I am within my rights to do whatever I fuckin' feel like right now."

"So it's like that, huh?" He smiled. It wasn't the nice kind of smile I was used to.

"Yep. Damn straight."

"You're saying you don't trust me?"

"I guess."

"Oooh. Wanna hurt me some more?" he chuckled. I had never noticed how much his composure and polish went out the window when he was angered. It was like looking at a different person. "So, I've got no issues with you on the trust stuff?"

"Nope. I've shared everything with you. I even told you about that shit with my brother. My girl, Isrie, doesn't even know about that."

"She know about Jamal?"

"Wha—who?"

"You know," he laughed with a glint in his eye. "Jamal Brown. Does Isrie know about Jamal Brown?"

I struggled to understand what Ivan was talking about and asked, "Jamal?"

"Ooooh. Short memory now? Y'see, I was going to keep my mouth shut and give you time, but I can get stupid too. Don't play dumb. I found his business card . . . in the back seat of my ride, no less. Been out having fun in my shit?"

"His card? But . . . I threw that away." I turned my van off, trying to make sense of this. I remembered putting the window down and throwing Jamal's card out that night after Slap Happy and the club.

"Guess you didn't throw it as far away as you thought. *Now* who's got trust issues?"

"It wasn't like that, Ivan."

"Uh huh."

"Fuck you. I wouldn't do something like that to you. He gave me his card, but I honestly thought I'd thrown it out your window. The wind must've blown it to the backseat. On the real. That's all . . . I swear. How come you didn't tell me you were going to be shooting with Sophia?"

"Baby, I know how you react whenever her name comes up. I was just trying to keep you happy and save you grief. Anything I do in front of the camera is work. That's all. I get paid to make things look real. You know I love you and only you, Deja . . . and I trust you. When you say nothing happened with that dude, I believe you, boo. And I'm really sorry about this going down like *this*. So, we've got everything out now and you've made me look like a fool. We're cool?"

"We'll see. Get back to work, Mr. Dempsey. I'm sure they want to see you at the press conference. We'll talk later."

"Promise?" he asked, taking my hand.

"Promise." I smiled cautiously as I felt his grip. I wondered if I should have told him about Jamal kissing me that night and decided to leave well enough alone. Had Ivan just twisted everything back to me by bringing up the Jamal stuff? I was tired—tired of worrying about Sophia and tired of my insecurity when it came to my man.

40

Isrie

"We could've roomed together, Isrie."

"Will you stop already? He'll be here. He's probably in traffic. There's plenty of time."

"Didn't you say he lives in Long Beach?"

"Stop it. I already told you how Michael is always busy." I nervously looked back at the long, winding line that had formed behind us, hoping to see his reassuring face. Deja's brother, Theron, had dropped us off at the San Pedro Pier in her van. I didn't want him going out of his way, so I didn't ask him to pass by Michael's apartment. I had tried calling once, but Michael's cell phone was turned off . . . again. He had directions, so I figured he would meet us there.

"Whatever you say, girlfriend. Whatever you say," she replied. Our matching discount luggage rolled in unison each time we inched forward. Ivan's agency's cruise was the first opportunity for the four of us to get away and for D-Square to finally meet my future.

My girl wore a zebra-print wrap dress on this unusually cool December morning. Her hair was put back in a ponytail. I sported my suede shirt jacket with some patchwork jeans. My hair was stowed away under my bronze-and-black scarf and shades shielded my eyes from the glare of the sun.

"Those seagulls are getting on my nerves," I muttered, looking up and hoping they wouldn't drop a gift on me.

"Sourpuss. Lighten up. They ain't even much worrying about you. That scarf probably makes a tempting target for them, though. Hella colorful."

"Like you should talk. Ms. Safari!" I nudged her with my elbow.

"You got me. At least you're smiling now. This is supposed to be fun, remember? I'm sure he'll make it. He might already be on the boat, for all we know."

"You're right. That might be why his phone's off." I doubted it, but went along with the fantasy my imagination cooked up.

After quickly tipping the baggage handlers, our suitcases were taken to our rooms, where they'd be waiting for us. Deja and Ivan were sharing a room on board. Until recently, she would have preferred things that way, but something had gone down courtesy of Sophia that had them taking a small step back. My girl blew off whatever had happened, but I sensed it was something big. Ivan also reserved a cabin for Michael and me. It would suck to be all alone in the tiny room for these few days at sea, I thought to myself.

In the reception terminal, I had the attendant check to see if Michael had been through there already. Nope. Both Deja and the attendant looked like they felt sorry for me, which I hated. At that point, I committed to having a good time whether or not Michael showed. A free cruise was not to be wasted by this sister. ID cards and documents in order, we headed up the ramp to the boat.

Ivan was already aboard and meeting with his people. It was a relaxation cruise, but as his agency had arranged everything, he still had business to attend to. All of the industries came together in this town, so I knew I'd see my share of celebrities before this was over.

On the main deck, someone helped with directions and pointed us to our cabins. A waiter was nearby, so I snagged a tropical drink to start this off right. Most of the agency party had been booked in the same section of the ship, so Deja and Ivan's quarters were just around the corner from me. Inside, Ivan's things were already neatly laid out on his bed, marking his territory. I hung out with Deja while she unpacked, peering out her portal at the dock outside, before agreeing to meet back up with her later to eat.

I was feeling pretty relaxed and loose from my drink, so I retreated to my room after checking my watch. I figured it was best to wait for Michael there. As I turned the handle on the door, I hoped to hear his excited voice, anxious to explain where he had been all this time or just to smell his scent. I got neither. At least my luggage was there to keep me company . . . and the cheesy music that was being piped in. I made one last call, this time to Michael's apartment.

"—ello?" The connection wasn't the best. It kept breaking up, but I knew a woman's voice when I heard one.

"Hello. Is Michael there?"

"Who?"

"Michael!" I shouted, "Is Michael there?" I had lost all patience.

"*Oooh!* T! Nah. He ain't here." I recognized the voice. It was Lloyd's woman, Charletta. "Llooooyd! Pick up the phone! It's T's girl!"

I paced for a few seconds, about to hang up when Lloyd came on the line.

"Yeah?"

"Lloyd . . . it's Isrie. I'm on the boat waiting for Michael. Do you know if he's on his way?"

"Nah. I don't know nuthin'. Y'all goin' fishin'?"

"No! I'm on a cruise ship, dammit! Look, do you know where he's at?"

"I guess he's on his way then," he replied in as cocky a manner as he could.

"Thanks for nothing," I said as I abruptly hung up. I couldn't stand his ass.

I must've dozed off after my little chat with Lloyd. The sound

of the boat horn startled me awake. It was an hour later and
the boat was pulling out. My scarf had slipped off my head and
my clothes still needed to be unpacked and stowed away. After
taking care of them, I crammed myself into the tiny bathroom
and freshened up.

It was warm now, so I combed my hair down and changed
into a tank top and denim shorts. When I caught up with Deja,
she and Ivan were just leaving their cabin to go to the lunch buf-
fet, but not before he got in a quick inspection of her tonsils. Ivan
wore a blue tropical Hawaiian print shirt that he hadn't finished
buttoning and white shorts. Deja had switched into an apple
green tank top with shorts that matched his.

"*A-hem.* Y'all two are really trying to make me jealous."

"Hey, girl," she answered, pushing Ivan's lips away as she
wiped the corner of her mouth. "What's the word?"

"Fuck him."

"Hi, Isrie. Where's your friend? Michael, right?" Ivan asked
as he looked down the hallway behind me, not catching on to
what was just said.

"He didn't show up."

"What? You want me to call the port? We're not that far out.
We could have someone fly him in if he missed departure."

"Forget about it," I halfheartedly laughed. "If he wanted to
be here with me, he would be. I appreciate your kindness,
though."

"Oh." Ivan was tense from my blunt answer and looked to
Deja to bail him out.

"Yep. Men can be asses, huh, Isrie?" Deja said with one of her
glowing smiles as she cut her eyes her boyfriend's way. "Ivan,
we're going to show my girl here a good time, so let's gets this
started. I'm hella starvin'!"

"Okay, then. After you, ladies," he said, motioning us on.

At lunch, the waiters were especially flirty to the people with
the agency party. I never heard so many bad pickup lines in
equally bad English in my life. I *was* flattered by them thinking

I was a model, though. I spotted a few faces from the music scene and from those UPN sitcoms, like Rodney Jerkins and LisaRaye, but tried to act nonchalant. As we sat around the large circular table, Deja scooted next to me to talk.

"What's the 411 on this Michael?"

"You probably think I've been making him up, huh? If I hadn't experienced the wonderful times with him, I'd be wondering myself. This is it, Deja. I'm through with him."

"Think it's another woman?"

"Yes! . . . No. Heck, I dunno. It's his job, I think—always gone on weekends, running late and stuff. I'm just fed up. He played me, girl. He played me."

"He might have a valid reason for not showing."

"Hmph. I don't want to hear it."

"If that's the case, there's plenty of *options* on this boat, girl," she giggled.

"There *you* go. Must be talking about men," Ivan said, finishing his light lunch of tuna salad and iced tea.

"That's the problem, Ivan. Not enough men being men," Deja replied, not enjoying his eavesdropping.

"Was that directed at me, boo?"

"You know I love ya."

"That's my baby." Ivan leaned over to give Deja a kiss on her cheek, but was interrupted by an arrival to our table.

"Mind if I join you guys?" I had never met this person, but I knew all I needed to know about her. It was that bitch Sophia, who Deja had issues with. I remember Deja telling me she worked for the same agency as Ivan, so it was only natural that she would be here. The girl was pretty. As pretty as her pictures, which is rare. Her plate was crammed with food. I hated women who could eat like that without it going anywhere. Maybe she's one of those purgers, I thought in a moment of cattiness.

"Actually, I do mind," Deja said in a direct manner. "The boat's not that small."

"Excuse me?"

"Do you need to move your extensions back so you can hear?" Deja asked, standing up from her chair and tensing as if to leap across the table. "Get . . . out . . . of . . . my . . . face. I understand you have a *job* and that it sometimes involves Ivan, but this is my time, with *my* man. The last thing I want to see is your conniving face and your fake smile."

Ivan, who was uncomfortable as hell and looking as if he were in a fog, stood up between the two and was trying to find the words to defuse things.

"You have some nerve," she snarled back at Deja. "As much as I've done for your pitiful career."

"Sophia?" Ivan was doing a horrible job, so it was time for me to end this.

"Yes. *And who are you?*"

"I'm the person that's going to hold your plate while my friend here goes off all up in your ass if you don't step. *Then* I'm going to dump the plate on you . . . and smile. Please try us." Ooh. The hood hadn't come out in me in years. Damn, it felt good.

Sophia looked at Ivan to say something, then looked back into my eyes. Deja was still standing, ready to spring while I just sat back and gave Sophia a cold smile. It took her a second to recognize her situation wasn't a good one. Ivan finally decided to speak, but Sophia was already storming off, plate in hand.

"Please. No more of this the rest of the cruise," he said to Deja. "I work with these people and can't have this kind of shit going down."

"Shit. You're acting like I was the one doing something wrong, Ivan. She's the one who went out of her way to get in my face."

"I understand that and I was about to handle things," he said, waving his hands in frustration.

"How? By letting her sit with us?" Deja was getting pissed. "All you did was stand there like a cat had your tongue. I'm not putting up with any more of her shit. Know this, Ivan! Know this!"

That bit of drama set the tone for the rest of the cruise. Deja distanced herself from Ivan, hanging with me more and more. I don't know if Ivan even noticed as he spent a lot of time with the onboard activities sponsored by his agency. That girl Sophia would be around and I know Deja didn't want to see her. I didn't want to be negative, but I saw nothing but headaches for my girl as long as Ivan failed to set Sophia straight once and for all. I knew the two of them worked together and stuff, but *Deja* was his woman and he couldn't be punking out whenever his ex decided to test a negro.

When we sailed into Mazatlán for the day, Deja came by my room just before noon to give me the rundown. Some more activities were planned on the beach, which included a sail out to some island in the bay. Deja wanted to go into town for a day of shopping and sisterhood instead, so she gave Ivan his pass.

"You know I couldn't go to another country without buying something," Deja said as we walked with bags in our arms later that day. "Even if I had to charge it all."

"Yeah, but how are you supposed to haggle over the price when you're using *el plastico*?" I asked with my made-up words and shitty accent.

" 'Cause that's all I got right now!" she chuckled. "Let's go see some more sights before we return."

"You sure you don't want to head back to the beach now?"

"Nah. It's cool."

"Don't be messing up your thing on my account, Deja."

"I'm not."

With that said, we went off to catch one of the Aztec shows put on for the tourists. After lunch and a few tequila shots, we returned with hours to spare. Ivan was on the beach by the volleyball net with some of the other beautiful people. Having just finished a game, he dusted sand off his shins and gave Deja a look like he was seriously missing his boo. He took a swig of his Mexican beer, then motioned for her to join him. She tried to ignore him and look away, but he continued to smile as if sending out telepathic waves that said, "I'm sorry." Sophia was nowhere to be seen.

"We spend so much time focusing on the parts of men that we love, but sometimes forget about the other parts till we have to deal with them." With the sand beneath her feet and her back to Ivan, Deja was having one of her reflective moments.

"Yep. That's the way love goes. Why don't you go see what he wants."

"You know what?" she remarked with a gentle smile and gaze his way, "I think I will. You coming?"

"No," I said, knowing I wasn't needed, "I'll take your bags aboard." At least Ivan was here so they could to work through their problems. I watched my girl take off her sandals before romping across the beach.

On the final night of the cruise, all of us attended the Captain's Dinner held in our honor. I had brought a special eye-popping number just for Michael, but stowed it away. I had already put on a turtleneck dress instead but changed my mind and went with my original choice. I was going to be looking good for someone at least. My hair, which I wore up, was beginning to wear on my nerves. Maybe it was going to be time for a change when we returned to shore.

At dinner, Deja and Ivan were the magical pair—she with her all-red ensemble and he with his all-black designer after-hours wear. One of these handsome twins that modeled for the same agency struck up a conversation with me even after I told him I was involved. As the evening wore on, something in the food didn't agree with Deja. Ivan excused himself from the celebration and escorted her to the infirmary, then on to their cabin for the evening. It was the last night on the boat, so I didn't want to just sleep the night away after dinner.

Ivan's agency spared no expense on this trip. I learned there was an exclusive party being held in the ship's club, so I headed off to dance and work off some calories. Inside, the theme was "Way Back," so as the expensive liquor flowed, the DJ was spinning nothing but hits from the seventies and eighties. We danced to stuff ranging from old George Clinton and Parliament Funkadelic to MC Hammer. Talk about feeling like a kid again. One of those twins shared the floor with me for most of the songs. Over the music, I could barely hear him, so we were content to smile and use hand signals. I'd be lying if I said I knew he was the one that I had talked with over dinner. Damn. The two of them looked *so* much alike. All I remembered was their last name, Alonzo.

After I'd had my share of nightlife, I politely excused myself and left to taste the chill of the midnight air on deck. I got lost on cruise ships anyway, so the scenic route didn't bother me.

The stars overhead filled the sky and cast their reflection on the mirrorlike waters below. Matching their glitter was Michael's gift around my wrist. This was to be my first time wearing it for him.

"I guess they let anyone on this boat."

I don't know where my thoughts were going at that moment, but they disappeared with a *pop*. The hairs on my neck bristled at the voice. It was like a splash of cold water had been thrown in my face. Torn between dealing with him or jumping ship, the wooden slats beneath my feet looked pretty damn good. "Are you stalking me or something?" I asked, gripping the railing and wishing I had my mace.

Ryan walked over, the bow tie to his tux dangling loosely. I instinctively moved away. "What are you doin'? Following me?" he asked.

"You wish. What are you doing here?"

"Just enjoying the party." He laughed, holding up a bottle of champagne. "I was invited. Everybody's that's somebody is on this cruise. We get our network on. You remember how it was when you rolled with me, baby." He took a sip from the champagne bottle. "One of these dudes hittin' it now? That dude from New York you were with at Infiniti?"

I sighed. "Please. Just leave me alone."

"And if I don't? Thought I forgot about that slap?" His tone made me unsettled but I was on the deck first, so I stood my ground.

"If you don't want another one, you'll get out of my face."

Ryan moved up on me quickly, placing a hand on the railing. "It would be a shame if you fell overboard, Isrie. They probably wouldn't know you're missing until morning, and I'm sure the sharks would have gotten to you by then."

I looked down at the icy black water, then back at Ryan, trying to determine if he was the least bit serious.

"Why don't you leave the lady alone, bruh? I don't think she wants your company."

Ryan whirled toward the voice, seeing a gentleman standing directly behind us. Rather than comment, he winked at me and stormed off. "She ain't worth it," he remarked to my savior as he bumped past him.

"Thanks," I said, feeling less worried now.

"You never told me what you did," the familiar voice said.

"Did you follow me from the party?" I asked the tall, rugged high yella brother as I released my grip on the railing.

"Certainly," he answered with a smug charm. "I thought we had one more dance."

"I'm through for the night, especially after this. Excuse me, what's your name again?"

"Marcus. And my brother is Matthew. Can't tell us apart, huh?"

"Well," I chuckled. "Actually . . . no."

"I'm the good-looking one," he laughed. "But back to my question. What do you do?"

"I'm a massage therapist." Don't ask me why, but right when I said that I thought about Kendra's situation.

"You've never considered modeling? I mean, you have everything."

"It's not something I'd be interested in. Thanks for the compliment, though."

"So, you're out in the cold because . . . ?"

"Because I wanted some fresh air to clear my head before I went to bed."

"Oh. I thought you might be waiting on someone."

"Like who? Certainly not that asshole you ran off."

"I dunno. Maybe somebody like Ivan."

"Ivan?" I asked, repeating what he had just said. "Why would I be waiting on him?"

"I don't know. Ivan and me don't really talk, but I saw you with him the other day on the boat. I just thought—"

I let out a belly laugh. "No, no, noooo. You probably saw me with him *and* my girl, Deja."

"The photographer? Yeah. She was there too. Ooooh, she and Ivan are—"

"Yes," I replied. I didn't think it was a secret.

Marcus covered his mouth as he smiled and gasped with surprise. "My bad. I had no idea. Sorry. She's a sweet girl."

"Yep. That she is. A beautiful, sweet person."

"Too sweet to be involved with someone like him," he muttered as if talking aloud to himself.

It was too cold and I was getting ready to say my good-bye and move on, but paused.

"Why do you say that?"

"No offense, Isrie. I'm not trying to hate on the brother or just saying it to try to get in with you, but Ivan's too much for your friend. The boy's out there bad." I didn't quite know what to make of Marcus or his not-so-subtle jab at Ivan, so I just stored it up in my head for future reference. Ivan was no angel, but Deja knew that going in.

"Alright. Thanks for sharing, Marcus. Look, it's getting late and I didn't plan on being out here this long, so—"

"Good night?" His face twisted up to reflect his disappointment at my ending our conversation.

"Yes. Good night." Marcus offered to walk me to my cabin, but I declined. He made a tempting offer, but quick fixes never worked and that's all it would've been. I shook his hand while thanking him for his company and the timely save. I didn't know him or his motives, so it was best to keep him at arm's length.

After going in circles a few times, I found someone to ask for directions. I was approaching my cabin from the opposite direction I was used to and that had been throwing me off. As things started looking familiar, I slipped my heels off and picked up the pace in the corridor. A quick shower before bed and I was going to be home the next time my eyes opened.

As I slowed to look at the cabin numbers on the signs, I noticed Ivan going back into his room.

"Ivan!" I called out, wanting to know how Deja was feeling. He didn't hear me. I heard her voice greeting him just before their door slammed shut. She seemed to be in good spirits by the sound of her giggles, so I had my answer. I knew exactly where I was now. My room was just around the corner. I couldn't help but hear the sounds of them carrying on as I walked past their door. I stuck my key card into my lock and tried to open the door. Nothing. Shit, I almost broke the handle. I had heard about cabin doors acting crazy on these ships, but this was too much. I inserted the key in and out and cursed to myself before I noticed I had the wrong cabin number. That couldn't be, I thought to myself. I had counted the doors down from where Ivan had gone in.

41

Isrie

"**Y**ou've been quieter than usual this morning, girl. Hung-over? Was your last night on the boat *chips* for you? Talk!"

Talking was on my mind alright, but I didn't know if Deja was ready to hear it. Ivan was hovering nearby like some kind of guardian angel, or perhaps more like a buzzard. When Deja wasn't looking, he gave me that same smile, daring me.

The night before, I stood outside the door I had seen Ivan go in . . . and waited. I wasn't sure what to think. I didn't know whether to mind my own business or go banging on the door for an explanation. Maybe it wasn't even him, I thought to myself in a cowardly moment. I had decided to turn and quietly walk away when I heard the voices and noises on the other side of the door again. To hell with that.

I banged on the door, not knowing what I was going to say. Everything went silent inside. I heard someone walking to the door and stepped to the side of the peephole.

"Yes?" I knew whose voice it was.

I pretended not to speak English very well and mumbled, *"You call?"*

I heard other voices now. Was it some kind of party or late-night meeting? The door opened a crack. I saw Sophia's robe first, then part of her face before I slammed the cabin door into it and forced my way in. Sophia fell backward from the whack to her forehead, her robe falling completely open, revealing her nude body. I thought I knew everything in that split second, but I was just plain stupid. The next sight hit me blindsided. Ivan was buck naked on his back on one of the beds with another girl between his legs *talking on the mic*. Ivan's hands gripped her head of long black hair and guided her down his shaft. Ivan was so startled by my entrance that he jerked forward to get to his feet, sending the girl gagging who had been on her stomach servicing him. The shoes that were in my hand dropped to the floor.

"You low-down, dirty son of a bitch," I said with a look that was equal parts shock and disgust. "What the fuck?"

Ivan struggled to come up with some words or smooth talk while reaching for his pants. The other girl, who I had seen in passing on the cruise, wiped her mouth and frowned at me. There wasn't even a hint of modesty from the ho, as she didn't move to cover herself. "She joinin' the party?" she asked of Ivan.

Sophia, furiously rubbing her forehead, returned to her feet. She took one look in the mirror and snapped when she saw the scratch I had put there. I grabbed her wrists as she charged at me, trying to dig her nails into my face. I wasn't expecting to be in the middle of a scrap at that time of night and went tumbling onto the table in the cabin. Sophia was screaming like a madwoman and wiggling to get on top of me. It took all my effort to hold her back. She didn't weigh much, but was stronger than she looked.

"Sophia, stop," said Ivan.

Like a puppy obeying its master, Sophia quit fighting instantly in response to his command. Even though she quit struggling, I didn't trust the bitch. I had gotten a foot up and hurled her back off me. I rubbed my back as I got up off the table. Ivan had closed the door to the cabin and was trying to help me up.

"Get your fucking hands off me!" I yelled as I snatched my arm away. He was looking cool, calm, and collected again like a switch had been thrown. That was my first time seeing that snakelike smile, though.

"Why'd you *really* come here tonight, Isrie? Curious? I could use a body like yours."

"You're a sick motherfucker, Ivan. Deja made a big mistake getting involved with a freak like you."

"Yeah, yeah, whatever. Deja is sound asleep right now in our cabin. I think you're just jealous of what me and Deja have," he said with a laugh as he gave Sophia a kiss and fondled her breast under her robe. She purred like a kitten. "And that's just what I'm going to tell her if you get any ideas about running to her."

"Like she'd believe you instead of her best friend."

"Oh, she would. She'll believe whatever I tell her. Hell, she thinks me and Sophia only have a working relationship now. Besides, I think you're just upset that your man dumped you before the cruise and you wanted to ruin her good thing. Y'know . . . misery loves company and all that other shit. I *think* you even tried to hit on me when we ran into each other in the hallway tonight. Yeah . . . that sounds good."

Slap!

I caught with him with one good one before he defended himself, grabbing me in a bear hug.

"You know you can still kick it with us tonight," he whispered in my ear as I screamed for him to let me go. "The three of us could use the company. Besides, I know you'd be good. And Deja wouldn't even have to know." Sophia was enjoying watching me squirm. The other girl was getting bored and removed her bra before snorting a line of coke that I had scattered across the table with my fall.

"Let me go!" I yelled again, stomping my heel down on his foot with all my might. I wished I had kept my shoes on for that, but it still made him release his hold. I made a run for the door and stumbled out into the hallway. There was no one chasing after me—only laughter, as if I were already an afterthought to them.

I was so traumatized and disgusted by what I had just witnessed that I fled to my room and remained there until morning. Nothing was really done to me physically, but his words and voice made me feel dirty and violated. I showered over and over again, crying uncontrollably.

As Ivan continued smiling, all I heard was that laughter in my head from the night before. He had been at Deja's side the entire morning as we pulled into port, daring me, as he had the night before, to say something. Well, we were home now and I wouldn't be a true friend if I let the illusions continue. I still wondered what Ivan got out of lying to Deja.

"No, I'm not hungover," I answered Deja slowly, finally coming back to earth. "I'm just ready to go home. Look . . . I need to talk to you about something. Last night—"

"Isrie, is that brother waiting for you?" Ivan asked, intentionally cutting me off. He had placed his arm around Deja and pointed into the crowd of cab drivers and people who had been waiting for their loved ones to return. I thought he had probably made that up to delay my telling her, but a quick look would only spare him seconds at best. I looked into the crowd we were approaching and saw him clear as day. Michael was walking toward me with a dozen roses in one hand and a big sign in the other that read, ISRIE, I'M SORRY.

42

Deja

"**D**on't he look sappy with that sign in his hand," Ivan whispered in my ear. "Whipped."

"Quiet, boy. I think it's sweet."

Isrie looked like she had something important to get off her chest, but that was before we saw Michael. I had never met him before, so I wasn't passing on this moment.

"Michael! It *is* Michael isn't it?" I said, running up to catch him by the arm. "You look just like Isrie described. To tell you the truth, I was beginning to wonder if you were for real, bruh."

"You must be Deja." He grinned with a look of recognition. He wasn't as muscular as my man, but Michael seemed solid enough. Really handsome in a subtle, mature way. Something about his mannerisms reminded me of the actor Leon, who I had run into a few times around town. He and Leon looked nothing alike, mind you, but his walk and bearing were smooth like that. Underneath his black sport coat this morning, he wore a gray turtleneck with black slacks and shoes. He really complimented my girl. A perfect pair *if* he had a legit excuse for dogging her on the cruise.

"That would be *moi!*" I answered with my usual bubbly enthusiasm before going stone cold sober on him. "You are in *big* trouble with my girl. I don't know what your excuse is, but these roses and this sign are a good start. *Hmph*. You may want to drop to your knees now too while you're at it."

He chuckled at my suggestion while continuing to smile. Isrie wasn't taking another step farther and just looked at Michael with a hard scowl. That's why I stopped him first. That's what friends are for . . . to help you out in difficult times and situations.

"Shit, I'm serious. You and I both know that was foul standing her up, but hey, I just met you."

I motioned Isrie over several times as the crowd of fellow passengers exiting the boat walked around us. She finally walked up. From what she had said about Michael on the boat, her face was showing a colder reaction at the sight of him than I expected. It was like something had changed her perceptions within the past twenty-four hours, but I hadn't a clue as to what it was. When two people are as close as we are, it makes it more frustrating when a friend does something you don't anticipate. I backed away after cracking a few jokes and nervously watched the two of them.

"C'mon. Let's give them some privacy," said Ivan. He had come up from behind and startled me.

"W-wait. Hold on a second. She might need a ride home."

"C'mon!" Ivan repeated with a little more force this time. He began pulling me away toward the parking lot by the arm. "They need some time alone. I'm sure your girlfriend is in good hands."

"Oh . . . alright. I guess you're right, Ivan."

"I always am," he said laughingly. "Would I lie to you, baby?"

"No. I guess not."

As Ivan and I began walking with the flow of traffic, our luggage in tow, I took one more look back at Isrie and Michael. They were talking, which was a good sign. I wondered what she wanted to talk to me about, but I was sure it could wait.

"Do you feel like breakfast at Roscoe's, baby?" Ivan asked as he gunned the Hummer to merge onto the Harbor Freeway. It was a cool, overcast morning—normal for this time of year.

"Nah. That medicine they gave me last night when I got sick made me sleepy, but it wasn't a restful sleep. I just want to check on Theron at home and take a quick nap. I need to do some work at the studio tonight." I still wondered what I ate that made me so sick.

"Alright then. I hope I didn't disturb you when I left last night."

"No. I didn't hear shit. Where'd you go?"

"It was still early, so I decided to take a walk. You know how I get in confined spaces for too long," Ivan replied. He opened his mouth to say something else then stopped.

"What?"

"Huh?"

"What are you *not* telling me?"

"It's no big deal."

"It is now. Tell me."

Ivan smiled to himself, then chuckled as if blowing something off. "Forget it."

"Want me to tickle you? I know how ticklish you are."

"Your friend was out last night."

"Who? Sophia?"

"No. Isrie."

"So."

"Yeah, that's just it. Nothing." With a thump from the speed bumps outside, we had merged over into the car pool lane.

"Something happened?"

"Nah. She was just a little tipsy, s'all. I ran into her in the hallway outside her room."

"Oh." Ivan started working the remote to his CD changer and turned up the volume to Jill Scott. I really liked her, but reached over to the knob and turned it back down. "Anything else?"

"Like I said . . . she was a little tipsy and said some things."

"Like?"

"I think she was thinking about her boyfriend. No biggie. The whole thing would probably embarrass her—if she even remembers it. I didn't go in her room. I just blew her off and told her to get some sleep. Forget about it. I already did."

"Oooh. Alright."

"I wouldn't have even mentioned it, but I don't like keeping secrets from you. We already ran into that kind of stuff when I agreed to do that photo shoot without telling you. I know better now."

Ivan gave me a kiss on the cheek, then turned the music back up. I closed my eyes to rest them and to try not to think about anything stupid. I knew right around where Ivan would be slowing down to exit, but I never heard the car slow.

"Where are you going? We passed my exit back there," I said, realizing that we were approaching the Santa Monica Freeway interchange.

"We're going to my place. Your brother might be using your van, so I'm going to let you take my whip again. Just bring it back whenever."

"You are too kind."

"You're the kind one . . . and I'm lucky to have you. What do you think about us moving in together once your brother's gone?"

"Moving fast, huh? Got a ring in mind?"

Ivan looked into my eyes and slyly answered, "Maybe."

Whoa.

43

Isrie

I hated Deja for what she did. By her going out of her way, I couldn't sneak through the crowd without Michael seeing me. It was even worse afterward when I looked back to see that son of a bitch Ivan yanking her away and leaving me to face someone I wasn't in the mood to deal with.

Michael looked as good as the day I first ran into him . . . literally. But that didn't change anything. His disappearing acts had worn on me and my being stood up on the cruise had pushed me beyond my limit. After my run-in with Ryan and what I had witnessed with Ivan the night before, I really wasn't in the mood to trust any man.

"What do you want?"

"To give these to you," he said, extending the fragrant roses toward me. "And to beg for your forgiveness."

I looked at Michael, leaving the roses hanging, and spoke clearly. "I'm sorry, Michael, but I'm not down with this. Go run your games on somebody else. Good-bye."

"No. Please. I'm not playing games," he said as he dropped the flowers to his side. I started walking around him, but he dropped his silly sign and stepped in front. "Listen . . . please. I know I fucked up, but I can explain."

"Yeah. I'm sure you can. That's just it. I don't want explanations anymore, Michael. I just want someone I can trust that's going to be there for me. I don't know if it's your career or if you're out there hoin' around, but either way I've had it. I deserve so much more and *I'm* willing to give so much more when I find that right person. Now move. I'm going home."

Michael didn't move, but he didn't block me either as I went around him this time. His head dropped, dejected. I wanted so badly to believe him and listen to his excuse this time, but I didn't—*wouldn't* allow myself the weakness of being swept up in his smile and personality again.

I concentrated on the rolling sound of my luggage wheels on the cement as I distanced myself without looking back. Michael shouted, "I love you, Isrie!" over the noise of the crowd. I pulled my suitcase faster to make the noise drown him out. I held back the tears as I made it to the parking lot. Yep. Deja and Ivan had left. I had no plans to get in any car with Ivan anyway, but I'd hoped my friend was still around for support. I saw two taxicabs driving up to the curb and began walking toward them. Michael had to walk this way to exit the place and I wanted to be long gone by then.

"Didn't think I'd see you again," came a voice from behind me.

"Oh. Hey—"

"Marcus. The name's Marcus," the twin laughed. "Forgot already? I'm *truly* hurt." He was looking flawless this morning as he pulled his monogrammed luggage behind him. "Need a ride?"

"N-no. I was just going to catch a cab."

"Can't have a beautiful thing like you paying highway robbery for a ride. What happened to your friends Ivan and Deja?"

My eyes flared at the mention of Ivan as my *friend*, but Marcus knew nothing of what went on. "They left," was all I replied.

"Shame on them and lucky for me. C'mon. Let me get your bag."

I saw Michael in the distance, coming our way. "Where do you live?"

"Rowland Heights."

"No, no. That's too far out of your way. I live downtown, near the Staples Center."

"So? I'll just take the Pomona Freeway home after I drop you off."

"Okay. Thanks."

"The pleasure's all mine." He smiled, his massive dimples popping up in the light of day.

"Wait." I had taken half a step off the curb and stopped dead.

"What now?"

"I just want to make things clear before we go. This is just a ride home . . . and nothing else."

"Oookay. I think I understand that. Your point being?"

"Nothing, nothing. I've just got enough complications in my life right now and want to make sure we understand each other."

Marcus looked at me intensely as if trying to understand my inner demons before his smile returned. "I'm not bringing you anywhere if you stop me again. Now let's get outta here."

On the drive home, Marcus was the perfect gentleman. I decided to make conversation. "So is this yours?" I asked about the silver Camry we were riding in.

"Yep. What did you expect? A Hummer?" he asked, taking a jab at Ivan. "I live within my means. That's why I live farther out . . . to get more for my money."

"So it's not all 'champagne riches and caviar dreams'?"

"Yeah. Right. What we do pays okay and comes with a lot of perks, but we're not rolling in the dough like some people would think. Only a select few got it like that. The rest—well, the rest perpetrate and live way beyond their means."

"I had no idea."

"Most people don't. Keep it quiet, though. We like to keep our *mystique*."

"So do you too?"

"What?"

"Perpetrate. You already said you don't live beyond your means."

"Sometimes," he laughed. "Usually, I just invest for the days when this pretty face and smile are gone."

The light conversation helped calm my nerves and I thanked Marcus when he dropped me off safely at home. Marcus offered to bring my bag and walk me up, but I rejected him once again and said a sincere good-bye. Why couldn't Deja have hooked up with this one instead? Or me even, I thought with a fleeting smile.

"Hi, Webster," I said as I walked into the lobby. Webster was bending over behind the counter this morning, but I recognized the scruff of his blond hair in passing.

"Good morning, Ms. Walker. I have something for you."

"Again?"

"Yup," he smiled as I slowed my pace and backed up to the counter. "He's got a *jones* for you."

"What did you say?"

"I—I heard it in a song before." Webster nervously reacted until my chuckle calmed him down. "Here."

Webster reached under the counter and pulled out a dark blue box wrapped in a ribbon that was about three shades lighter. I could tell there was a smaller package inside of it by the sound it made when I shook it. My stomach churned from some instinct that was kicking in. A small note card was taped to the top of the box. I opened it, scanning it quickly to confirm it was from Michael and nothing more.

"Here. I don't want it. If anything else is left for me from him, please refuse it."

"What? But—"

"Fuck him, Webster."

Messages were waiting for me on my answering machine. After putting my stuff down, I got a glass of orange juice from the fridge and sat down to listen to them. Most of the messages were hang-ups. The first message, where someone bothered to talk, was Michael's. It was left while I was on the cruise and I deleted it after the first few words. I had my finger on the DELETE button for the next message, when I pulled back at the last second.

"Isrie. It's Kendra. Remember what we talked about? Please call me right away. Okay? Bye."

I had put off thinking about Kendra's problems during most of my trip but the memory of her horrible encounter at the club came back faster than a crackhead wanting another hit. Had something else happened? Did Kendra tell her man? What if it was something worse? She left the message yesterday.

"Too much happening at once. Why me?" I asked aloud. I finished my orange juice, took my bra off, and changed into one of my long T-shirts. I looked up Kendra's number in my planner and prepared myself for whatever news she was going to give me. I quickly dialed up Kendra and was waiting for the ringing tone that never came.

"Hello?" I asked into the silence after waiting a few seconds.

"It's me," said Michael in a solemn voice. "You were dialing when I called. I tried calling you on your cell, but you had it turned off."

"Sound familiar?" I chuckled. I laughed, but was dead-on with what I said. "I don't want to talk to you right now, but I'm not lying when I say I have a very important call to make."

"More important than me? Us?"

"Yes. You had your chance to make *us* the main priority on the cruise, but you blew that off with your disappearing act."

"Okay. I deserve that. Did you get the package I left for you at the desk?"

"I saw the box. I refused it. The concierge probably has it now."

"What!" he shrieked into the phone, making me blink. "Do you know what was in that box?"

"No. What? Our future?"

"I'd like to think so."

"So, it's a ring?"

"Yes."

"It really would have been beautiful to have you with me on the cruise. To be by my side and put the ring on my hand . . . rather than leaving *a box* at the front desk."

"I know, I know. I wanted to be there with you. Things came up at the last minute . . . with my job."

"Your job. Again. If you have another woman, just tell me, Michael."

"I don't. You are the *only* woman for me," he pleaded emotionally. "Look, I need to talk with you. Really talk and clear things up. I'm looking into a career change also."

"We'll talk . . . but I have to go now." I sighed. As angry as I was, not all of it was his fault.

"Alright. I know when to back off."

"Give me a day or two."

"As you wish, Isrie. I love you. Maybe you can come by or we can meet somewhere."

"Okay."

Shifting gears, I hung up, rubbed my eyes, then hit REDIAL once I heard a dial tone. On the third ring, Kendra's man picked up. Hearing his voice made me tense, worried.

"Who this?" His voice was gruff and it sounded like I disturbed him.

"Hi. It's Isrie . . . Kendra's friend from work. Is she busy?"

"Nah, she ain't busy. She just got back from church. What's your name again?" I didn't remember his name either.

"Isrie."

After a few seconds of whispers between the two of them, Kendra came to the phone. "Hello," she said, as if a different person from the one who had left a panicked message.

"Can you talk?"

"Yeah. I had forgotten you were outta town."

"What's wrong?"

"I need to go to the clinic. I made an appointment for tomorrow. Please say you'll come with me. I can't go there alone,

Isrie." Her voice was bordering on a whisper. "I even went to church today. I never do that."

"Have you told anyone else yet . . . about what happened?"

"No. My man is wondering why I won't have sex with him. He thinks I'm cheating on him. I'm so scared, girl." Kendra was taking deep breaths to keep from choking up on the phone. "I— I think might have something . . . or be pregnant."

44

Deja

I was lucky that Ivan let me take his wheels as neither my brother nor my van was in sight. I did think it unusual for Theron not to be home when his big sister returned. My thoughts of him hightailing it out of town in my beat-up van faded when I saw his duffel bag in its usual place as I walked in. He had to go, but I was going to miss having family around. Isrie came close, but it wasn't quite the same as having your blood with you. I sent up a silent prayer that Theron's troubles with the military would be solved without him being locked up or a fugitive any longer.

After unpacking, I put on my Chris Botti CD and slipped under the covers for a brief catnap. I intended for it to be a nap, but my place was pitch-black when I awoke. The water bed shifted as I rolled over to turn my lamp on. The whole day had passed and I never heard Theron come back. A quick check of the living room told me I had been alone the whole time. I was a little hurt that my brother hadn't bothered to see if his sister had made it home in one piece. For all he knew, the ship could've hit an iceberg or something. Not really. He was probably wrapped up in some chickenhead's stuff at the moment that had him not knowing what day it was.

I was starving and fixed myself a big salad with the last of the croutons in the cupboard. It was almost ten at night, but I still had unfinished work waiting for me at the studio and was going to need an energy boost. I washed down two diet pills with a bottle of spring water. Money was a little scarce after not getting that *big break* Sophia had guaranteed with Ebony Emotions, and I needed to bust my butt in the studio tonight so I could get paid for some of my small jobs. As I finished my water, I gave some thought to the idea of Ivan and me sharing a place like he had hinted.

It was close to midnight when I arrived at my studio. Except for one homeless man looking for a scrap of food, Menlo was deserted as I turned off the headlights. I felt sad as I watched him walking down the sidewalk toward me. I wondered what his story was. Was he once a great poet? A construction worker? A banker? A proud father? Hmm. I wouldn't know my father if he came up and smacked me in the face.

Being alone, my first instinct was to clutch my purse to my side as I got out of the car, but I fought off my natural tendencies. I had only a twenty-dollar bill to my name at that moment. I motioned to the quiet man and handed it to him. I can be a saint, but I was really wishing I had some smaller denominations to hand him. *Sigh*. It was almost Christmas anyway.

"Bless you, child. Bless you," he said in a gravely voice, strained from exposure to the outdoors too long.

"I already am blessed," I replied with a big smile. "Don't have me catch you wasting that on some shit, okay?" My comfort level had returned.

"Oh, I won't." He smiled. "What's your name, pretty?"

"Deja."

"That's such a pretty name. I remember that name from an old, old movie."

"Oh?"

"Back when things were . . . better," he said, pointing to the smelly clothes he was now used to wearing. "My lady friend back inna day, Mitzy, used to say she wanted to name her daughter that . . . if she ever had one. Yeaaah. Those sho were good times. It's nice knowin' somebody named their kid such a pretty name. And that she grew into such a pretty lady too."

"Thank you."

"Well, pretty, thank you for the donation and your time. It was nice actually talkin' to someone without them runnin' from ya or tryin' to ignore ya. Be careful . . . and God bless."

"Good-bye." I grasped the glass door to the stairwell as the humble homeless man crossed the street. After hours, it was normally locked, but someone had forgotten this evening. Funny, my grandma used to call my mom Mitzy. I remember that from one Christmas when, as a child, I heard them arguing. As I pulled the door handle, I turned to look back across the street to see if maybe my new friend wanted a shower or something. But he was gone. He had disappeared back into the night from where he came.

After a brief chill swept over me, I locked the glass door behind me and walked up the creaky stairs to my studio. I pushed my key into the lock of my studio door, but it came open before I could turn the key.

"Oookay," I said to myself with a smile, thinking I knew where my brother had been all this time. The lights were on as I began to walk in. "Theron, you in here?" I yelled out. "I don't see my ride outside, bruh! You had better not let someone borrow . . . *it*."

I had taken half a step when I froze dead in my tracks. My entire studio had been gutted. My photo equipment that I had worked so hard all these years to collect had been jacked. All that was left was an overturned couch and a few props. The bastards didn't even have the decency to leave my photos on the wall. I heard a crunch as I tried to get my suddenly wobbly legs to move. The shattered picture at my feet was a rare one of me. It was taken at Del Amo Park by an old boyfriend way back when I was in photography school. The frame was twisted up as if someone had stomped on it.

The pieces of glass fell to the floor as I clutched my last remaining memory to my bosom, trying to hold back tears. The tears gave way to loud screams as I tried to cope the only way I could with the nightmare of my whole world being stolen. I don't know how long I stood there screaming, but I remember my throat getting hoarse and crumbling to my knees. Why? Why would someone do this to me?

Once I got up the courage to look around and try to make sense of it all, I began finding scuff marks across my floor like somebody was in a hurry and literally dragged pieces of my livelihood—no, my life out the door. I was still dazed when I found my telephone in the corner. It had been knocked off the hook, causing that nasty tone you hear when you forget to hang up. I clicked it twice to make sure it was still working, then called the police.

"I've been robbed," I said to the 911 operator with a weird kind of calmness. "I—I've been robbed."

LAPD arrived shortly. Two officers came first. One of them was the same redhead that had pulled me over in Ivan's ride and harassed me before. He had placed a call to the crime lab and was now looking around while his partner talked to me. I don't think he even recognized me. Just another black face to him.

"Does anyone else have keys to your place, ma'am?" The clean-cut black man was by the book, but seemed to have genuine concern for my plight.

"No, no. I have all the keys." I wasn't completely lying. I was so dazed, I almost mentioned Theron's having keys. His set was at my place, so in Clintonese I had all the keys in my possession. If I had mentioned Theron, he would be on his way back to New York the minute they ran a check on him. Damn him.

"Have you let anyone borrow your keys recently? I'm asking because it's obvious someone had access to your business without using force," he said, pointing to the front door.

"No . . . no. I can't think of anyone right now." The officer's face now shifted from concern to curiosity. "If you could please find my stuff, officer," I sobbed. "All of this stuff in here was my livelihood."

"We will, ma'am. We've got people checking into it now. Our crime lab will be here soon to fingerprint and look for evidence. From what you've described, that's a lot of special equipment. If

I were you, I'd follow up with my insurance company first thing in the morning to report this."

"Oh, no," I gasped.

"What?"

"I don't have insurance on the place."

45

Isrie

The clinic on Normandy was where Kendra had made her appointment. I had driven down Normandy many times and had never noticed the place. I guess I never was looking for a discreet place to be checked out by a doctor, though. It was my first day back to work after the cruise. Kendra had insisted we go during work so her man wouldn't think something was up. After playing cheerful and lying to everyone about how amazing the cruise was and how it went without a hitch, Kendra and I took an extended lunch.

Kendra neglected to tell me that she had already been here and was following up on her test results. I was guessing they had called her back and that was what spooked her. Shit, I would be spooked too. Most of the people in the place kept to themselves, but there were a few that thought we worked there because of our scrublike uniforms. Kendra was too shaken to say much, so I had to be the mean one and shoo them away. I was thumbing through a torn *Newsweek* that was four months old when the nurse came out and announced Kendra's name. I watched Kendra wince as if praying no one in the clinic knew her.

"You want me to go in with you?"

"You would?" she asked in a bashful manner I had never seen from her.

"Yeah. If you want."

"No. I'll be okay, I think. I might need you, though, so if you hear me screaming, come running. Okay?"

"Okay." I smiled because it was all I could do. She gave me a quick hug before leaving her hard plastic chair to join the impatient-looking nurse.

I had my cell phone with me and wanted to see how Deja was doing and why she had left me at the port with Michael like that the day before. I knew if I called her just then that I would get on the subject of Ivan and his threesome, and this was neither the right time nor place for drama on a phone. I needed to be strong in case Kendra flipped out. I still thought it strange that my girl hadn't bothered calling me, though. Maybe Ivan had spread his poison like he had promised.

The pages of the magazines went on and on as I waited for Kendra to reemerge from the long white hallway. While waiting, I met a nice elderly woman on fixed income suffering from leukemia. I gave the lady one of my cards for a complimentary day of pampering I knew she couldn't afford. After a while, I got up to stretch my back and to check on Kendra. Our extended lunch was beginning to run into dinner and I couldn't afford to lose my job for anyone.

"Excuse me?" I said before dinging the bell at the counter. I didn't know if they had rules about roaming the halls, so I figured I'd check first. Someone in the back of the office was just returning from lunch and was strolling in with a half-empty Carl's Jr. bag.

"Can I help you?" she asked, kind of pissed off at my interrupting her lunch. She quit frowning to stare at me for a second. "Hey . . . I know you."

"Oh, no," I thought to myself, thinking it was another person who had seen me on that TV show.

"Yeah, you that girl from Lloyd's place that day when I came by."

"Huh?"

"Y'know. *Lloyd*. T stay with 'im."

"Charletta?" I asked as the lightbulb went on upstairs. Her long hair that covered her ebony skin was gone now, telling me that it had been a weave.

"Yeah! You pretty good with names." She smiled, impressed with my memory. "What you doin' here?"

"I'm waiting on a friend."

"Oh. What's she—or he—*here* for?" she asked as if the clientele disgusted her.

"I don't know," I answered, smoothly lying through my teeth. "I just came to pick *her* up. I was checking to see if she was ready."

"How you and T been?" I wondered if Lloyd and she knew more than I did.

"Michael's fine. I'm fine."

"Haven't seen you around Lloyd's place."

"Busy."

"Oh. What's your friend's name?" She had opened the appointment book and was running the tips of her French-manicured nails up and down the list.

"Kendra."

"We have a Kendra Brown. That her?"

"Yes."

Charletta picked up the phone and called someone in back to check on Kendra. She nodded and mumbled as someone gave her Kendra's status. I was dying to hear what the person on the other end was saying as Charletta let out a snicker. Without even knowing what the snicker was about, my face scrunched into a scowl.

"She's about to come out. You can have a seat."

"Thanks." No screaming or crying was a good sign. Maybe everything had checked out. Kendra was still going to have a difficult time with the psychological scars and I was going to try my best to get her to seek counseling. I gave a courtesy smile to Charletta and went to take my seat again.

"Can I ask you something?"

I faced Charletta behind the counter again. "Sure."

"Why you always call him by his last name?"

"Who?"

"T! Who you think?"

"No I don't. I call him Michael all the time."

"That's his last name."

"What are you talking about?" I asked, now bothered by her tone.

"Michaels. That's T's *last* name. His name's Thomas Ross Michaels. That's why we call him T. *You* didn't know?" Charletta took some pleasure in knowing something I didn't. I felt like I was made of glass and somebody had just taken a hammer to me, shattering me into a million pieces.

"Are you sure?"

"Yeah, I'm sure. I remember T's full name from when he started staying over and Lloyd had to add him to the lease."

"Wha . . . wait. Michael . . . T . . . He moved in with Lloyd? The apartment's Lloyd's?"

"Yeah. Hallo! What were you thinking? T and Lloyd know each other from back in the navy. T's always out here in LA because of his job so he offered to split the rent with my boo. Uh, sumthin' wrong?"

"I—I—"

Kendra walked out slowly from her appointment just then. Her eyes told me things weren't okay. I stopped trying to make sense of these new revelations and walked off to help Kendra. Charletta was still talking but her words fell on deaf ears. Kendra wanted some privacy, so I walked her out to my car.

Michael Thomas Ross. Thomas Ross Michaels. My mind would replay the two over and over as I drove.

"Did you hear me?" Kendra asked.

"Huh? Yeah." The red light gave me time to focus on Kendra's problems again. She had broken down and was in tears. "So, it's not AIDS."

"No. Thank you, Lord. They recommended that I follow up,

though . . . for a recheck. Gonorrhea. I—I never had anything in my life." She sniffled. "Anything!"

"That's curable, right?" I didn't know much on the subject of STDs either.

"Yes. They gave me a prescription for some antibiotics. Th-that bastard! I could cut his dick off and stomp on it."

"You know how I feel already, Kendra. It's still not too late to report this to the police. Maybe they can still find him . . . before it happens to someone else."

Kendra began crying uncontrollably, losing all composure. It took all my concentration to shift gears in traffic and console her.

"What? What? What are you not telling me?"

"The counselors were speaking with me back there, Isrie. They . . . they're gonna tell my man because he's at risk as my sexual partner. I wasn't going to give them his information, but they made me feel guilty."

"They're just doing their job."

"Doing their job? How? By wrecking my home?"

"Aww, c'mon now. I'm sure he'll understand when you tell him the *full story*."

"No . . . no. He won't, Isrie. I know him. He'll say I was out hoin' around and brought something unexpected home."

"That's harsh. I was there that night. Look, I'll go home with you and make sure everything's okay between the two of you. If it's anything, you're going to need support and not finger-pointing."

"You don't know him," was all she said with reddened eyes. "You just don't know him."

My life and concerns were put on hold . . . again. But my day with Michael . . . Thomas . . . T—or *whatever*—was coming soon.

46

Deja

Ivan's warm touch beneath the cool sheets stirred me from the best sleep I'd had in a long time. His bedroom window was cracked. Outside, I could hear the morning waves of the Pacific. I had hoped my place being burglarized was all a bad dream, but I wouldn't have been in Ivan's bed if that had been.

I remembered how I wound up here. After a bunch more questions I had no answers to, I locked up the studio and sped home. Theron was still nowhere to be found and I was about to go crazy from the throbbing headache I had. Anxiety will do that to you. After no break-ins, robberies, or slip-and-falls, I had cut corners and let my business insurance lapse for just a second . . . and that was all it took. Frustration and not wanting to be alone led me to Ivan's door before daylight, where he welcomed me with open arms. I lay cradled in his embrace as he soothed me, telling me everything would be okay. I really wanted to believe him, for the thought of starting my business from square one was more than I could bear.

His words and companionship were all I needed, but Ivan gave me so much more that night. I guess he figured I needed my mind taken off matters. This morning, my thighs ached from involuntary pleasures as he had lapped up my honey in the dead of night.

"You want to get up?" Ivan asked, running his soft hand across my face.

"Do I have to? I just want to forget this happened."

"Did you leave the police a number to get in touch with you, baby?"

"Yeah," I said through a yawn. "Home and my cell."

"Good. So, they took all of your stuff?"

"Ivan, they cleaned me out. They even got my little safe where I kept emergency cash. If the police don't find my equipment, I'm fucked. Literally fucked."

"I'll help any way I can. You know that, baby." A reassuring kiss gently brushed my forehead.

"I know. Even in the middle of this hell, you make me happy."

"The son of a bitch who did this to you better hope the cops catch him before I do."

"Don't talk like that. I don't want you damaging any part of your gorgeous body. At least one of us is still capable of making a living. You don't want to be in the same boat as me. Trust me."

"That reminds me," he said, rolling over onto his stomach. The sheet slipped down to his bare buns. "Remember what I said before about us moving in together?"

"Yeah, but I couldn't afford to help you pay for this place, though."

"Actually, I was thinking about us staying at your place."

"*Mine?*"

"The view's great here. Especially now," he said, pausing to lick his lips as he surveyed my outline under the sheet. "But I pay way too much. I think I overextended myself a little."

"Even with your Ebony Emotions job?"

"Yeah. I won't see the real money from that until next year sometime. Besides . . . I don't need all *this* when I have you. For real."

"You've got me at a vulnerable time. We'll see." I was playing like I had some cards to deal, but I was dead broke and knew I needed Ivan now more than ever. My brother was going to be leaving soon anyway.

Ivan held me a little longer and I fell back asleep for a couple more hours. The steady rhythm of his heartbeat against my back sang to me in my dreams. I didn't realize it was missing until I heard my phone ringing in my purse. I looked at the time on Ivan's Bose Wave radio, and then caught my purse strap with my fingertip, dragging it to me.

It was the brother in black from my studio the night before. I quickly came to attention at the sound of his commanding voice, taking in his instructions. I nodded repeatedly as if he could see me through the phone.

"Who was that?" Ivan was wearing a pair of black silk pajama bottoms. Everything from the thin waist up was bulging as if he had just left a gym. I smelled what seemed to be breakfast coming through the now-open bedroom door.

"It was the detective from last night." I wrapped the sheet around my chest as I sat up. "He wants me to meet him at my place. There's been an arrest."

A crowd was gathered in the parking lot as we drove up. Ivan had to slow down and honk several times to avoid bumping some of the people too ignorant to move out of the way. It looked odd seeing the three police cars parked below my place. Two LAPD cars were positioned on both sides of the stairs and an unmarked white one was blocking my van. At least I knew Theron was back. Ivan hadn't come to a complete stop when I jumped out and ran to the detective. Someone was handcuffed and being stuffed into the backseat of one of the cars. My mind raced to thoughts of whoever robbed me going by my apartment in search of more and doing something to Theron. Another policeman saw me rushing toward his fellow officer and stepped in front of me. The detective motioned for him to let me pass.

"Detective, did you catch them?" I huffed. "Just tell me my brother's okay." I had given up on pretending Theron wasn't staying with me. Right then, my only concern was for him to be safe and among the living.

"Oh, your brother's fine, Ms. Douglas," he recited calmly. "Just fine."

"Wha—?" He led me with his eyes to the backseat of the sher-iff's car that had just been filled. "No," I gasped.

"Ms. Douglas, there's your thief. I believe you know him," he chuckled. "He *is* your brother after all."

There he was. The face I had grown up with, staring back at me through the metal grating that divided the front and back of the police car. Theron's face was fixed and nonemotional, the exact opposite of mine, which was twisting and turning in agony.

"This is a mistake, Detective."

"Nope. No mistake. We've also added assault on a police of-ficer to his charges. He wasn't too cooperative when we started advising him of his rights. We got an anonymous call that tipped us off. This is LA County Marina Sheriff's jurisdiction, so I had to call them and let them know we were doing a follow-up. You're lucky I don't arrest you for being an accomplice, but that didn't add up. I checked your *no insurance* story and con-firmed you had nothing to gain. Believe me, if you still had in-surance on your business, you'd be in the backseat keeping him company."

I shook my head at Theron, hoping for some sort of sign from him that he was innocent and that this was just a big misunder-standing. Theron had started wiggling around, as if his cuffs were too tight. I could see him cursing.

"So, how come you didn't tell us about Theron when I ques-tioned you earlier?"

"He keeps to himself. He—he had been in trouble in the past, so I just wanted to keep his name out of things." They must not have known about his military information yet. I couldn't believe that at this moment I was *still* trying to shield Theron.

Ivan had parked and talked the sheriff deputies into letting him through. He looked angry and ready for a confrontation.

"What's all this about, Officer?" he snarled.

"It's *detective*. Detective Grantham. And who are you sup-posed to be?"

"He—he's my boyfriend, Ivan," I answered for him.

"You know anything about her brother . . . Ivan?" Detective Grantham had shifted his focus and had pulled out a pen and pad.

"What's up, Deja?"

"Theron. They . . . they arrested Theron."

"For what? Because he left—"

"Stole my stuff," I said quickly, cutting Ivan off. I was regretting telling him about Theron's being AWOL from the Army. *Sigh.* Still being a big sister and protecting Theron. "They're claiming Theron cleaned me out."

"Just what were you about to say?" Damn. The detective was curious now.

"I was just about to ask what you think he did and what the fuck does this have to do with my girlfriend being robbed? This is crazy. You need to be out there looking for who really did it rather than trying to frame an innocent black man!"

"You," the detective said to Ivan with emphasis, "stay here. I don't like hotheads. Ms. Douglas, come with me."

I assured Ivan that I would be okay, then followed the detective up the stairs to my apartment. Two more officers were inside, taking pictures of my place. Theron's duffel bag had been opened and its contents dumped out on the floor in front of my sofa.

"Any of this look familiar?" he asked, sifting through the pieces of clothing . . . and other stuff.

"Lord, no," I whispered. Before me were two of my smaller cameras from the studio along with a wad of money that I knew came from my safe. Hell, it even had the same blue rubber band I had put around it. "No!"

I began trembling uncontrollably first, then came the pain in my eyes. I couldn't even cry anymore. How could someone I love so much do this to me? I bolted for my front door, thinking I could somehow make it down the stairs and to my brother's throat. Detective Grantham anticipated my reaction and caught me in the doorway before I did anything stupider than trusting Theron in the first place. As I fought to break free, he motioned for the squad car below to take off. My own blood had betrayed me and I watched him sulking in the backseat, heading to the police station to be booked. My grandma must be turning over in her grave.

I almost collapsed from stress and had to be led down the stairs. Everyone in the complex had come outside now to watch. I could see their faces as they whispered and came up with their own stories about what had happened to pass the time. Ivan met me at the bottom of the stairs, where I fell into his arms. I moaned like a wounded animal as I hid my face in his chest. My man stood there like the Rock of Gibraltar, holding me tightly.

"Shhhh. It's going to be okay, baby. I'm going to take care of you."

47

Isrie

I dragged my jacket behind me as I came through the front door late Monday night. I was yawning and really considered going straight to bed in my work clothes. Kendra had made it through the rest of the day after her unfortunate news, but I followed her from work in rush hour traffic anyway. We talked outside her place and she had decided to tell her man everything before the clinic called him. I was a little nervous about her telling her man without backup, in case he flipped, but she assured me she would be okay and begged me to leave. I told her to call me on my cell if she needed anything.

My answering machine was flashing, but it was going to have to wait till morning. It was a weekday, so at least one of those messages was probably from Michael. The lying sack of shit didn't know I was onto his game yet, so he'd keep until tomorrow. Why did I have such bad luck? The best man I ever met had turned out to be a complete fraud. Charletta had pointed me in the right direction without knowing it, but I still had to get down to the details for *my* peace of mind. With all the revelations coming to light about Michael/Thomas and Deja's man, Ivan, I'd started questioning there being any good men out there. It was almost enough to make a sister wanna turn lesbian. Nah! I liked the vitamin D too much. And besides, my dad was a good man, so I knew there was hope.

My place was cool without having to use the AC—just the

way I liked it. I took my white Keds off, then removed my shirt. Everything else stayed on as I let myself fall backward on my mattress with a *whoomp*! My heavy eyelids shut and I took one long, deep breath before welcoming whatever insane dreams awaited me on the other side of awake.

I thought I heard a soft tapping sound as my body went limp, but figured it was someone in another unit. As it continued, I tried to ignore it. When it got louder, I gave up.

"Shit. Go awaaaaaaaay!"

"Isrie. It's me." It was Deja. Something must've been up for her to be at my door this late. I was burned out and almost told her to go away. I couldn't do that to my best friend, though. Maybe she had found out about Ivan's true self on her own. "Did I wake you up?" she asked. I let the door swing open and walked away.

"No. I was on my way, though," I chuckled from the kitchen. Needing a quick jolt, I asked, "Want some coffee?"

"No, girl. I'm sorry about disturbing you, but I've been trying to reach you all day."

"Oh. Something came up. I just got back. What's wrong?"

Deja joined me in the kitchen as I boiled some water for a cup of instant. "My photography studio was hit. Everything was taken."

"No!"

"Yeah. I've been with Ivan and the police most of the day. I asked Ivan to come by here with me, but he was pretty drained."

"Oh . . . my . . . God. Come here, girl. It's going to be okay," I said, hugging her.

"That's just what Ivan said, but—but I don't think it will ever be okay. Isrie?"

"Yeah, girl?"

"Theron did it. Theron did it." Deja sounded like she was in a trance.

"Huh? Your brother? *What are you talking about?*"

"They arrested him. Isrie, he had some of my stuff in his duf-

fel bag . . . and everything. The police said they got an anonymous tip that led them to my place . . . and Theron."

"Look, I don't know him that well, but that sounds crazy."

"Maybe. Maybe not. I never told you this, but Theron's
AWOL."

"What? This—this is too much."

"He's wanted by the army . . . for stealing."

I quickly finished making my coffee. It was obvious there
would be no sleeping tonight. We walked over to my couch and
took a seat.

Jumping back into the madness Deja had just shared with
me, I asked, "Did you talk to your brother? What's his side?"

"Nothing. He just looked at me from the back of the police
car. That's why I came over. The detective said I can go by the
station tomorrow. I want—no, I *need*—to talk to him. You think
you could come with me?"

"Okay. If you want me to."

"This has been so hard."

"I can't even pretend to know what you're going through."

"But y'know, God won't give me more than I can bear." She
sniffed and wiped away a tear. "I just feel so betrayed."

"Yeah. I'm getting a lesson in that too."

"Huh? You and Michael worked things out, right? I mean, I
thought when we left y'all two by the boat—"

"Let's just say I reached an understanding with Michael. He
just doesn't know it yet."

"Oh?"

Changing the subject, I repeated, "So, you want me to go
with you to see Theron tomorrow?"

"Please."

"Okay. In the morning, I'll call in. You want to spend the night?"

"If I could."

"You know you don't have to ask, girl. Let me get you a pillow." I walked over to my closet and stood on my toes to tip a
pillow off the top shelf and into my hands.

"I don't think I can take any more surprises, Isrie. I may not have a place to stay in a few weeks if the cops don't find all my equipment and money that Theron took. Without that stuff, I don't have the means to make a penny. Ivan said he wanted to move in with me before Theron was arrested. I think I'm gonna do it."

"You can move in here, D-Square. Until you get on your feet."

"Thanks, girl, but nah. I think it's time Ivan and I move in that direction anyway. He's been so supportive and caring. I feel like a little kid for all the mistrust over Sophia 'n stuff."

Damn, damn, damn. I *knew* I should have told Deja the real deal about sorry-ass Ivan earlier, but I had been sidetracked with Kendra's situation and Mr. Change-A-Name-On-A-Sister. How supportive would I have been just then to hit her over the head with another bombshell? I decided to grin and bear it for now.

48

Deja

"Remember, D-Square. It's innocent until proven guilty."

"I know, but Theron's already torn his draws with me." I was using my grandma's phrase in the same breath as I was speaking ill of her grandson. She wouldn't have approved and the thought filled me with sadness and regret.

Isrie spent most of the night trying to cheer me up even though she was the walking dead. We had fallen asleep on her sofa right where we had been talking, and then were right back up at seven this morning. She rode with me by my trashed apartment for a change of clothes; then we followed the directions the detective had given us to the station on MLK. This was never a place I wanted to be. It was uncomfortable being somewhere I could have wound up if the detective hadn't believed me and thought I was working with my brother. *Brother.* Thoughts and feelings were coming to mind that should not go along with the word.

I was going to be allowed to talk with Theron this morning, but it was going to be from behind the glass. Isrie felt uneasy, so she stepped back against the wall to allow us some privacy. I was rubbing my eyes when Theron was escorted into the room. A few seats down, a woman was pleading in Spanish with her boyfriend, who was giving her the silent treatment from the other side of the bulletproof window. Theron looked like he hadn't slept either. His eyes were drooping more than usual. He still wore his wrinkled Nike T-shirt and jeans. I smiled to break the tension between us as he sat down across the glass from of me. Theron hesitated before picking up the black phone. Both of us struggled with what to say.

"Hi."

"Whassup, sis."

"Are you okay? They said you assaulted one of the cops."

"Hell, yeah. They come runnin' in on me, looking through thangs. Whatcha expect me to do?"

"Cooperate."

"Huh? These motherfuckers ran up accusin' me of stealing!"

"Isn't that what you did, Theron?"

"What the—? Is everybody goin' fuckin' crazy, *including you?*"

"Dammit! They found some of my shit, bruh! How could you? After all I've done for you!"

"I'm innocent! Look . . . they don't know about my other situation. You gotta get me outta here now, Deja. C'mon."

"*If* I believed you, how in the fuck am I supposed to get you out? With my good looks? I have barely a hundred dollars to my name, thanks to your no-good ass. You took everything, Theron! Everything!" If there hadn't been a glass separating us, I would have lunged at him. Instead, I lowered the phone from my ear and glared at him. Theron waved his hands quickly for me to pick back up.

"Shhh. Alright, alright. Calm down. *They might hear you,*" he said, looking nervously at the guard on duty. "I said it before and I'll say it again—I did not rob you, girl."

As Theron went on talking, I watched his mouth move but wasn't hearing him. My mind was playing over the conversation I had with Detective Grantham after Theron was taken away. Everything pointed to Theron, from the photography studio being robbed without forcible entry to my stuff being found hidden among Theron's things. Everything fit into place . . . and pointed right to him. And they didn't know about his history . . . yet.

". . . they're going to arraign me tomorrow, then ship me off to County. I can't go there, girl. You *know* I got enemies in the County. . . . Deja, are you listening?"

"What happened in New York?"

"Huh?"

"What . . . happened . . . in . . . New York?"

"I can't talk about that now. Why you bringin' that up? That's got nothin' to do with this."

"Because I want to know. Tell me the full details or I walk outta here now."

Theron fidgeted in his chair and looked at Isrie, who was trying to ignore the one-sided conversation she was hearing from my end of the phone. "You told somebody about the Army? You told *her*?"

"At this point, do you think it matters? I am so sick of the bullshit."

"I already told you it was about guns 'n shit," he said stressing it intentionally low.

"And?"

"And I didn't do it."

"Yeah. Kinda like you didn't stab me in the back and clean out my studio, huh, bruh?"

"Why in the fuck won't you believe me?! It's that pretty boy, huh? He's got you all twisted . . . even about your own flesh 'n blood."

"This isn't about Ivan. Besides, he's one of the few people trying to stick up for you, although I have no idea why at the moment. Tell me everything about New York."

"Nothin' much to it, anyway. One of my boys worked in the armory. That's where they keep our guns 'n shit. A lot of us in there got shifty pasts, some shiftier than others." He chuckled that familiar laugh of his. "Anyway, he and some other partners had a scam goin'. They were selling the older shit that was supposed to be disposed of, on the outside."

"And you were helping."

"Nah! Nah! It ain't even like that. I was just in the car when it all went down. I didn't know anything about it until that night. They wanted me in on it, but I said I wasn't down. See, the Army or somebody had been following 'em and waited for the transaction to go down."

"Oh, so you're innocent?"

"Exactly!" he answered excitedly. He was so desperate that he didn't hear the sarcasm in my voice. "They didn't see me in the car at first, so I made a run for it. Someone told me to stop and shot at me, but I kept goin'. They didn't see my face, so I made it back to the barracks, packed my bags, and jetted. You know how it is on the streets. I saw trouble and got as far away from it as possible. That's it. That's everything."

"Theron?"

"The police found some of my cameras in your duffel bag. And some of my money. I saw it with my own eyes. Is that what you were going to use to get away after Christmas?"

"No. No. They must've set me up!"

"They even thought I had something to do with it."

"Deja, are you listening?"

"Theron, they almost took me to jail for your foolishness."

"Sis, ya gotta believe me—"

"I've always gone to bat for you your entire life, bruh, but I can't anymore. I'm tired. And I just don't believe you."

"Dejaaaa—!"

I let the phone slip slowly from my hand; then I quickly walked off, crying. If I slowed or turned around, I knew I wouldn't have the strength to stay on the course I had chosen. Isrie lingered for a second, then ran after me. She later told me that Theron went ape-shit and started smashing the phone up before the guards restrained him and dragged him back to his cell.

49

Isrie

Deja was so bad off that she couldn't drive. I made her pull into the parking lot of the Carl's Jr. after she almost hit a young brother who was selling bootleg DVDs in traffic.

"Look, you need to calm down. Killing both of us ain't gonna help the situation, D-Square."

"It'd serve me right, though. You know how hard it was to leave Theron like that back there?"

"So, you really think he did it? Stole from you, I mean."

"I can't think anything else."

Deja was wired more than I had ever seen her. I persuaded her to allow me to drive from that point on. I stowed away my ill feelings toward Ivan enough to drive his truck, which wasn't easy. Once things calmed down, I was still committed to opening Deja's eyes.

We went by Deja's place, where I spent a large part of the afternoon helping her clean up. I put away most of Theron's stuff, otherwise it was going to wind up in the trash. Deja came out of her bedroom holding one of the two cameras the police had found.

"This is one of my very first cameras I bought," she said sadly. "You think I'm being too hard?"

I shrugged and said, "I dunno. I can't judge you on this, girl. Look, if you need bail—"

"No. Thank you though. I always can depend on you, Isrie," Deja smiled.

"You know." I laughed, trying to put a smile on her face.

"But this is something I *have* to do. I can't babysit him anymore. I *need* to be strong."

"You're hurting right now and I understand. I'll just leave that offer out there for you if you change your mind."

"I won't. I'm through." She wanted to believe that so badly.

Deja had calmed down by the time she dropped me off at home. Before she left, I gave her a few words of encouragement. As I watched Deja leave, a beat-up tow truck pulled out behind her. It had been parked just off property. The long day had my mind a little gone, but I could have sworn I had seen the same tow truck in traffic behind us when we left the police station. The city was full of beat-up tow trucks, I thought before dismissing the notion and heading inside.

I called Kendra immediately to make sure *things* were going smoothly between her and her man. They were having some difficulties after her coming clean, but were trying to work through them. She still didn't want to get the police involved in finding the guy or guys who had drugged and raped her.

As I ended my conversation with Kendra, my cell started ringing in my purse. It could have been Deja with some new developments, so I rushed over and answered it.

"Were you ever going to call?"

"Michael. There's been a lot going on with my friends. Things just took priority over you, s'all."

"Oh, I'm sorry. I've been going crazy waiting on your call. Something wrong with Deja?"

"Yeah, you could say that," I answered, almost forgetting that I was talking to an imposter. "But it's nothing I want to talk about with you. Personal stuff."

"When can we get back to our personal stuff? I miss you. I want to make love to you, girl. Can I come by?"

"No. It's been a long day, Michael. I took off from work today and need to go in tomorrow."

"Can I come by for a few minutes? Just to see you, I mean. I don't like things like this between us."

"Tomorrow."

"Tomorrow?"

"Yeah. We'll clear up everything then. Do you have plans for tomorrow?"

"Nothing I can't change."

"Good. How long has Lloyd been living with you?"

"About a year. Why?"

"I'm just wondering what your plans are for us, baby," I said to put him at ease and lower his defenses. "Isn't it about time to have Lloyd move out? If things are going to be as serious as you want them to be, then shouldn't we have your place . . . all to ourselves?"

Michael stuttered, "Yes, but, well . . . See, I have to give Lloyd more notice than that."

"Going out of town this weekend . . . to work?"

"Yes."

"Where?"

"All over."

"Such as?"

"East of here. Moreno Valley, Riverside."

"Oh. That's not far from my parents. Can I come along?" I asked like a squealing schoolgirl. "I promise not to get in the way."

"I'd love to, but I can't. Not this weekend at least. Important meetings with other regional coordinators."

"I see. Where are you going to be staying? Maybe I could pay you a visit or stay in the room."

"I'm not sure yet. I won't have the details on the hotels until Friday. I'll let you know." *You just did.*

"Look, let's get together tomorrow evening."

"Alright. Dinner?"

"That would be wonderful, Michael. We'll talk 'n stuff."

"I'd like that, Isrie. Want me to pick you up?"

"No. We'll meet. Heaven?"

He laughed. "Your favorite place. Whatever you wish. What time?"

"Eight?"

"It's a date then. So, I'll see you there."

"Of course . . . Michael." He couldn't see the smirk as I hung up. One day, I would have to thank Charletta.

50

Deja

Five minutes. Five fuckin' minutes. That was all the time I was inside my apartment. I guess that was all that was needed. I didn't even hear the alarm. Things couldn't have gotten worse . . . but they just had. How was I going to explain Ivan's Hummer being stolen right out from under me? Things were disappearing left and right on my watch.

I ran back inside to get the cordless and called the police from my doorway. I continued to scan the parking lot, as if I had misplaced Ivan's ride and it would mysteriously reappear. It hadn't been gone long, so the police had a good chance of catching the bastards, I thought.

"Please hold, ma'am." The precinct operator seemed in no hurry. If I had no further dealings with law enforcement for the next five years, it wouldn't be long enough. The operator, a middle-aged Hispanic woman by her voice, shortly returned. "Ma'am?"

"Yes. Is somebody coming out?"

"Is that a Hummer H2 registered to an Ivan Dempsey?"

"That's it! Has it turned up already? *Please* say it has."

"Ma'am . . . that car isn't stolen. It comes back as repossessed."

"No, it was stolen! Somebody just took it from my place."

"Ma'am, GMAC called it in to us. I'm looking at it on the system. They scheduled a repo on this vehicle two weeks ago. I guess they just located it. If you have any problems with that, I suggest you contact them. Can I help you with anything further?"

I wanted Ivan to explain how he had me driving around in his truck, knowing somebody was about to pick it up. Of course, if I had something I didn't want anybody to get hold of, that would be the easiest way of not having it around—by keeping it somewhere else.

"That son of a bitch used me," I thought aloud. Real cheesy. Was it Brotha-Fuck-With-Deja Week or something?

The trip in my noisy ride wasn't as pleasant as in Ivan's, but that was gone now. He honestly may not have known, but I decided to be devious rather than confrontational.

"Ivan! Open up!" I yelled from the hallway. Ivan's old car was downstairs in the garage, so he should have been home. After I pounded on the door a few more times, I heard the lock being turned.

"Hey, baby." Ivan looked like shit—something like that was usually impossible, but was clearly visible in the light of the hallway.

"What's wrong with you?"

"Nothin'. I'm just moving a few things around."

"Looks like you're moving more than a few things." Boxes that weren't there before were in the middle of his living room. Things were thrown into them haphazardly as if Ivan were in a hurry. That explained the way he looked, but there was more going on. I couldn't put my finger on it yet.

"Yeah, well, I said I needed to move, so I'm just getting an early start."

I hadn't even agreed that he could move in with me, but decided to get to what I had gone by there for. "Baby, your car was stolen," I said solemnly.

"What do you mean?"

"Ivan, I am *so* sorry. I was at my apartment. I went inside for just five minutes . . . and it was gone. I rushed straight over to tell you."

"Shit!"

"We need to call the cops. I meant to call them from my place, but I was so upset. Where's your phone?"

While pretending to search for the phone, I watched Ivan's anger shift. "No, don't call them."

"Why not?"

"I'm not worrying about that damn Hummer. Whoever took it can keep it. I'm just glad nothing happened to you." *The bastard.*

"You sure, baby?" I asked, batting my eyelashes.

"Positive."

"You're not mad at me?"

"No. I could never be mad at you, baby." Ivan stepped up and put his arms around me. I got a closer look at him, and his eyes. He was on something. I had allowed myself to be blinded early on and had been so clueless. I pulled away.

"What are you on?"

"Huh?" he laughed, trying to straighten up. "Girl, you trippin'."

"Coke?"

"Deja, I'm just a little stressed out. That's all. Stop that shit."

"Tell me!" I demanded. "Coke? Crack? Lord, tell me you're not a crackhead."

"Crackhead? Who the *fuck* are you calling a crackhead?" Ivan got up in my face. Sheer evil was in his eyes. I stood shocked at the monster before me.

"If the rock fits, smoke it."

My big ass went flying from his backhand. The stacked boxes cushioned my fall, but not much. Things came spilling out as I hit the floor. Some things shattered and other things rolled past me. A man had never laid a hand on me like that. I could feel the welt already forming across my face. God, it stung. I rolled out of the way, expecting another hit or kick, but none came.

"Deja! Deja! I'm sorry. I don't know what I was doing. You have to believe me. Here, let—let me help you up." Ivan had

gone from madman to crying idiot right before my eyes. If someone had told me this would happen, I wouldn't have believed it.

"Don't touch me. Don't fuckin' touch me." I got up on one
knee, then had to catch my breath. As I sucked in, I noticed some
of the scattered contents of the boxes.

"Come here." Ivan grabbed me anyway and yanked me to my
feet. I tried to push him off, but he held firmly. He tried to tend
to my new bruise, but I turned away. "Look, we're going to work
this out. Okay?"

"Let go of me, Ivan."

"Only if you promise this doesn't change anything between
us. I lost it when you made that crackhead comment. That's all.
I don't do that low-end stuff, baby. I thought you knew that.
Nothing but the best for me. And for you too. We're good together—you and I. Just the two of us . . . forever." I fought back
the trembling as Ivan held my face so he could kiss me. I wanted
to scream, but allowed him the kiss. This would be his last time
touching me in any way. "Let me make it up to you," he urged.

Ivan's breathing became heavier and I knew what he had in
mind for making it up to me. His hands had drifted down to my
ass and were gripping me as his tongue was now in my mouth.
The soreness on my cheek dulled any effects his kiss normally
would have had on me.

"Baby . . . wait," I said.

"Hmm."

"No. Stop. I need to get some condoms out of my purse."

"Oh. Okay," he said, finally relaxing his grip and allowing me
to breathe. His smile told me that he was so fucked up, he
thought he had actually swayed me with his words.

"They're down in my van. My purse is in the van."

"Fuck it. We don't need them anyway." His manhood, which
had given me so much pleasure recently, was hanging out from
the leg of his shorts.

"No. I'll be just a moment."

Ivan almost let me go. Almost.

"You can go get them, but I need a little sumthin' first." He grabbed my wrist, guiding me, urging me toward his dick. "You know what to do, baby."

I tried to reason with him, to talk him out of it. His eyes told me he heard nothing except whatever demons were whispering in his mind. He pushed down on my shoulder, bringing me to my knees. He was sweaty and dirty. The funk made me want to throw up, but I resisted as I took him in my mouth. While crying on the inside, I faked like I was enjoying myself. Ivan got his rocks off and I got off the hook.

"Now. Hurry up with those condoms."

Convinced by my actions, Ivan moved aside. I shut the door behind me, spitting to remove the taste from my mouth, and took one last look back. On his door, I now noticed the tape from an eviction notice that had been ripped down. I ran for my life to the elevator and paced on the ride down to the garage.

Looking over my shoulder in fear, I sped away. With shaky fingers, I dialed a number on my cell. I woke him up.

"Detective Grantham."

"Yeah. Ms. Douglas, right?"

"Yes, it's me."

"To what do I owe this pleasure? Especially at this time of night?" he asked through a yawn.

"I have a question."

"Shoot."

"You say an anonymous call was made to you about my brother?"

"Yes. That's what I said."

"Was it a man or woman?"

"A woman, although you never know these days. Why?"

"I know the people really responsible for stealing my stuff . . . and for setting my brother up."

A few choice things had spilled out when I crashed into the boxes. A lot of Ivan's junk, but also some pictures—several black-and-white photos of me and Ivan making love by strobe light on the chaise lounge in my studio. After developing them, I had never showed Ivan those pictures from that night out of embarrassment and had stuffed them in my studio filing cabinet. A round black object had also rolled out when I went down. It was a lens cap. The lens cap to one of my cameras that had been found in Theron's duffel bag.

The stupid bastard. Even stupider me.

51

Isrie

With all the happenings since returning from the cruise, I had yet to work a full day. My boss was getting tired of my excuses and I knew my position was in jeopardy. I couldn't tell her all the sordid details so I just had to take it while she lectured me like a child. Two days earlier, Deja had showed up at my door in the middle of the night, looking defeated. Without speaking, I let her in and showed her the bed. She lay beside me and cried herself to sleep. It wasn't till around noon that she finally woke up. I had been up since my usual time to call out of work. I fixed two big bowls of Golden Grahams for us and silently watched D-Square until she was ready to talk. You just don't know how it hurt me to see my best friend go through this kind of pain.

It was after *The Young and the Restless* went off that she broke down and filled me in on the night's revelations about Ivan and probably Sophia setting Theron up. I didn't give her enough credit, surprised as I was that she had figured out how Ivan had been broke and was stringing her along so he could lift all her stuff, get rid of Theron, and move in with her all in one swoop. She wasn't sure about Sophia's involvement even though she figured that was how her things were planted in Theron's bag and how her spare studio key was lifted from her brother.

I chose that time to tell her about Ivan on the boat with Sophia, the other freak and the drugs. That helped end any confusion she may have had about Ivan and Sophia still being a *team*. Hurt on top of hurt. And I had just dropped another shovelful onto Deja's head.

"Damn! Why didn't you tell me, Isrie?"

"I tried, I tried. Michael showed up when we were leaving the boat that day. Then you left with Ivan before I could tell you. The last few days have been like a whirlwind, so there was never a good time. It's like Ivan's two separate people. Scary."

"Tell me about it," she said with a fake laugh while pulling back her hair to reveal the hand-shaped bruise across her cheek. "I wanted to take a skillet to that bastard's head, but knew I needed to get out of there."

"You know if the police picked him up?"

"No. I don't. That's why I came here. I was afraid to be alone after that."

"Girl, you can stay here as long as you like. I just hope Ivan goes straight to prison, where they can pass his pretty ass around for cigarettes."

"Y'know, as crazy as it sounds, I don't wish that on him. Part of me still loves him."

"You don't sound crazy. I'm right there with you." Slightly changing the subject for my benefit, I asked, "What did Theron say? I know he must be glad to be out. Is he pissed at you for not believing him?"

"I—I don't know. I didn't see him."

"Oh. You still need bail? 'Cause I—"

"He's gone." She sniffled. "He's gone. They took him away."

"To the County?"

"No, no. I went by the jail first to try to get Theron out. They found out he was AWOL. The Army picked him up and took him back to New York to . . . court-martial him. He's gone, Isrie. Theron's gone."

52

Isrie

The plan had called for me to meet Michael at Heaven that evening, but that was never truly my intention. I made sure Deja was going to be okay before I left to handle my business.

Our date was at eight, so I started the drive down to Long Beach at seven, speeding most of the way to make sure I beat Michael on his way out the door. I gambled that he would be at his apartment and not leaving from somewhere else to meet me.

"I thought we were meeting at Heaven, Isrie," he said, trying to look his usual cool, calm, and collected self. From the small hairs on his shirt, it was obvious he was in the middle of trimming his goatee. Try as I might, the mention of my name on his lips still made me grin.

"Change of plans. You don't mind my dropping in, do ya?"

"Of course not. You don't know how good I feel seeing you." He expected a kiss and you don't how hard it was it was for me to simply walk by. Fortunately, keeping my mind on the deception kept me from losing focus.

The apartment was cleaner than it was on my last visit. "Lloyd's here?" I asked.

"No. He and Charletta went to the Magic Johnson Theatre."

As I looked down the hallway, I could see Michael's bedroom door closed while Lloyd's was open. Michael saw me looking.

"Why aren't you dressed?"

"I am dressed, baby." We both knew my vinyl jacket, black tank top, blue denims, and white K-Swiss, no matter *how good* I looked in them, weren't getting me into the restaurant. Without a warning, I made a break for Michael's bedroom and was at his door before he could say anything. As I turned the knob, he was running up behind me. I burst into the bedroom, expecting to see another woman. I was prepared to scream out "Where is she?" but no one was around. Just a lot of junk, *Playboy* magazines and a bunch of dirty clothes. The bed was the same one I had been in with Michael that magical night, but everything else was different.

"Isrie. What are you doing? What's gotten into you?"

"Outta my way!" I screamed. I ducked under his arm and ran to Lloyd's bedroom, where I saw what I needed to see. Michael had given up the chase and stood there, looking at me. "What? You don't want me in your room, Thomas?"

"You know."

"Yeah, you fuckin' liar. I know."

"Shit."

"Busted. Why the games? Were you trying to play me?"

"No, it's not like that."

"Oooh. Very original," I said as I walked around the smaller bedroom that was really his. It looked very *temporary*. "So how many women are you fucking? Besides me, I mean."

"None, Isrie. Well—"

"Bullshit! Be a man! I want the truth and I want it now."

"I'm married."

"Oh, Lord."

"But I love you."

"How can you say those sentences back-to-back?" Frustrated, I began walking out to leave.

"Please let me talk to you." He reached out in desperation.

"Don't touch me," I said as I raised my hands and backed away from him.

"I was going to come clean tonight . . . at dinner."

"I don't know why I should listen to anything else you have to say, except maybe for closure. Okay, let me hear it."

"Please. Come sit on the couch."

"I'll stand. Talk."

"How'd you find out?"

"A little bird told me, but not everything. I want to hear it from your mouth, Thomas. Damn . . . I almost called you Michael."

"I don't live here. I stay here when I'm working."

"Where do you and the Mrs. live? Somewhere out east? Rialto?"

"Y-yeah. Rialto. How'd you know?"

"I just guessed. Everything's starting to make sense—all the excuses, the *working* on weekends, standing me up on the motherfuckin' cruise. That's when you're with her, isn't it?"

"Yes. I don't love her, though."

"But you're sure sleeping with her, huh? You don't even have to answer that, you sorry piece of—"

"We have a kid together."

I closed my eyes. "Damn. How do I get into this shit?"

"It's complicated."

"It always is when a dog gets busted."

"We've got a lot of history. I've been with Maria since I was in the Navy."

"She's the one who cut you. Your scar."

"Yeah."

"She should have finished the job. Bye, Thomas. And Merry Christmas."

Michael . . . shit . . . *Thomas* was in tears as I went to leave. "I love you, Isrie."

"No, you love yourself. Otherwise you would have stepped to me like a man . . . and without all the lies and tricks, silly rabbit."

Thomas was up and cut me off before I left. We looked at each other for a while. I knew in my heart that I still loved Michael, but Michael was gone.

"Isrie, things shouldn't have gone on like this. I knew I wanted a future with you when I first met you. If I had told you everything then, you wouldn't have waited on me . . . and I couldn't risk that. Look, we can work through this. Don't give up on us. It'll take a little while to leave Maria, but—"

"Second string," I mumbled.

"Huh?"

"I can't be second string. I refuse to do it. Good-bye."

Like a wounded dog, Thomas opened the door and moved aside. He opened his mouth to say something, to try to plead one last time, but then went glassy eyed. I barely had time to move before he fell face-first to the floor. I didn't even see the lick to his head he had just received from an aluminum bat.

I watched the figure walk in with a push of the door and step over a groaning Thomas. "Bitch, I've been waiting for you!" he said to me.

"Ivan?"

The insanity of the situation made my heart skip a beat. Ivan's face showed nothing but madness and I knew it was wise to back away from the door.

"Deja's hiding at your place, ain't she, bitch? The two of you did this, called the cops on me. Well, it didn't work. I'm going to take care of your ass first; then I'm going after that fat bitch." Ivan stood there in a ripped T-shirt. He was dirty and sweaty as if he had been on the run. He must've followed me from my apartment over here.

Thomas, still dazed and probably suffering a concussion, tried to grab Ivan's leg. Ivan made him pay by busting him in the head again with the bat. This time, blood flew across the room as Thomas' head split wide open. I let out a scream, but had to cut it off in order to duck the next swing meant for me. I fell on my butt, then stumbled to my feet to run for dear life. All the while, Ivan was cursing to high heaven about betrayal and revenge as he took out his frustration on every object in sight. Maybe if I had told Deja about him sooner, none of this would be happening, I thought. I threw a book nearby at Ivan to slow him down. He laughed and swatted at it with the bat, sending it bouncing off the wall across the room.

"Ivan—"

"Shut the fuck up!"

"You can't do this!" I ran around the sofa, playing a game of cat and mouse. I knew I wasn't fast enough to make it outside without Ivan taking my head off first. "The police will be here any minute!"

"You'll be dead by then. What are y'all two? Dykes or something? That's why you got in Deja's head to turn her against me? Huh!"

Feeling brave for a minute, I lashed back, "You sick fucker! You're the one who used my girl, then stole all her shit. You and your trick Sophia, you fuckin' crackhead!"

"I ain't no crackhead! Shut up, shut up, *shut up*!" Ivan jumped over the sectional to catch me with a wild swing. He missed my head barely, but caught me on my shoulder, which went numb. I screamed and fell to the floor. Falling was the best thing I did, as Ivan flew right over me and landed in the hallway, falling awkwardly as well. The bat that was in his hand rolled away.

I wiped the tears blurring my vision, trying to ignore the pain and get up again. The madman slammed into me, sending me flat on my face on the carpet. I felt pain in my back and yelped as Ivan continued screaming at me for every wrong ever done against him. His musky scent made me want to puke, but I didn't have time for that. I had to get away before I wound up in a matching hospital bed with Thomas, or worse. I elbowed Ivan once to give myself room. Part of me wished Thomas would magically jump up to save the day, but he was unconscious, lying in a pool of blood.

"Help!" I screamed as Ivan grabbed my ankle and pulled me back to him. In the struggle, I rolled over and could see the hate etched on his face. I reached my hands out in one last desperate attempt to grab anything—anything to save me—and wound

up snagging the fertility god. There it was, even in the midst of this horror, smiling.

I realized then that it wasn't a fertility god, but a god of war. I asked it to forgive me for what I was about to do before I did its bidding, then let loose with a wild swing. The wood was solid and so was my blow. I'd struck Ivan right in the temple.

Ivan shrieked. He shot up in pain, allowing me to get another lick in. In an effort to protect himself, he curled up in a ball as I got back up to my feet. I didn't stop whaling until Ivan wasn't moving and I still kept the statue in my hand as I limped over to Thomas to check on him. I could see he was breathing, so I picked up the phone and called the police. As I dialed, I kept my eyes on the motionless Ivan. I then called Deja at my place to let her know it was all over.

As I waited for the police, I tended to Thomas as best I could. The front door was still open to the night air and cooled me as it blew on my sweaty face. I could hear the sirens, off in the distance at first but getting closer and closer. Ivan had begun twitching as if coming to. I moved Thomas' bloody head off my lap and walked over to Ivan, statue still in my hand. Just make a move, I thought to myself. When I saw the reflection from the police lights flickering on the front door, I smiled . . . and took one last whack at Ivan. God, I had wanted to do that since being on the boat.

Everything was going to be okay now.

53

Deja

My hands wouldn't stop trembling as I listened to Isrie's words over the phone. I wanted to rush down to Long Beach, but Isrie wouldn't give me directions. She claimed it was better that I not see the aftermath of Ivan's rampage . . . or the measure of revenge she took upon him before the police arrived.

I hoped that the police would be able to get a confession out of Ivan and manage to track down all my stuff. I wasn't banking on it, though. As cunning as Ivan had been in playing me, my things and my livelihood were probably long gone—scattered all over LA like some thick smog. Ivan had once told me he got paid to make things look real. He had it right. He made things look real, and I was the one who paid.

I was unaware I was crying again until the growling of my stomach interrupted me. I hadn't eaten all day. I forced myself up off Isrie's couch, where I had been watching TV most of the evening. In my purse, I fished out my diet pills. I really looked at the colorful logo of the Diet Zing for the first time since I had started taking it. Its rainbow label promised so much to all who took it. I laid my purse down and walked to the kitchen for a glass of water.

The phone rang again. I ran to it thinking it might be Isrie with more news.

"Ms. Walker?"

"No, this is her friend."

"This is the front desk. I have a delivery for Ms. Walker, but the lady refuses to leave it. Do you want me to send her up?"

"What does she look like? Is she a black girl with a big forehead? Beautiful? Looks like a model?"

"Uh, no, ma'am."

"Alright then. You can send her up." Sophia was still out there somewhere. I wasn't worried about her as much as what I'd do to her.

Before I could return to the kitchen, the burst of music from the TV announcing a news flash on KNBC came on. Some guy the police were searching for had been caught. He had spiked a woman's drink with the date-rape drug the night before. Luckily, he was caught before he could rape his victim. What's freaky was that he was caught on the parking lot outside the club we'd been at with Isrie's friend Kendra. As the phone number flashed on the screen for other possible victims to call, I praised the Lord that he had been caught and that something like that hadn't happened to me or somebody I knew.

After pouring my glass of water, I slowly, deliberately took my time turning the childproof cap. I peered down into the half-full bottle.

I felt my muscles tensing in my forehead and closed my eyes. I don't know how to explain what was eating at me except to say that something was. My hand began trembling again as I tried to pour two pills into it. The Diet Zing spilled onto the counter, with most of them winding up down the garbage disposal.

I nervously hovered over the sink for an eternity, looking at the spilled pills. I wiped my eyes, then my nose before reaching for the wall and flipping the switch. With a large crunching sound, the garbage disposal sprang to life. When everything in it was ground up, I dumped the rest of the pills and watched them disappear as well.

"Good-bye," I said with a smile, imagining that it was all the hurt I had experienced being flushed down the drain. "Good-bye."

With my life, it had been like that old Heavy D song: I

wanted somebody to love me for me. The crazy thing I found was that I hadn't learned to love myself yet

I was still crying, but it was different. Everything was going to be alright now.

There was a knock at the door. Isrie's delivery was here. I opened it cautiously at first, seeing an attractive Filipino woman with a box in her hand. Not dressed like a courier or delivery driver, she looked rather elegant. It wasn't my business anyway, as I was just accepting the package for my girl.

"Isrie Walker?" she asked, making sure she had the right apartment.

"Yes," was all I said before I felt the sting followed by a damp, wet cold. I backed away at first, startled. Dark eyes had suddenly narrowed as the woman curiously watched me. I began to panic as a red stain began spreading on my shirt. When I looked back at her I saw it. A large butcher knife had been hidden behind the box and was now in her hand . . . and coated with my blood.

"Don't mess with my husband," she said calmly, watching me as if I were a science project for her to observe. She didn't raise the knife again, but just watched. Black spots formed before my eyes. I tried to maintain my balance, but fell to my knees. My hearing went out as I put my hand under my shirt to try and stop the blood seeping from my stomach.

As everything faded to black, I remembered where I'd seen the woman before. She was leaving Isrie's spa the day I had gone by in Ivan's truck. It was more than that, though, as I knew she'd looked familiar that day too. I knew her face from a photo session. It was back when I was doing work at Fox Hills Mall. I had taken a picture of her, her husband, and a pretty little girl. Maria and . . . Thomas, I think . . . their names . . . were.

Grandma, I love you. . . .

Epilogue: Isrie

"Long time, no see," I said as the familiar droopy eyes perked up at the sight of me.

"How do I look?"

"The same . . . but happier."

He laughed. That same funny laugh. "Freedom will do that to a brother."

"Welcome back."

"Thanks."

"So, how'd that work out?"

"I was fuckin' lucky. My boy, who actually was doing the stealing, didn't let me take the fall. He came through during the court-martial. I still was guilty of running and the AWOL stuff. They could have given me more time than I got at Leavenworth. Hey, I should've never run, but old habits are hard to break."

"Want a cosmopolitan?"

"Nah. I don't drink that pretty shit. Just some water for me . . . with lemon." He reminded me of his sister with that order. He motioned for the bartender. The place was getting crowded and the volume was picking up.

"You miss her, huh?"

"Yeah. That whole situation wasn't right. I don't blame her for not believin' me. I've fucked up so often. It allowed me to face my shortcomings, y'know?"

"Why didn't you write?"

He looked into his glass as if searching for the answers in the ice cubes. "I wanted to 'man up,' girl. I didn't want to come to her only when I got problems. She needed the break, y'know? Where's she at anyway?"

"New York."

"For real?"

"Yep."

"Another photo shoot?"

"*Of course*. She's doing well. Some big shot with Ebony Emotions remembered her and hooked her up. I rarely see her."

"I wish I could have been there for her. Especially to smash that pretty boy's head."

"I took care of that," I said with a wink. "I'm sure she knows how you feel, though."

"So, what's new in your life . . . besides the hair?"

"You like my cut? The change was overdue."

"It's off the chain. The short look fits you."

"For real?" I asked, teasing it for effect.

"Yep. I don't screw around with people's heads anymore. I learned that the hard way."

"I've got other news. I've got my own business."

"Doing what?"

"Same thing as before. My very own spa. It's small now, but it shows promise."

"Must've cost some ends to start it up."

"It did. My daddy got a big advance on his newest novel and helped me out with a *loan*."

"Hmph. Daddy's girl."

"Ain't a damn thing changed," I giggled. "So, where are you?"

"Here and there. Trying to get a steady job. The dishonorable discharge makes it a little hard. People be thinkin' I'm a deserter or sumthin'."

"Here."

"What's this?"

"My card. Call me Monday. I figure I can get you on the cheap."

"This address. It's—"

"Yep. Deja's old spot. I knew the space was open since your sister blew up and moved on."

"Funny how things work out."

"Amen."

A song by the rapper The Game came on. Theron smiled, enjoying the beat. "C'mon, let's dance," he said as couples headed to the dance floor.

"But—"

"I know, I know. You don't like that hip-hop stuff."

"Actually I was going to say, 'Let me finish my drink,' Theron."

The two of us danced till the place closed down.

Epilogue: Deja

I was living in New York now. It was my way of shedding the pain. The paycheck and job didn't hurt either. Y'see, Hal Travis didn't forget me from that day at the Ebony Emotions shoot. After he heard about the escapade with Ivan, he approached me with an offer a sister just couldn't refuse. He had some contacts around the country and put together something for a woman of my talents.

After getting stabbed, I lost all the weight I'd been struggling to lose and then some. Of course, I gained most of it back. And you know what? It doesn't faze me. I learned there is a lot more to me than my dress size. I keep the scar on my stomach as a reminder.

Instead of getting a stay in prison, Thomas' wife wound up in a mental facility. From what Isrie told me, Thomas gave up his games to care for her once he recovered from Ivan's home run swing. Guilt is a *motha*.

As for dear Mr. Dempsey, I stayed around long enough to testify and to see him and Sophia cop plea bargains in exchange for reduced sentences. The last poses they struck were with numbers beneath their faces. For his attack on Isrie and Thomas, Ivan will still be gone for a good stretch. I just hope he doesn't drop the soap. The really strange thing is that, at trial, the homeless man I gave the twenty bucks to came forward as a witness. He had been roaming the street outside my studio and had seen everything. He told me that he wouldn't have come forward if I hadn't been so nice to him, reminding him of better days. I never did get all of my stuff back that was stolen, but I got at least got satisfaction.

Jamal stepped up, offering to comfort me . . . as a friend, but I felt it was just too soon. We talk from time to time about the day when he's going to make an East Coast swing on the comedy circuit, but I know in my heart that friends are all we'll ever be.

"That'll be all, Ms. Douglas," the magazine intern said as he wrapped up, bringing me out of my thoughts. The sexy, dark-skinned college graduate was a little young for me, but talkin' wasn't going to hurt a thang.

I watched him putting the camera equipment away and came over.

"That's a good model you got there." I said. "It's going to be phased out next month, though."

"What do you know about cameras, Ms. Douglas?"

"More than you, I'll bet." I put his camera to my eye and focused on him. "I used to be on the other side of the camera not too long ago. Don't let the pretty face fool you, son!"

Oh, I didn't tell you? I bet you thought my job was as a photographer. Yours truly signed with an agency and is now a model for plus sizes 'n stuff. Yep, D-Square is reppin' for her girls. Thought you'd be surprised. Hal Travis saw more in me than I saw in myself that crazy day long ago in Cali.

"Where are you off to now?" he asked.

"My crib in Brooklyn," I replied. I began snapping pictures of him. He tried to act cool, not used to being the subject. "Probably snag some Indian food and pop in a video tonight or something."

"That's it?"

"Yup. Tandoori chicken and Jamie Foxx in *Breakin' All the Rules*. I like my men funny."

"This is probably inappropriate to ask, but I'm going to anyway."

"Shoot," I said all silly-like, snapping another picture for emphasis.

"Would you mind some company tonight, Ms. Douglas?"

"No, I wouldn't mind." I lowered the camera from my eye. "And, please, call me Deja."

With those words, I stepped from behind the camera and got on with my life. Time to be my own subject.

Chips.

JWP Studios

Eric Pete is an award-winning author and one of the hottest voices in contemporary fiction today. His first two novels, *Real for Me* and *Someone's in the Kitchen*, have been featured selections of many book clubs across America. He has also contributed short stories to the erotica anthologies *After Hours: A Collection of Erotic Writing by Black Men* and *Twilight Moods: African American Erotica*. A graduate of McNeese State University, he resides with his family in the New Orleans area, where he is currently working on his next novel. Visit his Web site: www.ericpete.com.

Don't Get It Twisted

ERIC PETE

A CONVERSATION WITH ERIC PETE

Q. Don't Get It Twisted *is your fourth published novel. How have things changed for you?*

A. I think the obvious is that more people know about me. I'm glad my words are reaching them. The other thing I'm finding is that I have even fewer hours in the day. (Laughing) I could say that I now get my speeding tickets fixed, get free meals in all the best restaurants, and get to keep the DVDs I rent, but I'd be lying.

Q. *In your first novel,* Real for Me, *you alternated between a male and female voice. In* Don't Get It Twisted, *you write soley from the female perspective. How difficult was this for you?*

A. Of course, it wasn't as easy writing from a woman's perspective, but the feedback I've received from readers has been very positive. With any character, you have to let them speak to you. That part is no different, be it man or woman.

Q. *Would you say* Don't Get It Twisted *is a departure from your other works?*

A. Each of my stories is a departure from the one prior to it. I just like putting my characters in situations and seeing how they handle them. I'm just as surprised as my readers.

Q. *Where did you come up with the names Isrie and Deja? They are certainly unusual names. Of the two characters, do you have a favorite?*

A. In my books, I'm always coming up with unusual names, especially for my women. Both Isrie and Deja kind of just came to me. Deja is the name of this musical group I remembered from back in the day. I always liked the name, so I guess it hung around inside my head. As far as a favorite, that's like asking a parent to choose which child they love the most.

Q. *The issue of deception weighs heavily in this novel. Why do you think this topic is so popular with readers?*

A. I think a lot of people love secrets and the surprise experienced when the dirt comes to light.

Q. *What's next for Eric Pete?*

A. Just writing, writing, and more writing. If anyone out there (Cube, Will, Jada, Kelsey Grammer, Vivica) has read my stuff and wants to do a movie . . . CALL ME (Laughing)

Q. *Anything you want to say in closing?*

A. Yes. Thank you to the readers, for picking up this book.

QUESTIONS FOR DISCUSSION

1. What do you think of the title *Don't Get It Twisted* and how it relates to the story?

2. Which character could you relate to the most, Isrie or Deja? Why?

3. Did you ever suspect Ivan? Why?

4. What did you think of Ivan's relationship with Sophia?

5. If you were in Deja's situation, would you have put up with Sophia for as long as she did?

6. What did you think of Theron? Did you think he was guilty?

7. What do you feel is the overall message of this story?

8. Deja had pressures relating to her weight. What pressures do you feel Isrie had on her?

9. What did you think of the endings for both characters?

10. How do you feel about what happened to Michael/Thomas at the end?

11. Have you ever been in a situation where you didn't really know the person you were involved with? How did you find out? How did you handle the situation?

12. What's been the most extreme length someone's gone to deceive you?